TERMINAL OBJECTIVE

AN AMERICAN MERCENARY THRILLER

JASON KASPER

SEVERN RIVER PUBLISHING

Severn River Publishing
SevernRiverBooks.com

ISBN: 978-1-64875-489-0 (Paperback)

ALSO BY JASON KASPER

American Mercenary Series
Greatest Enemy
Offer of Revenge
Dark Redemption
Vengeance Calling
The Suicide Cartel
Terminal Objective

Shadow Strike Series
The Enemies of My Country
Last Target Standing
Covert Kill
Narco Assassins
Beast Three Six

Spider Heist Thrillers
The Spider Heist
The Sky Thieves
The Manhattan Job
The Fifth Bandit

Standalone Thriller
Her Dark Silence

To find out more about Jason Kasper and his books, visit
severnriverbooks.com/authors/jason-kasper

To Amy & Lucy

TERMINAL OBJECTIVE

REBIRTH

Casus belli

-Event of war

1

She was beautiful.

Absolutely, undeniably beautiful.

Her electric green irises were surrounded by dark shadow and smoky liner, the only makeup she permitted herself. Even that was more than she needed. Her heart-shaped face was framed by raven hair that fell in glistening waves around her shoulders. The first time I saw her, I thought she looked like a child cast out to sea, vulnerable and alone amid an ocean that she had no control over.

But that had been her first delegation.

Now, seated with one leg elegantly crossed over the other, streaking across hemispheres on a Gulfstream business jet, she looked like a different woman entirely. She was in control, a regal figure addressing her staff with total confidence. I reminded myself that I initially found her less than attractive, and now concluded this was probably due to a tacit understanding that she'd never be interested in me as a romantic prospect.

But sometimes opposites attract, which was the only reason that Parvaneh would talk to, much less hire or sleep with, a recently reformed gun-toting mercenary like myself.

I watched her with fascination and desire as she continued her briefing, thinking of anything and everything but her words.

"These are trying times for our Organization," she said. "The global market for drugs has exceeded a half trillion dollars per year and continues to rise drastically. We anticipate that within the next decade, illegal drugs will surpass global pharmaceuticals north of a trillion dollars annually."

Her back was against a glossy wood cockpit partition, and she'd opted not to utilize the flat-screen display mounted above her head. Instead it displayed a map of the North Pacific, our plane represented by a small jet icon streaking westward from the Canadian coast.

"Profit makes strange bedfellows, and in this era it has united crime and terror."

The few members of the audience shifted nervously in their seats. In the plane's forward lounge section, their discomfort was hard not to notice —this was about as spacious as private jets could be, but the forward-facing chairs still didn't afford much privacy. And apart from myself and Parvaneh, only five people were aboard.

Four were members of her delegation, two men and two women I'd met at the airfield that morning. All four had looked at me with a combination of disdain and contempt—which, I supposed, was understandable. My assignment to this delegation was the class equivalent of stuffing a gorilla into a tuxedo, except a gorilla could stay sober and keep its mouth shut. Both were challenges for me, and I would have felt infinitely more comfortable parachuting into combat than being stuffed into a confined space with the highly educated, politically correct team of diplomats. At least in combat, I could shoot people who pissed me off.

The fifth member of Parvaneh's delegation was Micah, her personal bodyguard.

He was watching me now, his eyes steely. Unlike everyone else aboard, Micah knew which end of the gun the bullets came out of. And as much as I hated to admit it, he was every bit as good in a fight as I was, a shared aptitude we'd discovered while under fire in Rio de Janeiro what seemed like a lifetime ago. But our similarities ended there. He was stern, crisply professional, and held me in utter contempt on a wide range of considerations, my disdain for authority chief among them.

I shot him a wink, and he looked away.

Parvaneh continued, "The distinction between drug producers and terrorist organizations has gone from distinct, to amorphous, to nonexistent. As a whole, this union is quickly globalizing into an ever more complex network that transcends all borders. Our policy is not to deal with terrorism or any of its offshoots, which, of course, places us in a perilous position as this new world order comes to fruition."

This statement got my attention, and for a moment I thought I'd misheard. But the truth was clear enough: Parvaneh, heir to the Handler's throne, was oblivious to her father's relationships with the terror networks. Of course, unlike me, she hadn't spent any time in the field, where the mercenary trade made such connections far more apparent.

"We receive continued indicators that our partners in the Russian, Serbian, and Chinese mafias are now operating with terrorist organizations including the Taliban, al-Shabaab, and Boko Haram. Even Al-Qaeda has established partnerships to facilitate narcotics trafficking for profit, decreasing their reliance on financial ties with wealthy sponsors in the Middle East. And as we have recently seen in Argentina"—she glanced at me sympathetically, an unspoken acknowledgement of my recent combat —"strategic partnership between the South American cartels and Hezbollah.

"This fusion of crime and terror has resulted in a new paradigm that severely threatens our business model in the short- to mid-term. Due to the nebulous essence of these connections between our global criminal network and terrorist organizations, and the increasing availability of highly encrypted communications methods, it is becoming difficult if not outright impossible for us to regulate, monitor, or administer organiza-tional relationships and revenue streams. Ten years ago we could easily enforce the Organization's ban on working with terrorist organizations. Today, it is nearly impossible."

It was always impossible, I thought, at least in any way but empty rhetoric. On the surface level, the delineation may have been clear. But I had no doubt the Handler maintained control over various terrorist activi-ties, a power likely handed down from his predecessor, whoever that was.

"And against this volatile backdrop, we have a bevy of threats both internal and external to our Organization. Internally, we had a recent conspiracy between my father's personal assistant and one of our top assas-sins. Externally, the threats facing our Organization aren't currently known. But a near-successful attempt on my life in Rio de Janeiro ignited the

3

recently concluded war between our Organization and Ribeiro's in South America."

Here it was. Every known conspirator, including Ribeiro, was dead. All my enemies were, save the Handler himself.

And one other man.

"Our only known enemy individual in this new threat matrix, the man who survived the downfall of Ribeiro's organization in the South American campaign, is Agustin Villalba."

The hair on the back of my neck prickled upright at the mention of his name. Oh, how I wanted that man dead. I'd come close, once, my shots probably missing him by inches before he vanished.

I saw Agustin now in my mind's eye, appearing as he did when I first met him. Well-dressed, well-built, with a dense beard and lucid chocolate eyes. Our first conversation had been during the Rio delegation, when I was banished from the primary negotiations along with the majority of security forces. As I stared out the top-floor window of a Botafogo high rise, I'd been asked a question that had haunted me many times since.

Do you see our Redeemer?

It was Agustin, pointing out the Christ the Redeemer statue atop a distant summit. He'd spoken to me in his perpetually calm voice, like a psychiatrist.

The next day, Agustin had personally led a kill team to wipe us out.

"He was the deputy operations officer until last year, when he was promoted to senior executive. He was a second-tier target, thought to be abandoned when Ribeiro was presumed to have fled South America."

When Ribeiro fled...only, as it turned out, he hadn't.

He had stayed right there, in the eye of the storm, letting the war swirl around him. Agustin had accompanied him until the end, when my team and I were closing in. Having left our wounded teammate Viggs unaccompanied for a brief jaunt uphill, we'd returned to find him strung up by his ankles, dangling from a tree in an inverted crucifix.

His throat was slit, the blood draining from his neck, and his body resembled a pale porcelain doll.

A message was written across his torso in fresh scarlet blood, the final punctuation mark scrawled across his tortured face, expression frozen in death.

4

DO
YOU
SEE
OUR
REDEEMER
?

"The member of our delegation with the most experience concerning Agustin is David. David, perhaps you could shed some light on your general observations on the man himself, and what his current activities might be?"

I suddenly felt exposed, on display before a delegation I knew nothing about. My lack of a gun compounded this feeling tenfold. Parvaneh had only offered me this slot yesterday, and my acceptance forever ended my duties as a warrior. Her sudden and unexpected inquiry made me acutely aware that my skill set revolved exclusively around pulling triggers, and I felt my face flush at being put on the spot in front of a group of people who unanimously hated me.

They turned in their seats to watch me, and I cleared my throat as I searched for words that wouldn't offend them or, more importantly, Parvaneh.

Finally I spoke, my voice uneasy. "These shitheads tried to kill Parvaneh in Rio. When their assassination attempt failed, Agustin personally led a kill team to finish the job. Maybe he enjoyed the hunt, or maybe his organization made a promise to kill her and he had to finish the job however he could. My best guess is a combination of both—but as for who they made the promise to, I can only speculate that there's a hidden sponsor behind the scenes. Maybe some new organization."

"That's impossible," a shrewlike woman scoffed. "There is no alternate reality in which our intelligence apparatus would not have detected the formation of a new entity seeking the throne."

I met her eyes, my brow furrowing in disgust. I considered whether to

5

respond with tact or the stream-of-consciousness candor that had both characterized and limited my career options to date.

I sided with the latter.

"It must be so peaceful in your heads, you know? Debating these issues thousands of miles from the fight in your"—I waved a hand at her—"neatly pressed blazers."

The woman recoiled and Parvaneh visibly winced, but no one stopped me, so I went on.

"Well, since you guys were sipping shandy while I was balls-deep in the jungle, let me fill you in: we didn't kill Ribeiro. Agustin did that for us, which meant Ribeiro's death was a power grab. Agustin's in charge now, and he wouldn't have made that move if there was nothing left to save. And without the assistance of a powerful sponsor, there *would* be nothing left to save. So, the obvious conclusion is that Agustin is now the ally of some bigger opposition. Whether that opposition is a group of disloyal factions or some new organization, I have no idea."

The woman gave me a sympathetic smile—she actually felt sorry for me—and looked away.

Parvaneh interceded, her expression a mask of formal professionalism that left no clue as to whether or not she'd be reprimanding me later.

"Thank you, David," she began uneasily. "This brings us to the way forward. For a half century, our closest—and by far the strongest—partners have been the Far North Coalition in Russia, due in large part to the relationship between their leader, Olexei, and my father.

"With Olexei succumbing to old age last month, leadership of the Far North Coalition has passed to his son, Konstantin. In the past, Konstantin has expressed interest in a, shall we say, *stronger* partnership between our organizations." There was a brief volley of suppressed chuckles among the delegates. "Through marriage." The laughter increased. "To me."

I looked around in bewilderment. Parvaneh had never mentioned a potential suitor to me, and nothing about the situation seemed the least bit humorous. Why were these people laughing?

She continued, "Since that has not and will never occur, the purpose of our delegation is threefold. First, to personally express our condolences for the loss of Olexei. Second, to transition the personal contact of our strategic partnership from Olexei and my father to myself and Konstantin. And third, to negotiate the reallocation of our global force distribution to better meet the emerging threat, whatever that is determined to be."

* * *

The initial brief lasted just over an hour, after which Parvaneh summoned me for my initial counseling as a member of her delegation.

We entered the aft section of the plane, where a low couch was flanked by the lavatory and two chairs facing each other across a small table. I took a seat as she set a file of papers atop the table between us, then closed the sliding partition door to seal us inside.

I watched her lower her lean form into the seat across from me and tuck a wave of dark hair behind an unadorned ear.

My God, this woman was beautiful.

She said, "It's time for your formal counseling."

Then she leaned across the table, and our lips met.

Hers were soft and warm, and I felt the tension melting from my body as surely as if I were drinking bourbon. This woman was addictive. She saw me for who I was, scars and all, and loved me nonetheless. The slight complication to our situation—namely, that I'd tried to kill the head of her transnational criminal syndicate, a man who happened to be her father—didn't matter to either of us in moments like these.

After we broke the kiss, I whispered, "I missed you, Parvaneh."

She smiled. "It's been less than twenty-four hours. You're going to have to exercise some patience."

Leaning forward, we kissed again.

She was right, of course, though only we knew that. Her syndicate's headquarters were deep in the British Columbian wilderness at a compound known as the Mist Palace. My quarters between missions consisted of a modest locked room amid the compound's impeccable and totalitarian security. When Parvaneh had appeared at my door unaccompanied by bodyguards, I hadn't believed her assurances that she could come and go undetected. So when she left my room after last night's visit, I secretly blocked the door from auto-locking.

And then, using my night vision device and risking everything between us, I followed her.

We broke the kiss again, and I saw that she was blushing. She set a hand on the table and I took it in mine, a pang of remorse pulsing in my heart. I didn't want to keep secrets from this woman, but for now, I had no choice.

"Was that my official counseling?" I asked.

"That was your *personal* counseling—or rather, last night was."

"Sign me up for another."

She gave a brief half-smile that faded when she said, "Your *official* counseling is three words: watch and learn. Normally you would first build an extensive knowledge of our Organization, allies, and enemies before accompanying a delegation. Since the timing of your assignment did not accommodate that, you must first observe how we conduct our business. Upon our return to the Mist Palace, I will show you the inner workings."

The inner workings. What an appropriate term.

Because I had learned, just last night, that within the Mist Palace, there was a hidden passage.

It wasn't much, just a short stretch of ancient mining tunnel, a remnant of the mid-1800s mining community on which the site had been founded. Its only entry points were so overgrown with foliage that they were practically invisible to anyone but an inquisitive child. After pushing my way through the brush, I'd had to crawl beneath a flat stone and through a hollowed-out slick of dirt to enter the rocky cavern providing access.

The tunnel hadn't led me far, perhaps two hundred meters, but I'd entered it just outside my guest quarters in the heavily secured compound, and exited it in a far more guarded site.

The Handler's garden. A fort within the fort, and the only place he went without bodyguard accompaniment. The garden was ringed with fifteen-foot stone walls topped with concertina, an impenetrable perimeter, or so I'd thought, until I'd exited the tunnel and found myself square inside it. I could kill him in this place, could revisit it until our paths crossed and he was alone. Then, I could finally earn the revenge that had been growing in intensity with every failed attempt to kill him.

I asked, "Do you really think this is going to work? Not us, but *this*. Me, on your delegation. Because even if I'm speaking with as much delirious optimism as I can muster, my relationship with your father is...complicated."

"Complicated?" She let out a soft chuckle, angelic in its merriment. "I'd have an easier time deciphering the Enigma code than the relationship between you and my father. It's not 'complicated.' It's chaotic, muddled, twisted..." She threw up her hands. "*Labyrinthine*. And he is only half the problem."

"What's the other half?"

She raised a suggestive eyebrow. "Half of diplomacy is asking the right question. So did you mean what, or *who*?"

"You're not suggesting that I'm part of the problem."

"I'm not suggesting, I'm insisting outright. The two of you are more similar than either of you is willing to admit, and you don't even know the best part." She paused for dramatic effect. "My father likes you."

My thoughts went blank, my mind grinding to a complete halt.

Finally I managed, "Likes me? I've tried to kill him."

"With far more success than any of his would-be assassins, I am assured. To my father, that makes you worthy of respect rather than disdain. I believe his exact words to describe you were 'fearless' and 'audacious.'"

"Well," I allowed, "maybe he has some modicum of taste..."

"Along with more emotion than any man with his amount of power should have. But I am heir to the throne. You know my plans to modernize, to end the ceaseless bloodshed, to legalize as many of our functions as possible to help people rather than squeeze every cent of profit out of them. Do you believe I can accomplish this?"

I thought for a moment.

"If anyone can do it, it's you."

"Then here is the rest of your official counseling. You must contribute to the transition of power by learning now, so that you may advise my directives when the time comes. That is why you are here. I want a warrior on my delegation, someone who has seen the battlefield and can advise on the application of force." She gracefully swung a hand to indicate the plane's main seating area. "The only person in there to have so much as fired a weapon is my bodyguard, and his expertise is in protection, not combat. Do you understand?"

I nodded.

"I told you last night that you had a tough transition ahead, from warrior to diplomat. And that I would be here for you every step of the way."

"Yes, you did." Swallowing back a lump in my throat, I aimed my index finger upward, waved it in a circle, and then pointed it toward my ear.

She raised a quizzical eyebrow. "I have no idea what that means, David."

"Is the plane wired?"

"No. Of course not." She leaned forward and whispered, "I wouldn't have kissed you if it was."

My jaw settled, and I said to her, "Humor me."

She gave a frustrated sigh, removed a phone from her pocket, and tapped the screen until a symphony of classical music began playing. Then she set it on the table between us.

Leaning over the phone, I whispered, "You wanted to know what really happened in Argentina. I need to tell you now."

She pulled her head back and shook it.

"That can wait, David."

"No, it can't."

I watched her forehead wrinkle—she'd asked me for the real story last night, and I'd put her off. Now I was demanding to tell her, and she couldn't figure out why.

So I began, "Your father was trying to have me killed."

I paused, certain she'd contest this, and braced to address her rebuke.

But she was listening intently, waiting for me to continue.

"You already know that I joined your father's private army to kill him. So here's what you don't know: I wasn't the only one. The team he gave me to command in Argentina had three other Outfit members trying to assassinate the Handler: Viggs, Cancer, and Reilly. The three of us were on paramilitary teams, and lost our brothers-in-arms when your father started wiping out everyone who served him. Our fourth man was Sergio, who unknowingly recruited an assassin targeting your father and was found guilty of negligence. My team was assembled to die in one fell swoop, and be written off as a combat loss."

"I don't mean to sound callous, David, but when my father wants someone dead..."

"I know. There's no 'trying' about it."

"Exactly. You wouldn't have made it five minutes in the jungle."

"If I hadn't changed our infiltration point at the last minute and then found a tracking device in my kit, you'd be right."

Parvaneh stroked her chin, recalling my mission debrief before the Handler's court. "So that's why you didn't report in for two days."

"Yes. Viggs was killed exactly as I said—that much was true." I lowered my voice even further, feeling a tingling sensation of guilt. "But the others are still in Argentina. Sergio, Cancer, and Reilly are alive, waiting for me to call their satellite phone. They're relying on me to secure their repatriation to America, and I can't do that without your help."

She rubbed her forehead. "You were right to keep this a secret from my father."

"I figured as much. Can we bring them back safely?"

Her lips were pressed together, and she looked lost in thought.

"Parvaneh," I pressed, "can we bring them back? Without your father sentencing them to die?"

She lifted her head high. "I *will* bring them back. Can they make it another few days on their own?"

"Now that they're not being hunted, yes."

"Good. As soon as our delegation returns, I'll arrange a message from the diplomatic network in Argentina. It will be addressed to me alone, stating that they have been recovered alive by our allies. Then I will personally oversee their return—and if I have a vested interest in their safety, my father will not interfere."

With these words, I felt like all the tension in my body was released at once.

"Thank you," I muttered softly. "Thank you, Parvaneh."

"But David," she began, her eyes hyper-focused on mine, "speak of this to no one else. I can guarantee the safety of your men, but only if I handle this delicately—and alone."

2

Alykel Airport
22 Miles West of Norilsk, Russia

We disembarked the Gulfstream jet into what I would optimistically call a frigid arctic shithole.

I'd zipped up my parka in anticipation of crossing the tarmac, and still felt like I'd fallen into a bathtub filled with ice. Astonishingly, no snow lay on the ground, but that was the only concession to a temperate climate. The landscape in every direction appeared to be primarily flat tundra, the sky and sun choked by a smoggy haze of gray clouds. I consoled myself with a single thought.

At least I'm not in New Jersey.

Our delegation walked toward an idling Mi-8, a huge, sand-colored Russian twin-engine helicopter that looked like a giant, predatory insect ready to pounce. Between the arctic climate and the Soviet-era aviation I was about to entrust my life to, I'd never so desperately regretted sobriety. Granted, that state of being wasn't voluntary; there had been no booze aboard our so-called luxury business jet, a shame since I'd have had time to tie on a half-decent buzz and recover before ending the transcontinental flight.

I was now a stranger in a strange land. And amidst the delegation's refined academics, there was but one individual I could publicly speak to about the current circumstances.

So, I fell into step next to Micah.

"Where in the hell are we?" I rhetorically asked.

He glanced halfway in my direction, never breaking stride. "A thousand miles from nowhere. And well within the Arctic Circle. Welcome to Norilsk."

"Is there a town, or..."

He pointed east. "About twenty miles that way."

The air around us was forty degrees Fahrenheit at the most, possibly under thirty, but it was made nearly unbearable by the helicopter rotors washing wind our way.

"And people live here?"

"This is the end of their summer, David. A three-month window without snow. In two months, maybe less, the daily high temperature will be below zero. But cheer up: for the most part, we only make this journey two or three times a year."

He then raised his voice as I strained to hear him over the thudding chop of helicopter blades we were approaching.

"Be grateful that the weather permits the helicopter flight. When a snowstorm forces ground movement—which is often—it's three hours cross-country in trucks modified for arctic travel. The tires are nearly as tall as you are, and riding in one is like hanging onto a rodeo bull."

We boarded the helicopter through the open rear ramp, and I practically began salivating before realizing why—most helicopter rides of my adult life occurred prior to or immediately following a combat mission, and I found the experience difficult to dissociate from my previously unbreakable addiction to adrenaline.

But there would be no fighting today, I thought, and resigned myself to feeling a sense of gratitude, however fleeting, for the waves of heat weakly emitting from vents in the helicopter's cabin.

Once the delegation was seated and our luggage brought onboard by porters, the helicopter ramp raised slowly and locked into place, encapsulating us inside.

Then the chopper lifted off, dipping its nose low as it throttled west and gained altitude.

I turned in my seat, looking through the porthole window between Micah and me.

I had to admit that there was an eerie, desolate beauty to the barren vista around us. The wrinkled earth was an endless span of sage green and desert brown, and a band of pale pink light ringed the horizon below a washed-out blue-gray sky. The arctic steppes were as vast a landscape as I'd ever witnessed, and I suddenly felt like a very small, insignificant visitor passing through a domain whose expanse I could only begin to comprehend.

The engine noise made the cabin too loud to communicate without shouting. A breeze hit our helicopter and the frame shuddered, causing an unpleasant lurch for the occupants. I said nothing else to Micah and stared instead at Parvaneh, who was reviewing her notebook on the opposite side of the bird. She looked focused and alert, jotting notes with a pencil until the big helicopter began its slow descent at our destination.

And contrary to what I would have expected from the secret world of mega-rich criminal organizations, our destination was staggeringly underwhelming.

When the helicopter finally landed and lowered its ramp, the view was of a simple dirt landing zone. It wasn't even as impressive as the Handler's inconspicuous airfield; instead, this was just a level clearing of permafrost. Three men greeted Parvaneh as she stepped off a ramp, and I could tell by their exchange that they were simply escorts. One offered an apology that Parvaneh casually dismissed, and then they led us toward a cluster of low-slung buildings that seemed to appear out of nowhere as we approached. Two stone obelisks stretched thirty feet skyward, the pinnacle of one crowned with a golden sun and the other a crescent moon. A worn path marred by tire tracks stretched between them, as if the twin spires marked some grand gate entrance to the compound.

But whatever their purpose, it was purely ceremonial: there was no gate.

I looked about with a profound sense of disbelief. The wilderness was beyond vast, everything past the compound seemingly untouched by man. Great rolling plains of short grass wrinkled into distant ridges, the first erratic clusters of tall pines appearing at the edge of a long field. The sky and the landscape beneath it were silent—no planes, birds, or animals in sight. This was the definition of a thousand miles from nowhere.

I turned my attention back toward the obelisks. Not so much as a fence separated the compound from the Siberian wilderness beyond, nor was there a road—my eyes traced the tire tracks fading beyond the helipad, disappearing into oblivion amid the tundra landscape.

An omnipresent hypervigilance born of PTSD tightened my chest, and a lump formed in my throat as I scanned for any discernible security measures.

In lieu of a fence, short guard towers were posted at periodic intervals around the perimeter. Each tower appeared to house a five-foot-long, tripod-mounted heavy machinegun topped with a massive thermal optic. A hasty glance revealed that the towers achieved interlocking sectors of fire around the compound, with just one problem.

None of the towers were manned.

I didn't see a single guard beyond sentry patrols roving between buildings.

Micah, of course, was the only one I could explain my concern to, yet he looked confident, relaxed. How could he be? The guy had probably forgotten more about running a personal protection detail than I'd ever know.

I approached him and whispered, "Micah."

"What?"

"What? Seriously? What the actual fuck, is what. There's no one in the guard towers. There's no gate; there's no fence. You're cool with your primary wading into this?"

He cast a sideways glance toward me.

"I thought you were a diplomat. You want to be a bodyguard now, too?"

"Don't give me that. It doesn't take a master tactician to see that this place is open to attack."

"Do I look worried to you?"

"No. But you should be, because—"

"David, do you want to learn something, or just complain?"

My stomach hardened. "Complain, mostly. Learning wouldn't hurt."

"Look at the towers again. Do you see the orbs?"

I looked to the closest tower and saw what he was talking about—the underside of its slanting roof held a reflective metallic sphere.

"So?"

15

"So they have long-range optics with day, night, and thermal imaging capability. All operated by technicians in the operations center"—he pointed to a circular building ahead of us—"who can zoom in close enough to read a license plate at a distance of two kilometers."

"If they know where to look. And some sniper in a ghillie suit could crawl half that distance in the span of daylight, when their thermals won't do them any good. That's close enough to put someone's lights out forever."

"This compound is at ground zero of a one-mile swath of ground sensors. A rabbit can't approach without disturbing them. And the machineguns in those towers are remotely operated. I've seen an operations center technician snipe a reindeer from the middle of its herd with a single eight-hundred-meter shot. If they need to dispatch a threat using their ground force, they drive those."

He pointed toward a row of trucks, likely the ones he had referenced earlier—they were recognizable as Toyota Hilux, but just barely. Apart from the word "Toyota" sandwiched between basketball-sized headlights on the grill, the rest of the vehicle was some Frankenstein-esque monster truck hybrid. The wheel wells extended two feet from the cab, elevating the door handles to my full height. A dozen of these trucks were spread equidistantly, facing the tundra like sentries.

Our party passed between the obelisks, and I scanned the low white buildings beyond. Some were windowless, while others had huge panes of glass overlooking the small kingdom. Solar panels were packed atop the roof of every building in sight, save one. Almost central in the compound loomed a log cabin of elegant construction, with what appeared to be a massive attached garage. I counted eight carports.

"Is that where the ruling family resides?"

"The villa is for the king alone. There are no families here."

"I don't follow."

"The Far North Coalition follows the Slavic model—no women or children at the compound. Their headquarters, and their work, is here. They return to civilization to visit their families in places like Yakutsk, Saint Petersburg, or Novosibirsk."

"That sounds awful."

"It takes immense discipline. But they believe it fosters strength—in themselves, and in their organization. You see why?"

"Because their wives are all banging out their friends back home?"

"Even the most proficient assassination attempt would have no choice but to target them in their hometown, where they still have considerable security. And that attempt may get the man, but it will never get the organization at its core. That is why the Far North Coalition has survived as long as it has."

The facilities seemed fine enough, but in comparison to the Mist Palace's cameras, fences, sensors, and omnipresent guard force, this place had all the security of a phone booth. I examined an exterior door as we passed—no digital keypad, card reader, or retinal scanner.

Instead there was just a normal keyhole with a simple pin tumbler lock.

"Even their locks are shit," I muttered to Micah.

"Remind me again what you contribute to this delegation?"

I looked to him with a slight smile. "Micah, my friend, we're in Russia. When Konstantin challenges us to vodka shots, someone's got to represent the Organization. And that sure as shit ain't gonna be you."

"Konstantin doesn't drink. No one here does."

"Really?"

"These are professionals, David. Not everyone is like you."

"Ah yes, the highborn nobility who disdain alcohol. Like Hitler, and Al-Qaeda. Neither lets the stuff touch their lips."

He ignored the quip, remaining silent as the escorts led us toward a building and held a door open for the delegates to enter. I took a final glance around the compound. At the far edge, a row of generators was lined up within the guard towers' protection but as far from the buildings as possible—a prudent measure, as I could hear the hum even from a distance.

Then I followed Micah through the door, which was mercifully closed against the cold.

The room we entered was an inviting lobby space warmed by crackling fireplaces and lined with plush couches and coffee tables. No sooner had we closed the door behind us than another opened, then the long-heralded Konstantin himself entered.

"My apologies for not greeting you," he said in a thick Russian accent as he embraced Parvaneh. "Something occurred which required my attention."

Konstantin's head was shaved—why, I had no idea. Personally, I'd have been trying to retain every shred of body heat I could in this frigid wasteland. And his demeanor was in no way indicative of some great criminal leader, or even a criminal leader at all. His tone and mannerisms were as slight as his body; he had an almost effeminate air, and wore a garish lavender dress shirt and sharp cologne more suited for a Miami nightclub than business. Judging from his demeanor, Micah and I were in greater danger of being on the receiving end of his affections than Parvaneh.

"When I heard about the attempt on your life in Rio—well, I was beside myself. Please extend my deepest gratitude to the men who saved your life."

"You can thank them yourself, *druzhishhe*."

She waved a hand toward me and Micah.

"Micah and David were single-handedly responsible for my rescue. David took three bullets saving my life."

Konstantin looked toward me, astonished.

"*Three* bullets?"

I cleared my throat.

"Two and a half, really. One was grazing—it's not a big deal."

"Not a big deal?" He gave a quick laugh, then spoke at a brisk cadence. "Parvaneh, I can see why you would keep both on your immediate security detail. Especially this one." He looked at me with an approving smile. "He is funny."

Parvaneh said, "I agree, Konstantin, but David is no longer a bodyguard. He is the newest member of my delegation, and is beginning to learn the art of statesmanship just as you and I have."

Now Konstantin reappraised me, seeing the inherent contradiction. There was no Ivy League in my voice, no finishing school in my stance. His eyes flickered toward Parvaneh. Did he sense that she and I had a romantic interest in each other? Did he suspect that was the *only* reason she allowed me to join her delegation?

And then my mind asked itself a question.

Was that the only reason Parvaneh invited me to join?

But whatever his conclusions, they were hidden beneath a veneer of what appeared to be genuine courtesy.

He gave a slight bow and said, "David and Micah, thank you, gentlemen, for allowing Parvaneh to have survived to attend this seventh visit to our humble accommodations."

Micah spoke before I could.

"Thank you, sir, for your generous hospitality. Each visit to your breathtaking land is more pleasurable than the last."

Konstantin's face twisted a bit at this last comment.

But then he shrugged indifferently and addressed Parvaneh. "I had a reception banquet prepared for the delegation, with a private luncheon for you and me. But with your saviors here? They must dine with us. David and Micah, I insist that you join us for our meal. Please, follow me."

And with that, the delegation was led through one set of doors while Micah, Parvaneh, and I followed Konstantin down a long hallway. Its walls were adorned with large gold-leaf frames that I assumed held the oil portraits of past leaders, but as we passed them, I saw the paintings were instead art—mostly semi-nude women whose depictions bordered on the erotic.

As he led our small procession, Konstantin asked Parvaneh, "So what is it that troubles you now?"

"Nothing that cannot wait until the session."

"By sunset there will be no secrets between us. Why wait?"

Parvaneh spoke quickly. "There is no question we face an entirely new threat. We are unsure, however, whether that threat is primarily a union of existing factions or some altogether new organization with funding and direction from some hidden sponsor."

We reached the door at the end of the hall, and Konstantin stopped with his fingers on the handle. Then he faced her.

"No question," he said dismissively. "There is a hidden sponsor, I am certain."

"What makes you so certain, Konstantin?"

I was only half listening. Our procession had stopped beside a decorative table holding a large glass bowl filled with what appeared to be miniature elephant tusks: four- to six-inch curved slices of ivory. There must have been twenty of them in the bowl, forming a decorative assortment that made me wonder what size beast these things came from.

I reached inside the bowl to touch one but was halted by a deep voice behind me, its Russian accent so thick it was almost incomprehensible.

"May I help you, my American friend?"

I turned toward the voice, and visibly jumped.

"Jesus!"

The man standing directly behind me—how he approached without being heard, I had no idea—was, to put it lightly, a giant.

Dark, uncombed hair spilled down over his collar, and a bushy, unkempt beard concealed what I could only assume was a square jaw. Even his scowling eyebrows were imposing.

Micah glared at me as Konstantin craned his head to see what I was looking at.

"Wild boar," he said cheerfully, seeming eager to explain. "The Far North has the largest and fiercest wild boar of anywhere in the world. When my council reaches gridlock on an issue, and we cannot determine how to proceed, we go on a boar hunt. And when we return, we are always able to reach a mutual agreement on our course of action. Something about being out in the timber provides a clarity that the conference room cannot. Our kills are our reminder to remain united always. Trophy animals go on the wall. The small ones' tusks are put there."

"These are the *small* ones?" I asked incredulously.

"Oh yes, David. We have some real monsters here in Siberia."

I glanced toward the bearded giant standing beside me. "I'm sure you do. What do you bring them down with?"

"My preference is 45-70 lever action. What about you?"

I shrugged. "I don't hunt."

"I would say you do, David. The look in your eyes tells me you have hunted men, and this is far more dangerous, no?"

"That depends on whether you're exaggerating the size of your boars."

He laughed again. "So funny, this one. Tell me, David. When one hunts men, what does one keep as a hunting trophy?"

"When the quarry shoots back, the only trophy is coming out alive."

He suddenly bolted into action, striding toward me. Selecting a tusk from the bowl, he grabbed one of my hands and slapped it into my palm.

My fingers closed around it as he clasped my fist in both hands, giving it a pat before releasing his grip.

"Then allow me to give you your first, David." He turned back to Parvaneh. "Now, where were we?"

She replied as if their line of conversation hadn't been interrupted.

"You said you believe this new threat we face is a new organization backed by a hidden sponsor."

"I can say with a great deal of certainty that it is. Allow me to show you something."

Then Konstantin swung the door open with a flourish, and we stepped inside the room.

My hands fell open in shock, the boar tusk tumbling to the ground.

An assembly of men lined the walls. They consisted of Caucasian Russians and Latinos, all armed. But before I could assess what weapons they carried, my eyes fell upon another figure.

Seated at a table, facing us and slicing a steak with only the briefest of glances our way, was a single man.

Agustin.

I stepped in front of Parvaneh, blocking her from Agustin and the armed men. It was all I could think to do, an instinctive act of physical protection, the last refuge of an unarmed man.

Micah, however, had no such restrictions.

He drew his pistol so fast that the metal was flashing in the light before I realized what he was doing.

But Micah never had a chance. Every bodyguard in that room was watching his hands, and had their weapons leveled with time to spare. And astonishingly, none took a shot.

Instead, the giant behind me had grabbed Micah by the shoulders and swung him effortlessly sideways. Micah's pistol tumbled to the ground as his skull made a sickening thud that inflicted a spiderweb crack in the wall.

Before I could so much as lunge for the pistol, Konstantin deftly snatched it up. It was replaced by Micah's body a moment later, when the giant dropped his limp form unceremoniously to the ground.

"Don't do this," I shouted, my eyes darting from the gun in Konstantin's hand to Agustin seated at the table. My arms were spread, trying to shield Parvaneh from the evil now staring us in the face.

Agustin calmly wiped a napkin across his beard and around the corners of his lips.

"Whatever do you mean, David?"

Then he set the napkin down, leaned back, and crossed his legs. In a reassuring tone, he added, "I am not going to harm anyone. You have my word."

Parvaneh flung my arm down, stepping forward to stand beside me.

"What is this?" she demanded of Agustin. "Now that Ribeiro is defeated, you seek to take his place?"

Agustin shook his head, as if explaining something to a small child. "Ribeiro had nothing to do with the unfortunate attempt against your life. The credit for that—and the blame in its failure, I'm afraid—belongs to me." He took a sip of his wine, registering her expression. "Oh, do not act surprised. Ribeiro denied many times that he had anything to do with the attempt. But the Handler is too wrathful to see reason. His mind was made up, and so he did what he did. Now, here we are."

Konstantin gave a sheepish grin, gesturing with Micah's pistol as he said in his cold, effeminate voice, "So now you see why I am certain of a hidden sponsor. Because I *am* that sponsor."

Parvaneh looked incensed.

"Your father and mine, Konstantin, had an alliance stretching four decades of cooperation and support. Now you turn your back not only on my family but your own?"

He shrugged, letting the pistol hang limply at his side. "My father's days were numbered. It was upon me to forge a new alliance. It was quite simple, really. When the attempt against you in Rio de Janeiro failed, there was no question that Ribeiro could not win the war that followed. No single organization could. But two major organizations aligning their interests, with help from the discontented syndicates, could start and win a revolution. So, we simply set that into effect." He grinned apologetically.

"This is just the beginning—there are many more alliances, though you'll forgive me for not disclosing our additional partners. The Handler's reign is over just as much as my father's reign is. And now that Olexei is gone, may he rest in peace, there is no longer any reason to keep the alliance a secret."

Konstantin gave an almost imperceptible nod, and the giant grabbed me from behind. My heart was slamming in my throat as I resisted his immense strength, but it was no use—he pinned both hands behind my back, forcefully taking control of me as he prepared to swing me into the wall just as he'd done with Micah.

"Don't you dare!" Parvaneh shouted.

"Relax," Konstantin assured her. "I need at least one of your people alive."

"Send one of her delegates," the giant ordered from behind me. Then he added, "Sir."

"No," Konstantin replied. "David is funny; I like him. He will not die today. Instead, he will be my messenger. I want the Handler to hear from a witness what happened here today, and what will happen yet."

"Good," I panted. "Good. You want to send a message. Kill me and send Parvaneh back—her words will mean more to the Handler than mine ever will."

"This is not about sending a message. We will fight this war until it's won. This, this is about removing an heir to the throne. I am finishing the job I started in South America, you understand?"

"Konstantin, Agustin...don't do this. I know you don't have mercy in your souls to spare her, but—"

"David," Parvaneh said quietly. I looked over in alarm—I'd almost forgotten she was there—and saw that tears were streaming down her face. "Do not dishonor me now."

Konstantin was still holding Micah's pistol, and he addressed me directly.

"You may take her body back. The Handler may bury his daughter. But that is the last mercy I will ever show him."

"She's more valuable to you as a hostage than a corpse, don't you see that?"

"This is where you are wrong. You cannot attack my people here, and I dare you to try. Once you are defeated, I am moving the Far North Coalition out of this frozen shithole forever."

I was at a loss for words. Agustin looked to me and said kindly, "You see, David? I told you I would not harm anyone."

Then he looked over, and I followed his gaze to see Konstantin extending the pistol toward Parvaneh's heart.

The giant twisted me to face her. I couldn't accept it, couldn't comprehend—the last woman I'd loved before Parvaneh was Karma. Her death had set me on the tortuous journey of revenge against the Handler, and now the cycle was repeating— everyone I loved taken away violently, dying before my eyes.

I'd never been able to cleanse the vivid memory of Karma's death from my mind, and I knew that I'd never be able to do so for Viggs's grisly murder either. I tried to pinch my eyes shut so I wouldn't have to witness Parvaneh dying too, but I couldn't—they were locked on her as she stood tall and unwavering, looking over to me with an almost serene detachment as she lifted her chin and spoke the last words she'd ever say.

"David, take care of my daughter."

Konstantin fired one shot, and Parvaneh fell.

I sagged in the giant's grasp, my knees giving out as he held me in place to see Parvaneh's body collapsed on the floor.

Then he twisted me away and led me back out the door. My last glance around the room showed a blur of faces—Agustin taking a sip of wine, Parvaneh's dark hair surrounding her pained expression, frozen in death, and Konstantin's eyebrows rising as he remembered one last thing.

"David!" he said.

The giant turned me to face Konstantin, who approached and knelt as if before a king. Then I saw he was merely retrieving something from the ground.

"You forgot something. A memento of your visit here, and a reminder of the fate that will befall your organization."

In his hand was the curved white boar tusk.

JUSTICE

Lex talionis

-Law of Revenge

3

The Mist Palace

The security detail escorted me briskly down the hallway toward the Handler's office.

No formal reception greeted me at the airfield, no honor guard waited to receive Parvaneh's body. Only a group of men to recover the body bag and a team of armed guards to take me into the Mist Palace.

He wants to see you, they'd said. *Now*.

No surprise there, and while I'd had a transcontinental flight to consider what I'd say to him, I'd come up with nothing. What could I possibly tell the Handler? I wanted to kill him, I now had a way with the secret path into his private garden, and the only impediment had been my relationship with Parvaneh.

Now she was dead. In the unholy union of Konstantin and Agustin, I'd seen a greater evil than even the Handler—and not, I reminded myself, for the first time.

When was this going to end?

I saw my enemies arrayed before me—there was nothing but enemies any longer. Konstantin and Agustin on one side, the Handler and his vicars on the other. My path to revenge had sprouted countless offshoots, the ledger of targets increasing endlessly.

And with the death of every person who needed to die came the loss of someone who didn't.

I saw myself mired in endless war, condemned to this fate. No matter which side the enemy was on, I was the same thing to all of them: a pawn to be manipulated, tormented at their will. A messenger, a killer whose only potential was my expendability. In this way I'd pinballed between criminal syndicates, the demons in my head running amok because I was always too busy chasing down someone else's.

The security detail led me around a corner, the final stretch of corridor to the Handler's office.

Where had this path gotten me? I had more enemies now, not less. Every advancement toward killing the Handler revealed someone far worse. Every victory on the mercenary battlefield was both narrow and fleeting, the only benefactors criminal kingpins who existed far from the wars they created.

And yet, what else was I to do?

Before Boss's team found me, I'd been on the literal brink of suicide, and for good fucking reason. Every night was a roll of the dice—whether I'd fall asleep, and, if so, when and for how long. The crushing weight of depression, the addiction to a darkness I'd never chosen. Or maybe I had; maybe that was the inevitable aftereffect of war. Maybe this was the fate of all combat veterans. Those of us who could resist the siren song of our pistol in those dim early morning hours were nonetheless condemned to a fate of fatigue yet inability to sleep, of emotional detachment yet constant hypervigilance, of feigning normalcy through medication prescribed or self-administered.

So the bizarre truth was that this mercenary underworld had kept me alive to date. It had been a sickening form of life support, and every time a cause for hope emerged—Karma, Parvaneh—it was taken from me in virtually the same breath.

And I kept returning to the fray.

What else could I do? There was no walking away from this criminal enterprise. At best, you could convincingly fake your death and start over... if you had something to start over for. But I didn't, not any longer. I hadn't since Karma's death, and now Parvaneh's. If I stepped outside the arena now, I'd kill myself. All the missions and murder and bullshit since I'd become a mercenary, and I was no closer to redemption than I had been at the start. Instead I was much, much further from it, a dark product of ever-worsening circumstances that I continued to choose.

As we approached the Handler's door, I saw his three chief vicars waiting outside the office.

Watts, Omari, and Yosef were his top advisors of defense, finance, and intelligence, respectively. All were being kept waiting outside while I was escorted in. Wasn't this grand, I thought. All three men hated me, and had made no secret of it. But while Watts and Omari made no effort to shield this sentiment from their expressions, Yosef appraised me with a different look entirely.

The Chief Vicar of Intelligence was so small he was nearly a dwarf, and a black yarmulke sat atop his balding head. Behind his rimless glasses were eyes of immense intellect, and they bore into me not with hatred but an almost malicious exploitation. I considered this for a moment, recalling that Yosef had been the only accomplice to my previous deep cover assignment. The Handler had kept that much secret even from his other two vicars, and Yosef's expression assured me of two things.

First, that another plan had been hatched, and I was to play a part in it.

And second, whatever was about to occur in the Handler's office was known only to Yosef.

I said nothing to the three vicars, and they said nothing to me. The guards on either side of me grabbed my arms and swept me past them in silence, escorting me through the final door to see the Handler.

* * *

His office was colossal, with high gray walls surrounding the ornate wooden desk at the far end. My view was partially blocked by the guards to my front, but I knew where they were leading me: to the fixed chair bolted to the ground before the desk, its wooden facets bearing leather cuffs to restrain visitors for additional security.

"Do not put him in the chair."

The voice was unmistakable. While the accent was a peculiar one somewhere between South African and European, the tone was of a man obeyed immediately and at all costs.

The guards before me parted in deference, and then I saw the Handler.

I felt an odd mixture of respect and disgust for this man, our relationship becoming more complicated with every operation I did for or against him. He stood before me, rangy at over six feet tall, moving one of his spider-like hands in a messianic sweep that caused the guards to release their hold on me at once.

I watched the Handler's gaunt face angle away from me, skewed Roman nose cast downward.

"Leave us." The security detail vanished behind me, and I saw the only other person in the office.

The Handler's personal bodyguard stood off to the right, a stout man whose hands were open and relaxed, hovering a few inches off his hips. I called him Racegun because of his holstered pistol: a 1911 heavily modified for professional-grade competitive shooting. I'd never seen him use it, but the fact that the Handler had chosen him to be at his side assured me that Racegun was very, very good with it.

The Handler still didn't meet my eyes, looking instead to Racegun. "You too."

Racegun nodded and blinked as if he required more detail, but the implication was clear enough.

"Sir," he began in his polished Southern accent, "I must urge you that I am never to leave you alone outside the garden—"

"GET OUT!" the Handler roared, his entire body jolting as if electrified.

Racegun's hand opened and closed beside his pistol, eyes ticking between the Handler and me as if trying to determine which option he feared more—the Handler killing him for disobeying, or me killing the Handler in his absence.

Finally he bowed his head with the words, "I hear and I obey."

Then he swept out of the room, shooting me a resolute glance that said *I will kill you if you try anything.*

I didn't respond, my eyes finding the floor instead. I felt too numb, too detached, my proximity to the Handler a haunting reminder of Parvaneh's loss.

The door closed behind me, and the Handler and I were alone, together. I was completely unrestrained.

Could I kill him now, before anyone intervened? Probably.

Then a more disturbing question entered my mind.

Did he want me to?

For the first time since I'd entered, the Handler locked onto me with his amber eyes.

And then I realized the true reason he had banished even his personal bodyguard. It wasn't to speak to me in complete privacy.

It was because he was about to cry.

His tears began almost as soon as Racegun departed, spilling from bloodshot eyes and running down gaunt cheeks.

In that moment, he didn't appear the monster who had killed countless people, many of them my friends. He was simply a man in severe grief, and my heart ached for him just as it would for any parent who'd just lost their child.

He spoke slowly. "Tell me, David."

"Tell you...what?"

He rubbed at his chest then, his voice raw with emotion as he repeated the words, more softly this time.

"Tell me."

I broke his stare, a stab of pain spearing through my stomach.

"She died quickly. She didn't suffer. I'm sorry."

"Who was it—"

"Konstantin."

"Konstantin," the Handler repeated, his voice a gasp. Then, more forcefully, he managed, "Agustin watched, but Konstantin ended her life. Is that right?"

"Yes. Yes, that's right."

A long silence stretched between us before he spoke again. "You were the only one who cared for her as I did."

Now my eyes tingled with the onset of tears, my heartbeat feeling suddenly irregular.

"I cared for her," I echoed.

He gave a brief nod of concession, admitting his understanding of what we wouldn't speak in words.

"Even as a child, she was born to rule. She was fascinated by the security, the visitors, the trappings of my kingdom. This was all a playground to her."

He folded his hands behind his back, looking upward.

"I feared she would resist such an upbringing. But she embraced it. She always wanted to know more, to better understand the throne, to prepare herself to one day assume it. I did not have to explain to her why she must rise to the position I now occupy; instead I only had to explain why she was not yet ready."

A trace of a smile played on his face, the expression eerily incongruous.

Then his face fell into solemnity, and when he spoke again, his wistful tone was gone, never to return.

"I am beset by enemies on all sides, David."

I didn't need him to tell me that; I was beginning to grasp the bigger picture in a way I never had. I'd often wondered why the Handler had suddenly decided to remove his would-be assassins in the Outfit—myself included—by forming my team in Argentina. He could have killed us whenever he chose; after all, he'd known about all of us for some time.

His attempt to wipe us out wasn't random in its timing, but rather because he was in a position of great uncertainty. Forces had been building against him for some time, starting with the nearly successful assassination of Parvaneh in Rio, and continuing with his betrayal from within when he sent me on my deep cover molehunt. The fallout had forced the Handler to kill one of his top assassins, Sage, and his personal assistant, Ishway, both trusted insiders who had conspired to kill him.

Now he had an unprecedented unification of enemies old and new, and had just lost a strategic alliance that was now working against him. By all accounts there was once an era where no one dared challenge his reign; now there was scarcely anyone who *didn't* challenge it.

He continued, "I have died with my daughter. But your work is just beginning. I need you to do what you do best."

I wanted to show him the respect he was due as a grieving father. But whether due to my attachment to Parvaneh or my innate hatred for the man himself, I couldn't.

"What is the point to this?" I said. Then I pointed to the chair behind his desk. "As long as your throne exists, it will be sought by evil. Someone worse will always want to take it from you, and the more I see of this under-world the more I realize that evil seems to prevail."

"Why are you so ambivalent to power, David Rivers?"

"If what you have is power, then I'd prefer to be powerless. And you didn't answer my question. What is the end state of any of this? To keep fighting off opponents, making profit off a global criminal network? The only person who could have reformed your organization was your daughter."

"It is not about reform, but revenge," he said. "Do you remember what I showed you in my cabinet, David?"

I glanced at the tall cabinet looming behind him, intricate carvings of Oriental dragons covering its doors. I knew what lay inside, nestled against a hollow of deep purple silk and illuminated by display lights that would gradually brighten as the cabinet doors were opened. He'd opened those doors for me once before, the first and only time I'd seen the contents: his personal nuclear device.

At the time, the sheer awe of standing in that object's presence had overwhelmed me. And I could revel in that awe because I'd narrowly prevented the device from being detonated in a civilian population center. I'd touched the device, my knowledge of the sheer power encapsulated within sending a tingling, orgasmic sensation rippling throughout my entire body.

But now, it stood as a reminder that no matter how tragic Parvaneh's death, the stakes were much higher than her death alone. The Handler had always been mad; now he was teetering on a complete meltdown, and he maintained possession of a weapon that could incinerate a number of souls limited only by its blast radius. I'd been told that it contained only a small payload. Cognitively, I understood that its modest size was at least some assurance that this was true. However, size and destructive power were extremely relative prospects in relation to highly enriched uranium.

And I, of course, bore the ultimate responsibility.

I'd recovered that uranium from Somalia, not knowing what was inside my cargo, and I'd eventually been told that the Handler was acquiring it to remove it from the black market. Only later did I discover that he'd weaponized it almost immediately.

He had an excuse for that too, of course, and I recalled him coolly dismissing my obvious concern.

The usefulness of such a device is in the threat, not in its employment.

Theoretically, yes. But in reality, the usefulness of that device was whatever its master said it was.

And with Parvaneh's death, that master had gone completely and totally insane.

Controlling my voice, I said, "Yes, I remember what's in your cabinet."

"Then know this: the killing will never stop. Whether I am alive or dead, it will never stop. I will set into motion a chain of events that will long outlive me. If this Organization does not rule, then no other will. I am prepared to initiate mutually assured destruction. So the end state, David, is survival. At all costs. Tantamount to that, at present, is revenge. Which is the one thing you are ceaselessly tenacious about. That is why I need you."

"You want me to kill Agustin and Konstantin."

"*Are you mad?*" he almost shouted. Calming himself, he continued, "Agustin, yes. In time. But if you kill Konstantin, David, I will see you ripped limb from limb."

I slid my hands into my pockets. The fingertips of my right hand came to rest against the boar tusk. I considered whether to give it to the Handler, whether to tell him about it at all. The security team who had frisked me had certainly been curious, but they ultimately gave it back to me.

I decided to not only keep it but to carry it on my person until Konstantin was dead. Now the Handler was telling me I couldn't kill Konstantin at all.

"What are your plans with him?"

"Unspeakable anguish. You will not simply be a killer, David. We will crush their organization to the last man, but first you will bring Konstantin to me, alive. For he will witness the complete and total destruction of his empire before I allow him to leave this world. He will suffer more than any man before him, and when he reaches his grave it will be shared with Agustin."

"I've seen Konstantin's compound. It is too remote, and too well-defended, for an attack."

"Konstantin's compound is prepared for an attack, yes. But my Directorate of Intelligence has a lead, David, on a place where Konstantin is not so well defended. I need you to develop this lead, and when the time comes I will bring the wrath of God upon him, and then I shall turn my sights on

Agustin. I need you to be more than a killer. You must be my instrument of revenge. For me, and"—his voice shuddered—"for Parvaneh."

My heart sank. I wanted to kill the Handler; he needed to die for his many sins.

But not before a worse evil was slain.

What if I died in the process of pursuing Konstantin or Agustin? The Handler would live as he always had, my revenge no nearer to completion than in the moments after he destroyed everyone I cared about.

But right now, the only thing I knew for certain was that I couldn't live with myself, couldn't meet my eyes in the mirror, if I didn't willingly and wholly fling myself into the pursuit of the men who had killed Parvaneh.

The Handler couldn't do it himself. For all his power and omnipotence, he and all his staff at the Mist Palace weren't fighters, if they ever had been. And out of the many armed warriors at his disposal, none had the drive to see this mission through like I did.

I looked into the Handler's tear-streaked face. "I hear and I obey."

He yelled, "Enter!"

The door behind me flung open, and I turned to see guards spilling into the room with Racegun leading the charge.

Racegun's eyes immediately fell to my hands, then performed a visual scan of the Handler to check for injuries. He swiftly marched to the spot where he'd stood upon my entrance, where he could maintain an angle of fire that didn't endanger his primary.

The rest of the guards surrounded me, one at each side grabbing me by the arms to control my movement as they awaited his order.

"Take David to the Intelligence Directorate for his briefing. He is to be granted any resources he requires to accomplish his mission. I will see the vicars now."

The guards led me out of the office. We'd almost reached the door when the Handler spoke again.

"Wait."

The guards stopped me in place, spinning me to face him.

"What were her last words, David?"

My eyes wavered as I tried to recall. The events in that room were a blur now, a horrid juxtaposition of violence and terror. I remembered Parvaneh standing tall but crying, Konstantin leveling Micah's pistol at her.

And then she'd looked to me with one last request.

"She told me to take care of her daughter, Langley."

The Handler said nothing in response, didn't dismiss me or acknowledge that he'd heard.

Instead he turned his back to me in silence, and the guards swept me out of his office.

4

---

200 Feet Above Ground Level
Two Miles Southwest of Yakutsk, Russia

"*Ten minutes*," the pilot transmitted over my headset.

"Copy ten minutes," I replied, releasing the transmit button.

I was sweating inside my cold weather gear, but that wouldn't last much longer—as soon as the pilot opened the rear ramp, I'd be immensely grateful for each layer, despite the so-called summer that was drawing to a close in Siberia.

Attached to my parachute harness was an inverted rucksack of enormous proportions, so heavy it was painful to stand with, and I was grateful for not having to walk far with it.

The packing list I'd put together was remarkably short. Aside from the cold weather gear I wore, there was no need for clothes: I'd be provided local garb at my destination. The same went for food and water beyond some basic survival rations in case my contact missed the first linkup. I packed a primary weapon, a sidearm, and a folding knife, though none were intended for Konstantin.

No, if Konstantin were that ill-protected, the mission wouldn't have to begin like this. The Handler's Organization wasn't interested in tipping its

36

hand by sending in a large element that could alert Konstantin to our plans.

That was where I came in: a single agent, parachuting to link up with a covert local intelligence cell. My edict was open-ended: find a time and place to capture Konstantin. No timeline. No budget constraints. The local intelligence cell working against him was skilled at what they did, I was assured; according to the Intelligence Directorate, they just needed a bit of assistance. And, of course, funding.

This explained the majority of my pack's contents: close to a half-million US in non-sequential rubles. That money, and, more importantly, the ability to access more, was to hasten the intelligence cell's discovery of a viable opportunity to capture Konstantin. And once that opportunity was discovered, I'd employ the remaining items in my ruck: namely, a ruggedized computer with satellite link. This was the lifeline, the connection that could bounce encrypted messages across hemispheres. Because while I would be the only set of boots on the proverbial ground at present, anything I sent could be dissected, analyzed, and interpreted by the Handler's Intelligence Directorate.

Once a chance to capture Konstantin revealed itself, a single message from me would bring the entire Outfit to whatever location I requested. As many men as it took, with as many resources as they needed. And *that* was when things would get "kinetic," as trigger-pullers were fond of saying. By the time they arrived, the intelligence cell and I would have acquired whatever transportation assets were needed to get the Outfit to Konstantin's location undetected. Then the shooters would launch an epic assault to capture the Handler's enemy alive and exfiltrate him back to the Mist Palace.

It was a prisoner snatch, pure and simple; but first, I had to anticipate where the bastard would be.

"*Five minutes*," the pilot said.

I started to reply as the plane suddenly lifted upward before diving a moment later to send my heart lurching into my throat. I had a strong stomach, but this flight was pushing my limits.

Finally I replied, "Copy five minutes."

To subvert the risk of detection by Russian radar, the pilot flew a "nap-of-the-earth" flight plan, meaning as low as he could operate the aircraft without slamming into a hillside. He'd actually need to climb to attain the 400-foot altitude I required for a safe exit. Without the time to deploy a reserve parachute, I hadn't bothered wearing one. Instead I had only the BASE rig on my back, which I'd packed as if I were jumping from a rooftop of that same height, but with one small exception.

Instead of freefalling from the plane's ramp—a distasteful prospect when there were only seconds to impact—I'd rigged my chute for a static line deployment, so it would open immediately when I jumped. The process was similar to my combat jump in Iraq, except with one plane and one jumper instead of four planes depositing 154 Rangers behind enemy lines.

"Three minutes."

"Copy three minutes, going off comms. Thanks for the ride."

"Happy hunting, Suicide."

Hurriedly removing the headset, I returned it to its mount, then donned a full-face motocross helmet, the interior padding wrapping snugly around my head.

Struggling to rise against the weight of the rucksack, I felt across my chest strap for the metal surface of my static line snap hook. Unclipping it from its stowage point on my harness, I lifted it upward before the plane rocked violently. I almost fell, but managed to steady myself against the canvas seat beside me before making a second attempt.

This time I succeeded in clipping the snap hook onto the steel cable overhead. Now my parachute's bridle was attached to the aircraft via a double loop of break cord, which would hold strong as I fell away from the aircraft. Once my parachute was fully extracted from the container with no more slack to give, the break cord would exceed its maximum tensile strength and snap. The snap hook would remain attached to the steel cable, the plane would be gone, and I'd be on my way to linkup.

And if any of that went wrong, I'd have about two seconds to curse my luck before slamming into the dirt outside Yakutsk.

A red light ticked on next to the ramp, and a metallic groaning sound heralded the ramp lowering to expose the Russian countryside beyond.

A brutally cold vortex of air entered the cabin, chilling me to my core as the roar of wind rose in volume. The sound stabilized as the ramp locked into place, creating a ten-foot platform outside the aircraft, and I felt the plane level off at my 400-foot exit altitude.

I waddled forward onto the ramp, fighting the rucksack weighing against my thighs and holding my right arm up to tease the snap hook along the steel cable. Stopping at the edge of the ramp, I looked down onto the Russian countryside.

I couldn't see much in the inky darkness outside the aircraft, but as my eyes adjusted I could make out rolling hills and fields, and clusters of black trees scattered around a flat, slick lake surface.

The red light extinguished, and a yellow one replaced it. This was my thirty-second indication, an insignificant amount of time unless you had what felt like a giant sack of bowling balls attached to your harness.

But the distraction of my ruck's weight wasn't completely unwelcome. It took at least some of the attention away from what I was being sent for, yet again: to kill.

Yes, there would be some intelligence gathering, but it was a means to an end. Embracing the darkness had made me a proficient killer, an audacious operative with a near-suicidal risk acceptance. Maybe the greatest good I could achieve would be killing them all. Konstantin, Agustin, the Handler, and his vicars. It wouldn't save me, but it would surely help a lot of people under their tyranny.

But this presented two mutually exclusive possibilities: killing them all, and killing them simultaneously. Because it would have to be simultaneous. Any action against Konstantin and Agustin served the Handler and his vicars, and vice versa.

I considered yet again how this would be possible. In Argentina, my team had been surrounded by cartel militia, Hezbollah, and the Outfit. It wasn't unlike the current situation. And the only way to win was to play every enemy against one another—we'd staged a three-way gunfight and escaped through the gap. Only this time I didn't need to escape. I needed them to destroy each other, and if I was collateral damage in achieving that, then so be it.

But first, I'd have to locate Konstantin.

I gave another look down the ramp, seeing that the plane was still over the trees. My drop zone was only a small field, and once the plane cleared it I'd have a three-second window to exit without landing in the trees. The intelligence cell had insisted on a "blind drop," which meant no lights or markings to confirm the drop zone or signal the pilot that he needed to abort the jump. Instead, they'd simply given us a location and a one-hour window that the drop zone would be manned to recover me.

I didn't even have the name of anyone in the intelligence cell, save a single callsign: Pesets, which translated roughly as "arctic fox." Whoever Pesets was, he was apparently the brains behind a pre-existing effort to oppose Konstantin's organization, even before Parvaneh had been killed. Prior to that, Pesets and his people would have been an enemy of both the Handler's Organization *and* the Far North Coalition—so their survival to date was impressive, to say the least.

And now that the Handler was determined to destroy the Far North Coalition, Pesets had gone from enemy to ally.

The yellow light flickered, then extinguished.

Then the green light flashed on.

With two shuffling steps, I leapt off the ramp and into the black sky over Russia.

No falling was involved in the exit—the effect of leaping from a high-performance aircraft at four hundred feet was like being tethered to a train that suddenly yanked you forward at full speed.

I was sucked out horizontally, the howling sky eager to snatch me from the back of the plane. The engines faded to the warbled rustle of slick parachute fabric unfurling, and I pitched backward on a pendulum swing under an open canopy.

I ripped at a canvas tag to release my rucksack, its weight vanishing before tugging at me a moment later from the end of its fifteen-foot lowering line. This reversed the pendulum swing, and I rocked forward as I took control of both steering toggles. I felt like I was falling fast, but I couldn't gauge my height over the field—I had no depth perception in the darkness, and pulled my steering lines to a half-brake position as a safeguard.

I thought I heard the *thump* of my rucksack making contact with the ground, but before this thought could fully register, I felt the earth pummel my body with a force that sent my brain spinning into oblivion.

* * *

I was on a knee at the edge of Fryar Drop Zone outside Fort Benning. I scanned the darkness for some flash of red light, maybe the headlights of the bus that would take us back to our barracks. Where was my night vision?

Then I realized that I didn't recognize the gun in my hands. This was no issued M4 assault rifle, but instead a much heavier weapon with two pistol grips and a massive curved box magazine. What the hell was going on?

Beside me was my aviator kit bag, stuffed to full capacity—that much made sense, I'd at least packed up my parachute after landing. And holy shit, it hurt to bend over. My ruck must have weighed over a hundred pounds; I must have just jumped a full load of machinegun ammo along with the tripod.

Someone knelt in the dark beside me. I looked over, but couldn't make out their features.

"Are you okay?" a voice asked.

I gritted my teeth. "Yeah. Where's second platoon's assembly area?"

My voice sounded muffled, even to me; I realized I was wearing a full-face helmet.

I pulled it off my head and repeated, "Where's second platoon's assembly area?"

"Who are you?"

"Private Rivers. Second platoon, weapons squad. Gun Six. Remy's my gunner."

No response. Shit, if this was anyone over the rank of private, I was dead. And I definitely didn't recognize the voice, though my head was ringing enough that it was hard to discern the speaker's age.

"Follow me, Private Rivers."

I stumbled through the darkness after the figure. I was confused; I couldn't see much in the night, my brain ached, and my thoughts were cloudy and confused. After I fell hard in the brush, the silhouette of a person took my aviator kit bag and hauled my parachute for me. I didn't know how much time had passed. I sensed that there were gaps in my consciousness when my view suddenly blinked from dark woods to the open sky of a clearing.

Then I came to as if awakening for the first time—but now, I was in the passenger seat of a car.

41

This was a problem. It was forbidden to transport sensitive military equipment in a personally owned vehicle, and there wasn't a single Ranger who would risk losing their beret and scroll for such an infraction. The headlights lit a dirt road lined with forest on both sides—we could have been anywhere.

"Where's my equipment?" I asked. "My gun, where is it?"

A voice with a Russian accent replied, "In the trunk."

I looked to the driver...and realized I was in serious trouble.

This was no Ranger at all. Behind the wheel, operating the stick shift between us, was a teenage girl. Asian features and a round face, dark hair pulled into a ponytail. I was only nineteen, but she may have been even younger than I was. That placed her perilously close to the age of consent, and...wait. I shouldn't even be thinking about that, because I was engaged to Sarah.

Wasn't I?

No, wait. She'd cheated on me with my best friend, and we'd broken up just before I graduated West Point. Graduated...had I? I couldn't have; I hadn't even told my chain of command that I was applying yet. But the memories were there, my classmates tossing their hats in the air as I sat immobile, knowing my ex-girlfriend Laila was in the crowd.

Suddenly it all came racing back to me.

I was an agent of the Handler, seeking a source named Pesets who had the network to locate Konstantin. I'd just completed my third combat jump...third, right? Iraq, Somalia, Russia...did the BASE jump in Chicago count, after I killed Saamir? Probably not, that was CONUS—so my third combat jump, and I was on a mission of the highest priority directly sanctioned by the Handler. I was supposed to link up with agents who would take me to Pesets, follow the trail to Konstantin, and then...

Wait a minute. First I had to verify who I was with.

I cleared my throat. "My plane had engine trouble. I had to bail out, and I don't know where I am. Is this Saint Petersburg?"

She eyed me warily.

"It is a little late for bonafides, yeah?"

I hesitated.

"So this...isn't Saint Petersburg?"

She rolled her eyes and spoke in a monotone.

"Saint Petersburg is far to the west; you are in the land of Yakutia where the snows fall...it has been enough now, really. You parachuted from ten meters above the ground and probably need medical attention. Your callsign is Suicide."

"Where the snows fall...?"

She gave a heavy sigh. "Almost all the year round. Happy?"

I sat back in my seat, relieved. "You know who you're taking me to?"

"Pesets. Yes, I know."

"Good. Now I need you to tell me about anything that could threaten my transport to Pesets. Checkpoints, surveillance, that type of thing. Is there any possibility you were followed?"

"I thought the jump had knocked you senseless."

"The jump was fine. But the landing..."

"Now I realize you are a moron."

I tipped my head to the side. "What did you say your name was?"

"You may call me Susan."

"Doesn't sound very Russian."

"My birth name is Syuzanna. But I am changing it to Susan when I reach America."

Ah, so there it was. Part of Pesets's terms were for this girl to be relocated to America after the job was done.

"If Pesets delivers Konstantin, then you can consider any of his requests granted. My employer is highly motivated to see this mission through, to say the least. So am I. Now, what can you tell me about the threats we face? How will we talk our way through checkpoints?"

Susan shot me a glare, as if that was the dumbest thing she'd ever heard.

"Konstantin has his tentacles so far up the ass of Yakutsk that we need not trouble ourselves with this."

"I don't follow."

"What I mean to say is that if we are stopped, with fifty kilos of rubles in the trunk and you being a moron, there is nothing that will save us. Every police and *bandity* has their pockets filled by the Far North Coalition. We get stopped, with parachute, monies, someone calls the people we try to kill. I give you three guesses to the rest."

My stomach fluttered.

43

"Then let's discuss what we can affect. How do we capture Konstantin?"

"Capture, very difficult. Killing is easier."

"If we kill him, things won't end well for me. So let's concern ourselves with capture."

"What?"

"Where. Do we find. Konstantin." I was doing a poor job concealing my frustration, to be sure, but I needed to find out as much as I could from my driver before she dropped me off. I needed to repeat the process for everyone I met from this point forward, because I wanted to see what confirmed or contradicted the intelligence briefs I'd received prior to infiltration.

And in part, I wanted to gauge what she knew.

She didn't seem to take offense. "He is at headquarters now. Somewhere outside Norilsk...but this is impossible to attack."

I didn't bother telling her that I'd been inside that compound—she'd only ask her own questions, and I needed mine answered.

"Because it's in the middle of the arctic tundra. I agree."

"So the action will occur in Yakutsk. Konstantin and many top people keep homes here, and visit often."

"Why Yakutsk?"

She braked and downshifted, making a right turn onto an adjoining dirt road without stopping. Once the turn was complete, she half-glanced at me, once more implying that my question was ludicrous.

"Suicide, is this a serious question?"

"Call me David."

"Fine, *David*. I give you three reasons 'why Yakutsk.' The first reason is money. The second reason is money. And the third—"

"Wait. Let me guess the third: money?"

"Russia produces one quarter of the world's diamonds. All but one percent of those come from Sakha Republic, and the capital is Yakutsk. Shall we discuss our gold mines?"

"Thirty tons annually. I've heard."

"Reported export, maybe. But like our diamond mines, the Far North Coalition takes its cut first. They must, to pay the government not to crush them."

"Are you suggesting there is corruption? In *Russia?*"

"I hope your intelligence collection is better than your comedy."

"Only slightly. But wait until you see how well I kill."

"I thought they were sending a warrior. Not just a killer."

"What's the difference?"

She cast a suspicious glance my way. "Killers have no humanity."

"Humanity isn't the calling card of the man I've come here to find. If we're going to defeat Konstantin, we'll need to fight like him."

"But not become him, David. Correct?"

I hesitated. "Correct."

But in truth, I'd do whatever it took to bring Konstantin to the Handler's justice. Parvaneh and I both knew I'd lost my humanity; before her death, she thought I could regain it, reconstitute it like the pieces of a Faberge egg given enough time and distance from war. But even if Parvaneh was right, that chance was now gone forever.

And Konstantin was going to pay for that.

By way of changing the subject, I asked, "How do Konstantin's people get here?"

"Private charter jet from Norilsk."

"And from the Yakutsk airport to their estates?" I asked.

"A convoy of armored trucks."

"You have pictures? Routes?"

"Photographs and routes, yes."

"I'll transmit them back and find out the exact ballistic specs of the vehicle armor, and what weapons will defeat it. What do Konstantin and his people do when they're in town?"

The car rumbled from dirt road onto pavement, but we were still surrounded by woods. We passed a road sign in Russian as she replied, "Theater. Ballets, the opera. In the summer they hunt bear and boar. Some nights he stays home with his wife, others he stays at a hotel without her."

"A hotel would be a perfect place to snatch him." God, how I'd love to do a hit on a hotel room.

"Perhaps not so easy, David. These are hotels for Russian mafia. Armored rooms, certain floors you cannot get a room unless you are *bandity*."

"What about Konstantin's home?"

"We call it the street of billionaires. Gated access, walls surrounding the homes. Security is good, but that is not the real problem."

"What is?"

"His schedule. Konstantin's trips are not so predictable. I have been living this double life since two years ago, and I still cannot tell you when he arrives next."

I watched her for a moment before asking, "How did you get into this racket?"

She looked at me strangely. "Racket?"

"The job. Intelligence collection."

"Teenagers get little suspicion. Teenage girls, less so. I know the corners of this city, how to move without acting like a spy."

I squinted at her, cocking my head.

"No, I get that part—and it's brilliant. But what I mean is, why?"

"Why what?"

"Why does a teenage girl in Siberia spend two years hunting a crime lord like Konstantin?"

Susan kept driving, her eyes fixed on some distant point outside the windshield. But she said nothing in response.

* * *

After we reached the top floor of a building with no elevator, Susan opened the door to her apartment, and I staggered inside with my ruck to find a cramped, run-down space. The only thing worse than climbing a flight of stairs with a ruck was climbing eight of them.

Stripping off my ruck and letting it hit the floor, I tried to zero in on a noise I heard as Susan locked the door. But it wasn't one noise, it was lots of them—the sounds of her neighbors in the adjacent apartments. Beyond one wall, a couple was loudly arguing in Russian. From another wall, I could hear a couple making love with equal vigor.

"Cozy," I said. "I love it."

She pointed to the side and said, "My room."

Through an open doorway, I caught a glimpse of an acoustic guitar sitting at the foot of her bed.

"You play guitar?"

She ignored me, shifting her finger to a threadbare mattress in the corner of the kitchen. A moth-eaten blanket lay atop it in a heap. "Your room."

Fair enough.

I examined her in full lighting for the first time. Her features were Asian, but her high cheekbones and strong jaw were distinctly Siberian.

I folded my hands together, addressing her with curt professionalism.

"We'll need to set up an evacuation plan immediately. I'll need to assess the—"

"I know this, of course." She opened a cabinet, allowing me to see a brown bottle with a rag emerging from its neck. "One. I torch the apartment."

Then she jerked a thumb toward the next room. I peeked through the doorway into a closet, where a ladder was propped against the wall beneath a roof hatch.

"Two. We take the ladder to roof."

"And three?"

"Three. We jump."

"We...jump?"

"There is a lower rooftop across a two-meter space. The fall is eight stories if you miss. So, try not to miss."

She retrieved a hiking pack from the next room and tossed it to me.

"Split the money from your bag with this one. We stage them by the ladder."

I nodded toward the roof hatch. "Can I go up there and take a look?"

"I do not like exposing my escape route. You will figure it out."

"How do I know which building to jump to?"

"The other buildings are taller, except one. I am sure you will manage."

"Then what? After we jump, of course."

"Then you keep pace with me. Fire escape to street, then my second place. No need for you to know where—this way, you cannot talk if caught."

"What if *you* get caught, and not me?"

"Then there is nothing that will help you."

"Do you have any early warning systems?"

"Systems? I have little old woman on the first floor who sees everything. If anyone looking suspect enters, she will call. There is no elevator here—"

"I noticed."

"—so we will have maybe three minutes. Less if they are running." She placed her hands on her hips, squaring off to me. "Now can we discuss Konstantin, instead of ourselves?"

"Fair enough. The solution to predicting Konstantin's movements is an inside source. Do you guys have any prospects?"

"Better. We have a source."

"Just one?"

"Yes," she said scornfully, "*just* one."

"That's a start. What's his access to the Far North Coalition?"

"He is a soldier, but a trusted one. They use him when Konstantin comes to Yakutsk. But he learns of these visits only on the day they occur."

"Good. That could still be helpful. Let's go over the rest—what other sources of intelligence do you have on the Far North Coalition?"

"The source is it."

"Is what?"

"Everything."

I raised a hand to my ear, as if having trouble hearing what she'd said.

"I'm sorry, it sounded like you just said Pesets is basing your entire targeting effort off a single human source."

"He is."

My mouth went dry. I swallowed, bit my lip, then ran a palm over my face in an attempt not to spontaneously combust with rage. Finally I spoke in as measured a tone as I could manage under the circumstances. "I just flew halfway around the world, and jumped over Siberia to land so hard that it knocked me back in time. I brought you a small fortune in cash, access to a lot more, and I carry the radio link that will bring an entire army to bear against Konstantin. I'm reporting directly to the highest possible authority. And you guys have exactly one... alleged...source?"

"Not alleged," she replied casually, seeming amused by my discomfort. "He is as reliable as it gets."

"No, a single person is as *un*reliable as it gets. I don't care who he is or how you found him." I felt an uncontrollable urge to begin pacing, but the space was too small to do so. Instead I crossed my arms tightly, bile forming in the back of my mouth. "Without any other sources of intelligence, we won't even be able to corroborate what he tells you. For all we know, he's feeding you misinformation as a double agent."

"He is not. I trust him."

"That's another problem. Trust breeds complacency, and we don't have room for any of that right now. What does he want in return?"

She shrugged. "To move to America. A new beginning, same as me."

"What else?"

"A house. Money to start over. He will be forever hunted by the Far North Coalition for his betrayal."

I cocked my head and then shook it, almost in disbelief at her naivety. "If he delivers what you say he can, he will not be hunted forever. Because after my employer is done, there won't *be* any Far North Coalition. But let's not get ahead of ourselves. Our first order of business is to expand the number of intelligence sources."

"There are no others."

"Not yet. We'll have to locate and recruit additional sources. That's what I'm here for."

Susan threw up her hands in resignation. "You are not getting this, David. The Far North Coalition survives for a reason. The spine of this is family ties. The people with top access are related. Blood does not betray blood."

"What about your guy—is he related?"

"He is the next best thing. The family has known him since childhood."

"How did you find him?"

"I have known him since childhood, too." Her posture went rigid with her response, and I sensed I hit a nerve somehow. Not wanting to push my luck, I switched topics.

"All right. If your source is the second coming of Christ, how come he hasn't been able to deliver advance notice of Konstantin's location yet?"

"It has only been three weeks since he gets access to computer. It is on network of Far North Coalition. It has a USB drive—"

"Perfect. I'll send for a USB device with malware that will allow remote access. All he has to do is plug it in once, and a bunch of hacker dorks will tell us everything we need to know."

I thought she'd be impressed, but she shook her head dismissively.

"This will not work," she said. "Network computers will not open any device without encryption. And not just this; the encryption is custom to Far North Coalition and their mafia friends. So we must get one of these USB devices."

Impatience was eating me alive.

"Fine. Then where is the nearest USB device that will serve that purpose?"

"Nearest does not matter. What you need is least *defended*. And I have found a Russian mafia safehouse where men come and go with computers. We will find a USB there."

"Tell me about it."

"It is a farmhouse, far outside town. Three men are there at all times. After sunrise, I can get you close to see for yourself. Then we can recruit some soldiers. There are former army men living here. Your money can buy their services, and their silence."

"I don't trust their silence, and I don't need their services. Three men in a farmhouse? That I can freestyle."

"Freestyle?"

"Wing it. Do it myself."

She blinked, surprised. "Alone? They said they were sending a warrior, but—"

"They sent something better: me. And the longer we wait, the greater the chance that my infiltration is reported and everyone increases their defenses. Better to do it soon, let everyone assume it's not an outside party. Now, when can I meet Pesets?"

She squinted at me, a twinkle of mischief in her eyes. "When you get the USB, you can meet him."

"Fine. For now, I'm going to contact my people and explain the malware we need. Set up a meeting with your agent for tomorrow, then get me all your photographs of Konstantin's security here in Yakutsk. Vehicles, people, places, along with all your notes. I want to send it all to my headquarters by sunrise. After that, if there's time, we can sleep."

She gave a heavy sigh, turning to a cabinet and retrieving something from inside.

"That will take time. We shall need this."

Then she turned to me, a bottle of vodka in her grasp.

I felt my shoulders relax. "Thank God; you've got vodka."

"Of course. This is Russia."

"That's what I thought. Konstantin doesn't drink."

She set the bottle on the counter and procured a pair of glasses. "I am not surprised. You cannot trust a man who does not drink."

"Susan," I said, "I think you and I are going to get along just fine."

5

The following night was clear and dark, a ceiling of stars with minimal interference from manmade light. I saw only a few dim orbs from lamps or fires in the surrounding farmhouses, and the brisk air smelled of wheat and cattle manure. Other than the barking of dogs in the distance and the hum of a farmhouse generator, the night was nearly silent.

I was in the woods outside the small building that Susan had assured me was a Russian safehouse. An estimated three men were inside, all armed, along with unspecified mafia supplies, though I was only interested in a USB drive. The hit would be simple enough, at least in theory, and my daytime reconnaissance had confirmed two suspicions that became my first and second courses of action for this mission.

First, the remote farmhouse utilized an outside generator to supply its power. I could simply disrupt the generator, wait for one or more men to come out and investigate, and start schwaking people. Not a bad option.

But a power disruption would cause them to be on high alert as they investigated the issue, so I'd sided with option number two: exploit the outhouse.

I correctly assumed the presence of an outhouse meant regular departures from the back of the building, after which the man in question would have to re-enter. Interdicting that man for a silent kill near the outhouse allowed me to take his place on the return trip, to say nothing of exponentially increasing my chances of success by removing an enemy fighter from the ranks before they realized a fight had begun.

And if that plan failed, then I'd just shoot my way in.

This was less of a fantasy than it sounded, namely because I'd chosen the right weapon for the job.

Given the option to jump into Russia with whatever weapons I wanted, I'd chosen a folding knife and suppressed 9mm pistol as secondary weapons. For my primary firearm, I'd sided with a Saiga-12.

The stock, pistol grip, and back of the Saiga's receiver were Kalashnikov-modeled, so they looked almost like an AK-47. But the wide, stumpy barrel and forward grip and immense magazine were those of something else altogether: a gas-operated semi-automatic 12-gauge shotgun.

I'd chosen this as my primary weapon because I knew only one thing for certain—I'd be working out of some kind of safehouse, so I wanted something brutally effective in close quarters. If an assault rifle could clean house, then this Saiga would knock the fucker down completely.

But that shouldn't be necessary. My patience observing the house from the woods had paid off: I'd already observed the outhouse routine once. There wasn't too much to see—a man had ambled out the back door with his AK-47 slung over his shoulder, used the outhouse, and returned. As far as I could tell, the only re-entry procedure to the farmhouse was a triple knock. That much I could replicate, and then the fun would begin.

Or so I thought.

The nighttime temperatures were somewhere around freezing, which wasn't bad for this area—even Siberia had a summer, and this was it. My cold weather gear was sufficient to keep me from freezing to death. But being stationary for well over an hour by this point had taken its toll, and my fingertips tingled with numbness.

At long last, a gleaming rectangle of light appeared and vanished as the back door opened and closed. Now a single figure was marching solemnly to the outhouse, completing the last trip to the restroom he'd ever make. As before, he had a rifle slung around his back, the barrel pointed downward. I tucked the Saiga behind me on its sling, drew my suppressed pistol, and waited for him to enter the outhouse.

Once he did, I slipped out of the woods.

I closed the distance to the outhouse at a brisk walk, uncertain how long my quarry would take and wanting to be in position by the time he exited. Soon I was beside the outhouse, pistol at my side, waiting for the door to open.

The smell was unbearable, and I willed him to hurry. I'd joined the Army with visions of jumping out of planes and shooting people. Now I was waiting beside a Siberian outhouse, the last conceivable circumstance I would have ever envisioned myself in. If I'd given the matter any thought, it was probably the *last* circumstance I'd ever choose to be in.

After a shuffling noise inside, the outhouse door swung open. This was my cue—I waited to hear a single footfall on the ground, stepped sideways around the side of the outhouse, and cleanly leveled my suppressor at the center of the man's head. I pulled the trigger once.

The subsonic round impacted his skull with a *thwack*. He collapsed forward, hitting the ground in an awkward sprawl of limbs. No follow-up shot would be required— his body had settled without so much as a post-mortem twitch, the most anticlimactic kill I'd ever made. No matter; things were about to get fun in the farmhouse.

I holstered the pistol and readied my Saiga, the semi-automatic shotgun feeling reassuringly heavy in my grasp. Then I paused to insert foam earplugs—shooting a 12-gauge in a confined space threatened to impair what little hearing I had left.

I approached the farmhouse with the Saiga at the ready, now less than a minute from putting the weapon into action. The prospect brought a thrilling rush through my veins.

There wasn't a lot I was naturally gifted at. I'd never been an academic whiz kid, finding very little subject matter of interest and dedicating the minimum possible effort to achieve passing grades. Sports had never been my forte—sure, I liked running and working out, but team sports had always seemed beyond pointless. My disinterest was probably a good thing, because on those rare occasions when I did have to participate, I was terribly uncoordinated. As of my high school graduation, I'd never found a single thing to be passionate about.

Then I'd joined the Army.

And in the post-9/11 military, I'd found what I loved: adrenaline.

Sure, I could claim it was combat alone. But outside of deployments, I got my fix through skydiving and BASE jumping. When those started to wear off, I was able to push it further, jump from lower altitudes, deploy my parachute at the last possible second. Still, combat provided the greatest rush of all.

The more combat I was exposed to, the less functional I was in the normal world—stuck in a peaceful setting, my PTSD would have been debilitating if I didn't compartmentalize it so well. I couldn't sleep, existed in a constant state of muscle tension, and my brain operated at a ridiculous level of hypervigilance at the most inappropriate times. Sprinkle in a debilitating emotional detachment from other humans and chronic depression for good measure, and I was a virtual poster child for the war-weary generation of vets that nations produced with every major conflict.

But PTSD was a product of evolutionary psychology for a reason, and while I was no scientist, I knew one thing for certain: everything that worked against me in normal society made me highly functional in combat.

That reptilian alertness that made public places a nightmare in the normal world made me incredibly resilient in situations of high risk and split-second responses. The permanently degraded impulse to sleep allowed me to operate for extended periods at high functionality. And the lack of empathy for other members of my species made me proficient at killing with little hesitation and no remorse.

Going to war and earning a real PTSD diagnosis was like going to an Olympic training camp as a sprinter. The sprinter would fall apart if forced to a wheelchair, just as the warrior could fall apart when returned to peacetime. The sprinter excelled on the track, and the warrior excelled in combat —it was a matter of setting.

And I was about to enter the setting for which I was more suited than anything else in life.

I stepped up to the back door of the farmhouse, then vertically hoisted the Saiga so its barrel was pointed straight up, the muzzle just below chin level.

Holding the main pistol grip with one hand, I knocked three times with the other.

Murmured voices from within, the squeak of a chair.

Footsteps approached the door, but it didn't open.

Well, this was unfortunate. Was there some secret password I couldn't hear from the woods? I couldn't be sure.

I rapped my fist on the door three more times, pausing between each knock for emphasis. A deadbolt unlatched, then another bolt slid open. I angled the Saiga forward ever so slightly, aiming for head level with the buttstock pinned under my arm.

Finally the door pulled open—but only six inches, the motion stopped by a guard chain.

A set of ice-blue eyes appeared, thick eyebrows wrinkling in confusion before the man shouted an alarm.

"*Nas atakujut—*"

"Surprise!" I called cheerily, giving the trigger a firm squeeze.

The Saiga rocked with the blast, buttstock jumping between my rib and bicep. A blast of flame burst forth from the muzzle, momentarily blinding me. As I cocked a knee upward, my vision cleared to see a jagged hole in the door where the buckshot had ripped through. The man's head was dropping out of sight, his skull bearing a fist-sized pit of carnage.

I kicked the door in.

It hit the man's body, and I shoved a shoulder into it to force it halfway open as I lowered the Saiga inside.

Remaining in the doorway was a move of tactical idiocy, but I wanted to get the drop on anyone in the first room before they had time to react to seeing their doorman's face turned to jellied gore.

One man was leaping up from a corner table, AK-47 in one hand, and I took a reflexive shot that transformed his left shoulder into a cloud of flesh and blood. Good enough for now, I thought, swinging my weapon across the room toward another man staggering backward with his arms flailing.

I didn't see a gun on him, but you couldn't be too safe with these things. My first shot opened up his stomach, bowling him forward to eat my next load of buckshot to the top of his head.

And with that, the first room was clear.

Actually, that wasn't entirely true—as I stepped over the doorman's body, the man by the corner table was screaming and sliding on his non-injured side, fumbling for the AK-47 with one hand. The other was splayed out to the side at an awkward angle. My shot to his shoulder didn't amputate his left arm, but it may as well have.

His scream ended when a load of 12-gauge buckshot ripped through his sternum, and I advanced through the room toward a door at the far side.

That's where the good stuff was, I knew at once—the door was metal, with a keyhole on its handle. Always a good sign when you're seeking the interior entrance for something they wanted to protect.

I thought I heard scuffling beyond, but I couldn't tell for sure. Stopping at the side of the door, I knocked three times for effect.

A barrage of rifle fire pierced the metal door. Guess there was someone inside. But the man within wasted close to a full magazine in a panicked stand. He was probably trying to buy time for reinforcements—good, because I'd gladly service his backup force with the same care I'd taken with the three men in the back room.

I blasted the upper door hinge, then lowered the semi-automatic shotgun to blow off the lower hinge as well. Keeping my back tucked behind the wall, I drove a hard mule kick backward and felt the door fall inside the room.

Then I whirled in place, bringing the Saiga to my shoulder and slowly sidestepping to visually clear the space. The man within was clearly an amateur, but sometimes amateurs could be the most dangerous.

And this one, I quickly found out, was exactly that.

In an alarming flash of movement that surprised even me, he leapt into view like a marionette. His attempt at taking me by surprise worked; I had just swung the Saiga barrel to his chest when his AK-47 sputtered three rounds into the wall next to me and went dead with a *click*.

I halted my trigger squeeze, taking in the man's features for the first time. His bearded face, already pale, now went white. He was pudgy, clad in long underwear, and with a glance to a bed with its blankets askew, I realized I'd woken him from his slumber.

"What's the matter?" I asked. "Reload."

He said something in Russian, shaking his head. But his eyes darted to a table where a trio of AK magazines were stacked.

Beside them was a computer with a USB drive plugged into it.

"Da, da, comrade," I said reassuringly. "Go ahead; I'll wait."

With that, he spun toward the table and fumbled for a fresh magazine. He clanged it into the empty magazine, then tried and failed to remove it. Setting the fresh magazine back down, he stripped the old one and...what the hell, I thought. This was taking too long.

I blasted him between the shoulder blades. The load of buckshot ripped through his spine and decimated his heart on the way out, and the man's body crashed onto the table before rolling sideways to the floor.

Then I reloaded the Saiga with a full ten-round box magazine, hearing the roar of a vehicle engine approaching the front of the house. I snatched the USB drive from the computer, knowing I could easily escape out the back door and lose any pursuers in the woods.

I had just the slightest moment of debate, and in the end the process of brutally killing people felt cathartic after Parvaneh's death. I wanted more of it. Hell, I'd just crossed the globe to get here, and who knew how long the effort to locate Konstantin would take.

I could have a little fun, couldn't I?

Stepping over the slicks of blood, I entered the front room and unlocked the door, pulling it open an inch. Then I tucked myself into the blind corner beside it, hearing the vehicle approaching, the sound of gravel spraying beneath its wheels.

Kneeling in the corner, I heard car doors opening and slamming. A rush of footsteps toward the entrance. Sure enough, these clowns were going to charge right through the main entrance.

The first man entered, then a second, moving quickly in an effort to reach the back room to protect the computer. I hit the lead man in the small of his back, the second in his rib, and then swung the Saiga toward the front door where a third and final man was desperately trying to reverse his forward momentum.

He saw me with terrified eyes, and contorted his arms to bring a pistol to bear on my corner. To his credit he was actually pretty quick; but to my credit I already had the Saiga's barrel lined up with his profile, and ripped another blast that shredded through his pelvis and caused him to drop in place.

The car peeled out on loose gravel—I considered giving the driver a parting gift through his rear windshield, but decided I'd pushed my luck more than enough for one night. Waiting for the reaction force had scored me three kills in about five seconds—actually, that wasn't correct. It scored me three *wounded* enemy in about five seconds. I'd need just a few more seconds to turn them into definitive kills.

Rising from the corner, I tried to ascertain which man was closest to shooting me only to find that none of them were. One was motionless, possibly dead already. Another was in no danger of returning fire, groaning with his pistol lying out of reach. The third, who'd been quick on the draw in responding to his two fallen comrades, was bleeding out from a severed femoral artery and too weak to move but watching me with an expression of disbelief.

He couldn't believe his fate—the Russian mafia had been operating in this area uncontested, protected from on high by Konstantin's Far North Coalition. Now they'd just had a safehouse and a reaction force knocked out in the span of a few minutes by some mercenary they'd never seen before.

I walked over to them and dispatched each man with a head shot.

Reloading again as I walked into the back room, I stopped before the computer and raised the Saiga barrel toward my face. The muzzle's black metal was a portholed cylinder, its edge carved in a shark's-tooth pattern so it could be held in place against doorframes when a breach was necessary.

Scalding heat radiated from the muzzle, its warmth like the glow of a campfire as I breathed the intoxicating scent of burning gunpowder and hot metal. A ghostly white wisp of smoke spun upward, and I blew it away from the barrel like a Western gunslinger who had just vanquished his opponent in a quickdraw.

Then I lowered the Saiga, removing my earplugs and giving a final rearward glance at the carnage in the farmhouse.

"Well, that was fun."

* * *

"What happened back there?" Susan shouted from behind the wheel, whipping her car in a right turn onto a main road. "What took so long?"

I rubbed my right shoulder, tender from the Saiga's repeated recoils.

"Relax, I was only in there a couple minutes."

"How many men did you kill?"

I considered the irony of having a teenage girl yelling at me like an enraged babysitter. But in her defense, I had to think about the answer to her question for a moment—always a sure sign of a great mission, particularly when you went in alone.

"Let's see," I began, "there was the doorman plus two in the back room,

59

another with the computer in the back. Then three from the response force, so...four plus three is seven. Right? Seven."

"This is not..." Susan stammered, "this is not any good." Then she braked for an intersection so hard that I lurched forward against the seatbelt.

"What's wrong?"

"What is *wrong*, David, is that one dead mobster would be a big deal to these people. Three in one night is maybe worth it for the USB. But they will search until they find someone to blame and kill." She flexed her hands around the steering wheel and spat, "*Seven?* Seven dead men brings a search party, and not just Russian mafia. Konstantin will send people to help them. They will punch out the insides of Yakutsk to find who did it."

Before the response could leave my mouth, she accelerated so fast that it threw me back against the seat.

"Actually," I said tentatively, "I forgot about the outhouse guy. So, eight kills."

"*Sran' gospodnja!*"

"What's the problem? You've got a good safehouse."

"It is a good safehouse until these people take a microscope to Yakutsk. With seven dead *bandity*—"

"Eight," I corrected her. "The outhouse guy, remember?"

"—they will not stop looking for who did this."

"Unless I stacked those bodies, we wouldn't have this." I held the USB drive so she could see it, then pocketed it again. "What if I ran out the back instead of ambushing those last three guys, and one of them shot me from behind?"

Her thin eyes narrowed further as I continued.

"Besides, we had an arrangement. I get the USB device, and you introduce me to Pesets. Now, when can I meet him?"

Now she actually smiled, the expression unnerving.

"What?" I asked.

"You already have."

"*You're* Pesets?"

"You sound disappointed.'"

I looked to the dashboard, sucking my teeth with my tongue and trying to be patient.

"Seriously, Susan," I began. "Seriously. When can I meet him?"

"I told you. You already have."

I felt my body temperature rising and tried to force diplomacy into my voice.

"You don't strike me as dramatic enough to name yourself 'arctic fox.'"

"*Pesets* means arctic fox. *Pizdets* means something is fucked up. So, the arctic fox is a Russian symbol for something that is fucked up. I picked it because Konstantin rules this land as a king, when he should be dead."

"I hope you're joking. Because my employer—fuck, Susan, I, fucking *I*, have business to settle with Konstantin. And if I don't deliver him alive, then—"

"He raped my mother."

The words stopped me cold.

She continued, "His men held her down, and he raped my mother. And when he was done, they killed her."

"What about your father?" I asked.

"He died when I was young."

"So you're an orphan," I said. "Just like me."

She looked at me contemptuously.

"I doubt your parents met so gruesome a fate in America."

"You're right. They didn't. But Konstantin took something from me too."

She twisted her head away, saying nothing.

"He killed someone I was in love with. Right in front of me, as his men watched."

She was unmoved, gazing straight ahead through the windshield, so I continued.

"He gave me something before he did it. Do you want to see?"

This piqued her curiosity, and she looked at me with inquisitive eyes.

"He gave you...what?"

I reached into my shirt collar, pulling the leather thong necklace off my head. Holding my fist between us, I let the boar tusk pendant drift in a pendulum. Her mouth was open, eyes riveted to it as if she were succumbing to a hypnotist's watch.

She reached for the tusk and I snatched it away, dangling it before her awestruck eyes.

"When Konstantin is dead, I'll give this to you. You have my word, Susan."

She glowed at this prospect, until I added, "But not before."

Then I put the necklace back on, tucking the boar tusk back into place against my skin.

"Very well," she conceded. "When we return, you put malware on the device. Tomorrow, I give USB to the agent."

I felt the USB device in my pocket. "What kind of transfer? Are you guys using a dead drop?"

"We meet face to face."

I winced. "That's dicey."

"Dicey?"

"Dangerous. What if he's followed? What if you're seen?"

"Our system has worked just fine before you came here and started piling up bodies. It will work tomorrow."

"Good. I want to meet him."

"Absolutely not!"

"Why not? If this guy's our only hope, if I'm going to be killing for him, then I want to look him in the eye and know what we're working with."

"He...he could identify you, then. If he is caught."

"Konstantin's seen my face already. And my death will not stop my employer."

I wondered why Susan was fighting me on this point. It wasn't like I was going to expose her source. But I took her sudden silence as acceptance of my demand, however begrudgingly.

Her frustration about the farmhouse hit was slightly more understandable, though I still didn't care. After Parvaneh...hell, after all of it—Boss's team, Karma, my inability to kill the Handler despite dedicating my life to that sole task—I was ready for payback. To slaughter, to punish, to administer wrath any way I could, and as painfully as I could. I didn't particularly care if I was killing mafiosos, Konstantin's servants, or Agustin's people. To me they were all fair game.

And truth be told, the fight made me feel *sane*. I was unquestionably maladjusted in normal society, and with each mission I lessened my chances of ever readjusting to regular life. Maybe those chances were gone already; maybe they'd been gone for some time.

So it was strangely refreshing to be back in a situation where my many idiosyncrasies, all the physiological results of exposure to combat, worked in my favor rather than sabotaging my every action and relationship as they did back home.

I looked over at Susan, who was steering with both hands flexed tight against the wheel.

"So, you guys have pizza here in Yakutsk? Because I'm starving."

6

When our lone source entered the apartment the next afternoon, I saw at a glance that he wasn't much older than Susan.

He may have been nineteen at best, with gangly oversized hands and feet that he had yet to grow into. He had dark hair, thick eyebrows presently compressed into a scowl, and intense brown eyes that ticked from me to the counter, where the vodka bottle—considerably drained—rested beside our two glasses from last night.

Susan said, "David, this is Roma."

Before I could introduce myself, Roma's face contorted in an emotion I couldn't immediately place.

He jabbed a finger at me, glaring at Susan as he spoke. "*Kto on nahren takoj,*

Syuzanna?"

Then I placed the emotion, and everything became clear.

It was jealousy.

"I'm David," I answered.

"I said nothing to you," he shot back, turning to Susan and speaking in Russian.

No wonder she had been reluctant to introduce me. She hadn't wanted me to know that her source was also her lover. Her concern was, of course, misplaced—few forces on earth were more motivating than the sex drive of teenage boys, and I had no doubt that Roma would take risks in the pursuit of Susan's interest that would make even me blush.

Susan replied in English, "David is the contact they sent. He will help us."

"I'm the guy," I added, "who can bring in an army of shooters to take down Konstantin for good. And take you and your girlfriend—"

"Syuzanna is my *fiancée*," he said hotly.

His response elicited a painful tightness in my throat. In that moment, the sight of Roma and Susan reminded me of myself and Karma. I existed in a perilous line of work— Karma had briefly lived on that edge, and died for it. Now Susan was on the same edge, risking her life in a game of chance in which I held the only real knowledge of the dangers.

I swallowed. "I will bring you and your *fiancée* to America when this is all over. My employer will take care of the details for your relocation to a place of your choosing, including a new house."

"As long as I give you Konstantin."

"That's right, Roma. As long as you give me Konstantin."

"How soon can you bring this...this 'army' of shooters?"

"Once you can give me some actionable intelligence, they can be wheels-down within twenty-four hours."

He nodded. "There is going to be a big meeting in Yakutsk. Soon. I do not know precisely where."

"Konstantin will be there?"

"Yes. They do not bring this much security for nothing, I will tell you."

"Who's he meeting?"

Roma frowned. "Someone named Agustin, I think."

My heart dropped into my stomach.

"Agustin...what?"

"V something. Villalobos, Villanueva, something like this."

"Villalba?"

He snapped his fingers. "Yes. Agustin Villalba."

I felt my pulse speed up. Just bagging Konstantin would be a massive achievement. If we could get him *and* Agustin in one fell swoop, it would be beyond extraordinary.

And what better opportunity would we have? None, so far as I was concerned. The Handler had promised me every possible resource, and I fully planned on mobilizing the entire Outfit on Russian soil when the moment was right. With me acting as the lone, undetected agent, and the Outfit deploying for a highly classified, no-notice mission, we could conduct one epic mission before the word got out.

But you could only do something like that once; if we surprised Konstantin with such a massive raid, then the odds of repeating that success with Agustin went down exponentially. He'd go underground, employ body doubles and counterintelligence, do anything and everything that Konstantin had not.

With Konstantin and Agustin in one location, we could hit them with everything we had—and by getting both at once, I'd be left to take down the Handler for good. All I had to do was stroll through the hidden tunnel that Parvaneh had inadvertently revealed, catch him in the garden alone, and kill him. Game over. With Konstantin and Agustin gone, no more impediments stood in my way.

Warily, I asked, "You're certain about this, Roma?"

"I am certain. If USB works, you will soon be certain as well."

"What else do you need?"

He shook his head. "Just some time to be alone with the network computer."

"Guns? Money? People killed?"

"No. Just the USB device. But I will tell you," he said with a wily grin, "you had better hold up your side of the deal. Me and Syuzanna get a new start, in America." He quickly added, "In Colorado, to be exact."

"You can get a new start in Monte Carlo for all my employer cares. Money isn't an issue for him, the information about this meeting is. You need *anything* else to get it, I want to know first thing."

I handed over the USB and Roma took it, turning it over in his fingertips as if examining it closely. But his eyes were locked on Susan.

"Ten seconds," I said, causing him to break his stare. "Plug that into the network computer for at least ten seconds, then remove it. After that, destroy the USB device before anyone finds it on you. Any questions?"

Roma pocketed the USB device with one hand, using the other to give me a dismissive wave. "I will get it done. Not for you, but for Syuzanna."

Then he stood wide, posturing for Susan's benefit. I should have been concerned with his teenage theatrics, and considered warning him against overconfidence in the events to come.

But instead, for reasons I couldn't explain, I felt an undeniable gut instinct that Roma was going to deliver.

7

I awoke suddenly that night when Susan kicked me in the ribs.

"Get up!" she cried. "They are coming!"

I scrambled to my feet, throwing on my boots as Susan strapped on her hiking pack.

By the time I got my ruck on, she was holding a lighter to the long rag leading into a Molotov cocktail, igniting the fuse.

She nodded toward the ladder.

"Go, David."

I took the bottle from her, angling it so the burning rag hung free rather than extinguishing against the side of the bottle.

"You go."

She didn't argue, wheeling in place and darting up the ladder.

I briefly wondered how much warning she had, or whether she was overreacting to a false alarm.

But I didn't have to wonder for long.

Through the apartment's paper-thin walls, I heard footsteps racing down the hall. Five men, maybe six—I felt my eyes drop longingly toward my mattress, where the Saiga rested fully loaded.

It was calling to me and I wanted to answer that call. I could blast every fucker who entered the apartment, then toss the Molotov cocktail on my way out. This was an opportunity to kill people who oh-so-desperately deserved it, then make good on my escape.

But wanton killing had gotten us into this situation in the first place, and so I reluctantly flung the bottle at the front door just as the footsteps closed with it.

The glass shattered on impact, spawning a wide pool of liquid blue flame that splashed against the wall, the floor, the door. A blast of heat hit me like a shockwave, and I fled toward the ladder.

Susan had already vanished, and I climbed the rungs toward the open hatch. My head cleared the roof under a freezing night sky just in time to see her sprinting toward the edge and taking a flying leap off it.

Pulling myself onto the rooftop, I ran toward the edge to find her ruck-sack abandoned at my feet. She was waving urgently from the adjacent lower rooftop, and I looked down to see an eighty-foot fall in the narrow gap between buildings.

Stripping off my ruck, I grabbed a shoulder strap in each hand and twisted my upper body sideways, hurling the ruck as hard as I could. I reached for her hiking pack the second I released my own, and glanced to see that she was darting out of the way to avoid being hit by the huge projectile. It had barely cleared the edge, but what the hell—it wasn't like I was tossing a baseball here.

I repeated the maneuver, flinging her hiking pack with all my might. It sailed over the edge, traveling slightly farther than the first and rolling to a stop past Susan as she put my ruck on.

I could hear the crackle and hiss of flames through the hatch as I darted away from the edge, skidding to a halt and reversing my direction of movement to charge back the way I'd come. Thanks to BASE jumping I had plenty of experience with timing the final running steps to coincide with a concerted leap off the edge, but it hadn't prepared me for landing on my feet a few seconds later.

I timed my last running footfall to strike just short of the edge and launched myself into a wild, arcing freefall toward the opposite roof.

But as I sailed over the six-foot gap to the opposite rooftop, easily clearing the far edge—to my credit, the distance of my jump beat Susan's— it became apparent that I had an obstacle to contend with: Susan's hiking pack.

My boots struck the roof, and I tried to tuck into a sideways roll as I would for a hard parachute landing. But my forward momentum didn't translate well to this effort, and instead I bounced a shoulder off the roof and was launched on top of her bulging hiking pack, my sternum and abdomen absorbing most of the impact.

Every ounce of life-giving oxygen felt as if it were being expelled from my body in the same millisecond, and I rolled sideways off the hiking pack and onto my back. I tried to will myself to move, to grab the pack and run, but my body responded with a choking suck for air that yielded nothing but a hollow suction and a rising sense of panic.

Finally I was able to move, but just barely. The hiking pack was heavy and I still couldn't breathe, so every effort was like holding my breath while moving in slow motion after being sucker-punched in the gut by a professional wrestler.

The end result was me half-crawling, half-dragging the hiking pack toward the distant handrails of the fire escape. Susan was nowhere to be found, and since she'd put on the first ruck I threw off the opposite roof, she now had the ruggedized computer that served as my vital link with the Mist Palace.

And as I crawled forward with agonizingly slow progress, it became clear that she'd left me to my fate. My mind was screaming for oxygen that my lungs remained unable to breathe as I processed a singular thought: *well, isn't this a peach.* Exactly what this mission needed in the eleventh hour before we found Agustin and Konstantin's meeting location—to have my safehouse compromised, my radio stolen, and to be abandoned by my single direct contact in the whole of Russia.

Just then, Susan's face appeared ahead of me, between the rails of the fire escape leading down over the opposite edge.

She clambered back into view, racing toward me and squatting beside me. "This is your fault, imbecile."

Then she scooted backward, dragging her hiking pack toward the fire escape and leaving it there to repeat the process with me. I tried to assist her with my weak attempt at crawling, but my mind was entering a gridlock of sheer panic because I was suffocating.

Then I managed a thin inhale, and the barest hint of air entering my system revitalized me. My brain was screaming at me to remain stationary, to suck in oxygen until my vital signs had come close to returning to normal. But this was an emergency, and by the time Susan had released her grasp on my shirt, she'd dragged me most of the way to the fire escape.

I reached forward to feebly grip a handrail, and Susan picked up the hiking pack beside me and dropped it off the side. It clanged to a stop on some metal landing below, and she hoisted me up by the shoulders as I struggled to find my footing. After a second breath of air, I managed to begin my descent with Susan clanging down the rungs on top of me, her feet stepping on my hands when I didn't move quickly enough for her liking.

By the first landing I was able to fill my lungs; by the time I donned my ruck and descended to the second, adrenaline was able to compensate for my diminishing oxygen debt.

Then Susan pushed me out of the way, moving quickly as I struggled to follow her to the streets of Yakutsk.

* * *

We were on the move for twenty minutes—not an inordinate sum of time, but it seemed considerably longer when carrying rucks full of cash and equipment. Finally we entered an alley, and Susan knelt beside a padlocked cellar door and inserted a key.

She flung open the two doors and we descended stone stairs into a dank cellar, dark except for the flashlights we procured from our rucks.

I whispered, "Where is this place?"

"The basement of a bakery owned by a friend of my mother. We will be safe here. Comfortable, no; but safe."

"Good."

"Good? David, do you not feel even a little bit bad?"

"No."

"Guilty?"

I thought for a moment. "Not really."

"You should. You just cost me my home."

"Your home is in America now, because we'll see this thing through."

"Our chances are much worse now. They know my name, and they will be looking for me."

71

"Does this mean that they know your connection with Roma?"

"No," she admitted. "He was always careful with his visits."

"Then we're still on. Any chance you saved that bottle of vodka on the way out?"

"This is not funny."

I knelt beside my ruck and began setting up my communications equipment.

"What are you doing?"

"Making contact," I said. "I need to report our new location and that we were blown out of our safehouse."

"Safehouse? How about my home, and everything I own?"

"Either. Both." The ruggedized computer screen glowed to life, and I quickly typed a new message.

But to my surprise, an alert notification flashed—I had a new message from the Mist Palace.

"That guitar belonged to my father," she said as I began reading the message. "He taught me to play..."

My eyes were leaping across the text, first in disbelief and then in jubilance.

"...so in addition to almost getting us killed, you have cost me the one thing that even your employer cannot replace."

I smiled, and then let out a laugh that grew wild, unrestrained, until I had to force myself to quiet down. I felt weightless, as if I would float away at any second.

"Oh, this is funny to you? Let me go to America and fucks up your entire world, then—"

"It's *fuck* up. Fuck, singular. And forget about all that. It worked."

"What?"

"Roma's emplacement of the USB drive, the malware to enable remote cyber access."

"Of course it worked. We knew it would, yeah?"

"Not this well, we didn't. My people obtained the time and date for Konstantin and Agustin's meeting. We've got just over two days. The shooters are mobilizing now, and their plane launches in a few hours. You and I will need to receive them."

"This is great!"

"There's just one problem: the location is a coded site. *Krassny Sem*— Red Seven. Does that mean anything to you?"

"No. But it will to Roma. The Far North Coalition has coded sites all over Yakutsk. If Roma does not know, he will find out."

"Ask him."

"It is unwise to send this information. If they connect my apartment with this phone number, they will be listening."

"What do you suggest?"

"I will send him instead to my own coded location. We can ask him to his face tomorrow evening."

"Where?"

"Well not at my apartment, thanks to you. Since that location is no longer safe."

That was an understatement. I guessed that the apartment was no longer an apartment at all—just a smoldering heap of ash, along with at least part of the adjacent units on the top floor.

"I feel like I've apologized for that multiple times—"

"You have not. We will meet him at the street market, you imbecile. A public place where we can speak without attracting attention."

8

We arrived at the street market in early evening. The sky was a peculiar cornflower blue in the narrow gap between sunset and nightfall, the hue bleached out by the glowing orange-yellow streetlights bleeding through the mist. It was just below freezing, colder than any night since I'd parachuted into Yakutsk. But that brought its own advantages—namely, the opportunity for coats, hoods, and hats that more or less concealed our faces.

I wore my suppressed pistol beneath my coat and had pocketed my folding knife. Together they were the last vestiges of weaponry that I'd jumped into Siberia with: the Saiga had gone up in smoke with Susan's apartment. And while I had all the money in the world to buy guns, Susan had been adamant that doing so in the wake of eight dead mafiosos and one torched safehouse would be too high profile.

Street vendors lined both sides of the sidewalk, their wares ranging from clothes to food. Pedestrians strolled the walkway, carrying shopping bags in mittened hands and bartering with salespeople.

Susan and I walked with arms interlocked, which she insisted would help us pass the fleeting scrutiny of any passersby who cared to examine us. The bottom of her face was hidden beneath a scarf under her hood, and to her credit we garnered no overtly suspicious stares. All I had to do was keep my American-accented voice to myself, and we were home free.

We came to a stop at the edge of a long row of clothing for sale, and Susan pretended to browse the hats.

Roma approached from the opposite direction, his face ringed by the hood of a green coat. His cheeks were flushed—I assumed with cold, until he spoke.

"I do not care who you are. If you put my Syuzanna in danger again, I will kill you."

"Keep your voice down," I said quietly. If he blew this handoff by running his mouth, I was going to show him what real danger was. "*Krassny Sem*—Red Seven. What does that mean?"

He edged closer to me. "It is a safehouse. With a conference room. *Prospekt Lenina 74*. Susan knows this place."

Susan nodded. "I can show you."

"Wait for further instructions," I said to Roma. "We'll be in touch."

I turned to leave when Roma shoved my shoulder blade from behind.

"I mean it, asshole. If you get Syuzanna hurt, then I will hurt you."

God, how I wanted to strip off my ridiculous puffy coat and fight him on the spot. This was just what we needed, some stupid teenage ego mucking up what should have been a two-second handoff.

"Come on, Susan," I said, giving Roma a hard final stare.

He didn't return it.

Instead he was looking at some fixed object over my shoulder, and I turned around to see a pedestrian stopping abruptly to stare at us.

The man's eyes widened at the sight of Roma, and then he looked to me and Susan before he took off running in the opposite direction.

Roma stammered, "He...he saw me..."

I didn't ask questions, and I didn't announce my intentions. I could see in Roma's face that he'd just been burned, and we were about to lose any chance of cornering Konstantin and Agustin in one place.

That opportunity was almost within our grasp, so close I could feel it. I could almost taste the victory in the cool night air. And I wasn't going to let it slip away.

I took off after the man, running toward the receding figure I'd only glimpsed for a second.

But that second was enough.

He was racing away down the main strip of the market, disappearing past a group of shoppers as I bolted after him.

A man and woman shopping saw me coming and darted out of the way, but the group behind them didn't, and I shouldered through their ranks while roughly shoving a teenager out of the way.

Then I accelerated to a full sprint. My opponent had a thirty-foot head start on me, long enough for me to close the gap if he tripped, or for him to escape completely if I stumbled.

My boots pounded across the pavement, and I swerved around an elderly shopper. The sky was thick with chilly fog, turning the street lights into blurry gold orbs. Tables on either side were heaped high with folded clothes, mannequin torsos bearing thick coats, and vertical displays where winter hats of all colors rested atop pegs.

The area on either side of the market strip—a street to the left, commercial storefronts to the right—was alternatingly visible and blocked by long rectangles of blue tarp erected as a windblock. If my quarry ducked sideways out of the market at the right moment, I could lose him entirely.

I shoved a man in a fur hat out of my way, realizing only as I did so that his black coat bore a police badge.

He shouted something at me in an authoritative tone—and while his words were in Russian, I could reasonably assume he yelled some variation of "stop." And while I could have tried to drop him with one or several well-placed blows, I couldn't afford to take my eyes off the man trying to distance himself from me.

I was at maximum running speed, my lungs aflame with freezing air. The cop was shouting behind me, his voice far too close, and bystanders were darting out of the way to accommodate his pursuit. Even if I could outrun him, he was drawing too much attention—as soon as another cop heard his cries, I'd have more peace officers stacked against me than I could handle.

Darting between cars at a street that bisected the market, I saw that the man I chased was looking left and right, seeking a place to exit the walkway.

Within seconds I was going to lose visual or, worse, drag the cop toward a man I desperately needed to silence. As I entered the market on the far side of the street, I passed a wooden stand whose compartments were filled with frozen fish. I yanked it sideways to the tipping point, sliding past before it crashed down behind me.

A sudden gasp rose up from the bystanders followed by the sound of a stumbling crash, and I glanced back to see the cop sliding face first amid a pile of frozen fish bodies.

I laughed as I returned my eyes forward, but the smile vanished from my face as I realized the man I was chasing was gone from view.

Christ, no. I sped forward, feverishly looking around the last spot I'd seen him for any indication of where he went. Short of his figure, I had no idea what I was searching for, no indication whatsoever to guide my instincts. I searched bystanders for puzzled expressions that would indicate his direction of movement, maybe someone pointing after him. But there was nothing; he was simply gone.

Wheeling sideways, I looked down an alley lined with a row of 55-gallon drums that blazed with flaming trash. My eyes were drawn to a single dark object on the ground beside one of the cans, and with my target gaining ground with every passing second, I decided that object was as good of an indicator as anything.

I bolted down the alley, seeing that there was indeed a partially open door leading into a building. Reaching beneath my jacket, I tried to draw my pistol as my eyes took in the object on the ground.

It was a discarded glove.

At once I knew I was still on his trail. He'd stripped one glove off, and my mind screamed *gun*. He had a pistol, and was waiting in a hasty ambush.

I fumbled for my pistol beneath my coat, desperately trying to reverse my momentum before I skidded to a halt before a partially open door. But I had too much speed to stop in time; I tugged at my pistol to find it snagged beneath my coat, and I was still fumbling for it as I crossed the doorway.

I entered a storage room piled high with crates, and standing among them was the man who'd escaped me.

His bare hand was empty, and in his gloved hand he wasn't holding a pistol at all.

It was a cell phone: he'd taken off a glove to dial.

His eyes registered immense fear at the sight of me—until it dawned on him that my pistol was caught beneath my coat.

He raised the phone to his ear.

I abandoned the attempt to draw my pistol. Instead I charged the three steps between us and tackled him to the ground before he could speak.

He landed on his back with a thud, my body atop his as the cell phone clattered on the floor. For a moment he considered grabbing it, then stopped, thought better of it, and boxed my ears with both hands.

"Fuck!"

I headbutted the bridge of his nose with all my might, and although I connected the blow he still managed to throw me off him. He was scrambling forward as I leapt atop his back, seeing the phone lying just beyond our reach.

To my horror, the phone's screen was glowing—the call had connected, and the other party was probably listening to the muffled sounds of struggle.

He was trying to scream, trying to shout Roma's name. Only my gloved hands managed to delay the inevitable, my left hand pawing at his mouth, my right failing to choke him from behind. Neither would succeed for much longer. If I was going to stop this, it had to be now.

I aborted my choke attempt, drew my right hand to my mouth, and bit the glove to strip it off.

I couldn't get to my pistol from this position—hell, I'd failed to draw it in time when I was upright—so I reached in my pocket instead and yanked out the folding knife.

Flicking the blade open, I slid the knife around his neck, then angled the sleek point into the notch of his jugular and plunged the blade inside.

I was still atop him from behind, so this act physically felt like I was stabbing myself. Psychologically, I probably was.

His entire body jolted as if I'd hit him with a taser. He emitted a wheezing, gargling sound that was truly hideous. I'd never heard anything like it: it was the soundtrack of oxygen-processing organs never meant to work in open air. His blood shot out in scalding spurts to the rhythm of his pulse, in fast succession at first, and then slowing as his vital organs started to shut down.

If I could have made this quicker for him, I would have. But I could think of no means of doing so short of an act of butchery that I didn't have it in me to carry out.

So instead I remained in place, holding his dying body as tightly as a python while keeping the blade far in his throat. His blood soaked through my jacket sleeve to my forearm, as though I'd dipped my arm up to the elbow in a vat of boiling motor oil. The slick, viscous contents of his veins formed a growing disc of scarlet that expanded across the floor beneath us.

When I was certain the man was dead—a blurrier line than I would have expected, given the time it took for his body's minute spasms to finally end—I withdrew the knife and stood, taking care to keep my feet out of the pool of blood. Walking around the body, I carefully knelt and picked up the phone, raising it to my ear.

A voice was calling, "Deniskov? Deniskov?"

I ended the call.

Turning back to survey the dead man before me, I considered my options.

I should have searched him, recovered all possible intelligence from his body. Taken his wallet, made it look like a robbery.

But I couldn't stomach the thought of patting down the blood-soaked corpse.

My right jacket sleeve looked like I'd painted it, the man's blood darkening the navy material to black. Then I recalled that a cop had chased me while I was wearing this overcoat, and I'd since turned myself into a walking forensic exhibit, with my coat as its centerpiece. And the possibility of the man's phone containing a tracking device rose steadily in my mind.

In the end, I left the man's body where he lay. Stripping my overcoat, I deposited it along with my coat, gloves, and knife into one of the drums of burning trash in the alley. The phone went in last.

The fingers of my left hand were going numb as I clumsily prepared a wad of cash. The process would have been easier with both hands, but the stains on my right weren't going to wash off anytime soon. My black sweater was the only protection from the cold, and while the man's blood across the right sleeve only darkened the fabric, it was beginning to freeze against my skin.

Stepping into the cold, I made my way to the first clothing stand I could find in the market. With my right hand buried into a pocket, I used the other hand to pass the vendor the stack of folded bills. Then I took a huge red coat from the torso of a mannequin, donning it over my sweater. Next I took a thick stocking cap from a pile, pulled it over my scalp, and put on a pair of mittens before sliding the coat's fur-lined hood over my head.

The vendor carefully watched my selections, stripping bills from the stack by way of making change.

By the time he finished counting and held the difference in rubles out to me, I was already slipping into the crowd.

* * *

Susan and Roma, of course, were gone.

I walked alone, retracing the steps toward Susan's cellar hideout. As I walked, I rapped a gloved fist hard against my chest as if trying to clear my throat. In reality I was reminding myself that although the scene with the knife had been horrific, it was nonetheless necessary to preserve the mission. But the man I'd killed was doing exactly what I would have done had I been born into his circumstances, just as he would have taken my actions if the roles were reversed.

This placed him in the unspoken cabal of most men I'd ever fought. Never in Afghanistan or Iraq had I encountered a 9/11 mastermind, or even a terrorist who threatened my countrymen directly or indirectly. Instead I fought the foot soldiers, some battle-hardened insurgents and some farmers who picked up their family AK-47s and ran toward the sound of the guns because someone had invaded their country. Wouldn't I do the same if America were occupied by some foreign force?

In every case we clashed, in gunfights and rocket or mortar attacks, meeting in a confrontation that was always lethal to one side and sometimes to both. In every case we were executing or reacting to the orders of power brokers situated far from the battlefield, both literally and metaphorically. In every case, the people who ordered the conflicts from far-flung corners of the globe had never seen the battlefield themselves. And when I peered beyond the lines of race, religion, and nationality, I oftentimes had more in common with the people I was fighting than I did with the policymakers I served.

The man I just killed was one of those cases—just a soldier, doing what he could to preserve the integrity of a mission he never questioned. No different from me.

Except in this case I *could* question the mission, but find myself justified nonetheless.

I hit my chest again, then again. Inside the thick padding of my cold weather coat, I felt the boar tusk, the symbol of Konstantin, pressing against my sternum.

A greater evil, I told myself. I was doing this to stop a greater evil. I'd begun this entire journey of vengeance to stop the Handler, and found instead forces much worse. As a nineteen-year-old in combat, I'd expected to be fighting true terrorists and never had. Now, as a mercenary, I was paradoxically engaged in a battle against the worst terrorists of all: not the occasional religious zealot or cell of operatives, but those who sought the strategic perpetuation of terror against civilians on a global scale.

My psyche continued to log the trauma of violence against my fellow man; I'd pay for this later in loss of sleep, in hypervigilance, in flashing memories of the man's death at random intervals triggered by environ-mental factors I couldn't control.

But this was a burden I'd gladly bear, that I *had* to bear, in order to stop Konstantin and Agustin. For once in my life I was uniquely positioned to fight true evil, and the Handler had seen that in me. And while he still had to die for his many acts of evil, I'd first have to leverage his assets into dismantling this united opposition of terror. Once that was done, I could worry about him.

Giving a final glance about the street, I cut into the alley and approached the cellar door. Kneeling, I knocked three times. I heard a scuf-fling sound, followed by the inner board latch coming undone.

I entered quickly, descending the stairs and closing the doors behind me. Then I secured the latch, turning with surprise as the dim glow of a single flashlight revealed that Susan wasn't alone.

Roma was down there with her.

"What happened?" he asked.

"I dealt with it. Whoever that guy was, he's dead now."

"How can you be certain? If he speaks my name, I cannot return to—"

He went silent as I pulled off a glove and held my right palm toward him, fingers open to reveal a hand turning frostbite-black with dried blood.

Then I lowered my hand and pulled the glove back on.

"I'm certain. He was trying to make a phone call. I stopped him. They're going to find his body with a knife wound to the throat. I burned all the evidence, aside from what I'm wearing. Will the meeting still occur?"

Susan looked to Roma with concern. Surely they'd already discussed this in my absence; but Roma chewed on the corner of a thumb, considering.

"Yes," he said, after a brief pause. "Deniskov was a foot soldier. His death could be due to revenge, or something personal…"

Susan added, "To many things, since there were not seven bodies piled about."

"Eight," I corrected her.

"They will not cancel a high-level meeting over this," Roma said confidently.

"Good. Then get your ass back to work, and whatever you do, don't act any different. Susan will call you to stage a linkup shortly before the meeting occurs. Be sure you make it to that pickup. It's the only way I can ensure your safety."

"Why?"

"Because the wrath of God is going to descend on that meeting, and the only survivor will be Konstantin: something worse than death awaits him. That much I can promise. Now go."

Roma must have been sufficiently humbled with the realization that I'd had to kill a man over the scene he'd made in the market, because he gave Susan a kiss and prepared to leave. I could have chastised him but didn't. He was a stupid kid, and if there was a lesson to learn he'd pick it up without any help from me. Besides, he wasn't going to have to live with the memories of that knife kill for the rest of his life. I was.

Susan locked up after he left, leaving us alone in the cellar.

I sat cross-legged on the filthy ground, feeling almost dizzy from the avalanche of events. My eyes were unfocused, watching the floor as Susan said, "I got you something from the market."

"Oh?" I said absently.

She handed me a bottle of vodka.

I gratefully accepted, twisting off the cap and taking a long pull. Wincing with the immediate burn of alcohol, I handed the open bottle back to her.

"What now, David?"

I held open a hand for the bottle, and she took a sip before returning it. Then I drank again, hoisting the vodka in my hand. "Vodka is step one. Next I'm going to send my report. And then..." I thought for a moment, then looked up to see Susan staring at me.

"Then what?"

I took another sip of vodka and passed her the bottle, flexing the fingers of my blood-soaked right hand. "Then you and I are going to stage some trucks."

9

Magan Airport, Russia
14 Miles Northwest of Yakutsk

I surveyed the forklifts from the corner of the warehouse, watching Susan direct the placement of their huge metal shipping containers along one wall. Each container was marked with magnetic panels bearing the logo of the ACG Group, a shipping company based out of Saint Petersburg, as was the cargo jet they'd just arrived on.

The warehouse was one of several available for rent just off the dirt tarmac of the Magan Airport, a half-hour drive from Yakutsk proper. The warehouse wall opposite the shipping containers was lined with the vehicles that Susan and I had acquired.

We'd rented two types, comprising ten vehicles in total: six LADA 4x4s, which were compact SUVs, and four panel vans called GAZelles. Both had a five-speed manual transmission, and had been produced in such great numbers as to be nearly ubiquitous not only in Yakutsk but in Russia and several export countries as well.

They weren't the most powerful vehicles on the market, but they were both easily attainable without attracting suspicion and virtually unnoticeable on the road. I'd made the decision to prioritize secrecy over capability, and rented enough of the vehicles to account for breakdowns of the mechanical or combat-inflicted variety.

As the forklifts rattled back out of the warehouse, Susan approached me.

"Two more containers to go?"

She nodded. "Two more. Now let me see it."

I grinned, pulling the boar tusk pendant from beneath my shirt and showing it to her. Once again, her eyes fixed on it. "You are a man of your word?"

"Always."

"Then today is the day I get it."

"Today," I agreed, "is the day."

Then she seemed to second-guess herself. "*If* your employer can deliver what he says."

Tucking the boar tusk beneath my collar, I replied, "He won't just deliver. He'll *over*-deliver. Trust me."

"How are you so certain?"

Regardless of Susan's experience to date, I considered how to explain the Handler to someone who'd never met him, much less a teenage girl.

"Konstantin may be a monster, but he's a child compared to the man who sent me. My employer is the greatest power of all."

Susan's face wrinkled up, and her expression became pained. She spoke slowly, as if I were a child who just didn't understand.

"David. The greatest power of all is our humanity."

"Not today it's not." I suppressed the sudden urge to ridicule her clichéd platitude. "Look, you want to understand my employer? Take your hatred of Konstantin and combine it with mine. Then double it. Multiply that by insanity, add in billions of dollars and a private army of special operations troops with a whole lot of experience and a whole lot of fireworks." I turned my eyes to her. "What do *you* think is going to happen, Susan?"

She patted me on the shoulder, a sympathetic gesture that was wildly out of place given the circumstances. Before I could decipher her intention, she looked away and said, "Well, I cannot believe the day has finally come. After two years of work."

"Will you miss being Pesets, the legendary arctic fox?"

"I will not stop being Pesets."

"Oh?"

"I will take this victory with me. I have decided that when I start over in America, I will take the name of Susan Fox."

"Susan Fox," I repeated. "That's got a nice ring to it."

She smiled, and I found myself involuntarily mirroring the gesture. But Susan was probably smiling because she knew Konstantin wouldn't survive the day as a free man, or because she was thinking of her new beginnings in America.

I, on the other hand, was smiling because today would be a combat day, a day to fight with the Outfit.

Because I would be accompanying the assault.

This hadn't been so much of a request on my part as a demand. A case could be made either way—if I was commanding a mission, training or otherwise, I wouldn't be too keen to have a former Outfit guy like myself leaping into the ranks. But I'd flown to the far side of the world, parachuted into Siberia, and assumed a whole lot of risk in getting them the information they needed. The least they could do was let me get a little action alongside them.

Ultimately, of course, the Handler got what he wanted. And when I told him the mission would be better served by my presence on the assault, well, the order had been made.

My mind was already drifting toward what would happen upon the successful conclusion of this mission. Once Konstantin and Agustin were gone, I could facilitate the return of Sergio, Cancer, and Reilly from their weeks-long seclusion in Argentina. This would take a little tap dancing with the truth, but nothing I couldn't handle. I'd been mentally reciting their satellite phone number in my head for weeks now, keeping it fresh in my mind, not daring to write it down for fear of leaving evidence that could endanger them. After this mission, I'd finally be able to call my team and tell them exactly where and how to make contact with the Outfit.

Once I singlehandedly facilitated the defeat of the Handler's enemies, he wouldn't refuse my demand that my former teammates be repatriated into the US. Maybe even back into the Outfit ranks, if they so chose. They'd be no further threat to the Handler.

But I would.

Because as soon as those men were safe, the Handler wouldn't be.

The arrival of the forklifts broke my train of thought, and Susan moved toward them to direct the placement of the final two shipping containers. Once they'd deposited their load and rattled back out of the warehouse, I closed the roller door after them and gave a final check that the lone personnel door was locked.

With that, we were secure: locked inside the windowless warehouse, now lit only by harsh overhead lights.

Susan called, "Come on out, my love!"

One of the GAZelle van doors slid open, and Roma stepped out. Predictably, he'd been given the day off while higher-ranking people scurried to accommodate the meeting. And wisely, he'd been fearful that a forklift operator might recognize him.

"All right, you two." I pointed to the far end of the row of shipping containers. "You guys start there. I'll start here."

I pulled a step ladder up to the nearest shipping container, unlatched the top, and slid it off before peering inside.

Uncomfortably nestled atop piles of equipment bags were a half dozen pissed-off-looking men squinting up at me and cradling weapons.

I spoke in a mock Russian accent. "Welcome to Mother Russia, comrades."

"The fuck?" one of them muttered back. "Russia, really?"

"Really."

They began clambering out of the shipping container, handing down their gear as I moved my step ladder to the next container.

Susan and Roma were doing the same down the opposite end of the row, and as we worked our way toward the middle, the Outfit shooters began staging their gear in the center of the warehouse, neatly lining up equipment and weapons to prepare for an emergency assault.

They were moving quickly, dressed in tactical fatigues and appearing quite grateful to have a mission ahead after the long transcontinental plane ride.

I'd settled for their arrival to Magan Airport to avoid raising too much attention. If the surrounding terrain had permitted, I would have preferred conducting an airfield survey and finding a sufficiently flat field far from civilization to land the Outfit's transport plane.

But while that may have been possible somewhere amid the tundra landscape of Konstantin's compound, there were far too many elevation changes and forests outside Yakutsk to land anything but a helicopter. And a multi-day, multi-phase infiltration was out of the question: the clock was ticking, and if we didn't interdict both Konstantin and Agustin now, we may never have another chance.

So the Magan Airport cargo terminal had been the best possible compromise. It wasn't as high visibility as the airport in Yakutsk proper, and we'd only have a short truck movement to our final staging area.

To prevent detection of a strike force infiltrating the heart of Konstantin's empire, we'd taken every possible precaution. At the Handler's level, knowledge of the operation was restricted to the vicars and their immediate staff. At the Outfit's level, the entire deployment was an emergency readiness exercise—pack your bags, you're flying somewhere for a comprehensive full mission profile with live ammo. That type of thing happened all the time.

And at my level, the Outfit shooters were concealed in a two-stage Trojan Horse: first, they landed in what appeared to be a commercial cargo jet flown by Outfit pilots. Second, they hid inside the shipping containers for transport from the plane to this warehouse.

A huge black man with a shaved head approached me. His fatigues looked like they were painted over his thick, muscular frame.

"You David? Callsign Suicide?"

"Yeah."

"I'm Orlando," he said. "Outfit commander."

Shaking his bear paw of a hand, I said, "Good to meet you. Hope you're not planning on riding shotgun today."

"I can and I will. You just saying that because I'm black?"

"No, I'm not saying it because you're black. I'm saying it because you're the blackest guy I've ever seen."

"Why, thank you."

"And in Siberia, you'd draw less attention in a gorilla suit."

"You done?"

"Yeah."

"You tell my guys, David. Tell the brothers: if you're black, get in the back."

"I don't want to do that."

"Unless you're the commander, because I'm fucking awesome. Ready to tell us what we're here for?"

"I'm ready."

"Listen up!" he shouted. "David's going to give us our warning order."

The shooters went silent at once, and the front rows took a knee as Orlando and I approached the formation.

I looked at the faces of these men lined up behind their equipment— the operators, the shooters, the expendable ones pitted against enemy forces or each other at the Handler's will. On the surface they were in it for the money, the adrenaline; beneath all that, these people were warriors, pure and simple.

I vaguely recognized a few faces in passing. My time at the Outfit had been short—a train-up complete with freefall jumps before I conducted a high-altitude parachute infiltration into Somalia with my partner. I'd returned alone, which was cause for suspicion among some. The Handler had immediately summoned me for a compartmentalized assignment within the Mist Palace, invoking everyone's ire. No one at the Outfit had heard my name again until Argentina, when they'd been sent to eliminate my reportedly rogue team.

Now I was facing a full strike force, the sole contact for a no-notice international readiness exercise that was about to prove to be anything but. And some of the men here had recently been placed in harm's way, had fought for their lives in Argentina due to the actions of my recon team.

I could see suspicious eyes upon me, and feel the collective seething mass of suspicion emanating from nearly everyone. Whispers were passed between them, junior shooters noticing their superiors' reactions to my presence and asking who I was. After hearing the hushed response, their eyes too steeled with mistrust.

I considered how I'd feel in their position, realized no sugarcoating was necessary. Just give them the dope, same as you'd want.

"Gentlemen," I began, "welcome to Russia. You are now in the eastern Sakha Republic, a few miles west of the capital city of Yakutsk where today's objective is located. You were sent here under the premise of a readiness exercise solely to preserve the security of this operation.

"The Organization's highest-value targets are Konstantin Kiselyov of the Far North Coalition, and Agustin Villalba, who heads the South American alliance formerly led by Ribeiro. These men are, as we speak, forming a strategic and historic alliance in opposition to the Organization. Chief among their objectives is to maximize criminal profit through union with terrorist organizations. Konstantin and Agustin represent high-value targets numbers one and two for the Outfit."

The shooters were watching me with dull expressions. They'd heard all this before, probably had the faces of those two men burned into their minds through the targeting matrix they saw daily at the Complex.

"And today, both of them—along with their top staff—will be meeting in six hours, exactly 3.2 miles from where we now sit."

This sent a wave of murmurs and movement through their ranks as people craned their necks to be sure they hadn't misheard.

"Your mission is to conduct a raid with three objectives: the prisoner snatch of Konstantin Kiselyov, the assassination of Agustin Villalba, and the execution of every single individual present, all in ten minutes or less."

Now they were certain they hadn't misheard, and a moment of utter silence preceded the eruption of cheers and applause.

Orlando made a hand-slicing motion across his neck and yelled, "Shut the fuck up!"

They did, at once, so I continued.

"The Handler's top priority is to capture Konstantin alive. Before you get too disappointed, know that whatever the Handler has planned upon Konstantin's delivery will be far worse than getting his head canoed by a full magazine on the objective.

"Aside from Konstantin's live capture, the rules of engagement are terminal protocol from this second until we are wheels-up from our departure airfield. That means the use of deadly force against local law enforcement is authorized. Use of deadly force against host nation military is authorized. And every individual present at the meeting, except Konstantin, is to die in place."

They didn't need me to tell them how historic this mission was. Whether the operation succeeded or failed—and we all desperately hoped it would succeed—this day would live on in Outfit lore for as long as there was an Outfit.

"You heard the man," Orlando barked. "Let's get to planning."

And for the next four and a half hours, we did.

Our convoy pulled out of the warehouse, pausing for Susan to close and lock the roller door behind us. Then we proceeded north around the airport's perimeter, making our way to the lone road leading toward Yakutsk.

I caught a glimpse of the Outfit's jet now stationary on the tarmac. The two pilots would have a boring wait until our return, but when we were ready to exfil, we'd need to launch in a hurry.

The point vehicle was a LADA 4x4, its operators responsible for navigation on the way to and from the objective. The trail vehicle was a GAZelle panel van with a crew-served machinegun to dissuade any pursuers who might attempt to follow us off the target.

In between were the other eight vehicles, each loaded with equipment and Outfit shooters prepared to conduct the raid deep inside Yakutsk. Orlando had decided to ride shotgun in the second vehicle, skin color be damned. I was in the seat behind him and now outfitted with a kit and M4.

I'd be trailing the assault element, which would be the first to dismount vehicles at the objective. The shooters would conduct simultaneous explosive breaches of front and side entrances and enter the building.

Then the support element would establish blocking positions around the building's perimeter, with Susan and Roma acting as translators if needed. This support element was tasked with isolating the objective, which included halting all intervention by law enforcement or bystanders by dissuasion or firepower. Since the sudden invasion of a trained death squad of shooters tended to imbue people inside with the courage to fling themselves out of windows in an attempt to escape, the support element would also pick off anyone who managed to flee the building.

Meanwhile, the assault team would conduct free-flow clearance toward the conference room, eliminating all security forces on the way. They'd inevitably face a final locked set of doors that would be blown up in short order.

And then, the shooters would enter the conference room.

Ordinarily this would be the simplest part of the operation—these men had drilled close-quarters battle so frequently as to be world-class at the practice. You could take any number of Outfit shooters, mix them in any order, and force them through a blind doorway leading into a house or a shopping mall, and the result would be the same.

The shooters would alternate direction with each man as they flowed inside, cutting left and right and moving to points of domination that allowed them to visually clear whatever was on the other side. Then they'd seamlessly mold their organization to the building's floor plan, from consolidating into a massive stack to breaking into elements as small as two men until every square foot of the structure had been physically or visually cleared.

So the clearance of a single conference room should have been so simple as to not warrant further discussion. But as usual, the Handler had to complicate things: his edict to capture Konstantin alive meant that advanced measures had to be undertaken. This changed the conference room clearance to something akin to a hostage rescue. Target distinction was critical, with the shooters attempting to kill everyone but him upon entry. A number of men were equipped with nonlethal munitions, from tranquilizer pistols to tasers, and tasked with incapacitating Konstantin and evacuating him from the room.

Once he was extracted, the assault leader would announce terminal objective: every remaining occupant in the conference room was to be killed.

Not just killed, Orlando had clarified, but *definitively* killed. The Outfit shooters would move from body to body, blasting heads apart whether the person appeared to be dead already or not. Agustin would get the greatest courtesy of anyone remaining, which was to say an attempt would be made to photograph his face before dumping a half dozen rounds into his skull at near-point-blank range.

That would take thirty seconds or less, after which the shooters would begin exfil, flowing out of the room and following the snatch team that had raced Konstantin toward the building entrance. As a final assurance that no one would survive the assault, Orlando would leave a satchel charge before following his men out of the building.

One minute later, as the men were reloading the trucks, the satchel charge would explode and take with it any possible survivors, however unlikely.

From there it'd be a short trip back to the Magan Airport. At this point, the Trojan Horse act was over and done. We'd be in commercially branded vehicles, sure—and if anyone tried to stop those vehicles, they'd be killed. The Handler simply didn't care about the fallout, so long as Konstantin was alive. The force would race to the airfield, ditch the trucks on the tarmac, and race onto the open ramp of their waiting aircraft.

And once the last man was aboard, the plane would begin its taxi to the runway. There'd be no tower clearance, no waiting in line to launch. The pilots would announce their takeoff, ensure that a collision wasn't imminent, and throttle down the runway. The transponder would be switched off to become invisible to civilian air traffic control, and the plane would set a speed record for the few hundred miles to Russia's eastern coastline and international waters.

We'd fly over the Bering Sea to a layover in Anchorage, Alaska. Konstantin and I would transfer to the Handler's Gulfstream for a short flight to the Mist Palace. Susan and Roma would board a charter jet staffed with a few members of the Intelligence Directorate, who would provide them with papers and escort them to their new life in Colorado. And the Outfit would continue to their home base, returning to the Complex with their mission complete.

At least, I hoped every part of our exfil occurred according to plan. Because if there were any mechanical issues with our cargo jet, we'd have to recover the pilots before resorting to an emergency plan: transferring our force into two long-haul trucks, then staging outside Yakutsk until the Handler covertly sent another plane to recover us—all while the Far North Coalition tore apart the city looking for their missing boss.

The first truck in our convoy reached a paved two-lane road and transmitted.

"*Checkpoint One, right north onto Route Red.*"

"Leopard Six, copy," Orlando replied. At this point the dialogue was little more than a formality—the road we'd just turned onto was the *Ulitsa Maganskiy Trakt*. It didn't just comprise the next leg of our route; as the lone road leading to Yakutsk, it practically *was* our route. By the time we turned off it in twenty minutes, we'd be deep inside the city and minutes away from dismounting to conduct the most historic raid in the Outfit's history.

Orlando looked over his shoulder at me.

"What'd you have to do to piece together this score, David?"

"A little targeting legwork. Putting a few bad guys in the dirt, greasing a few palms with rubles."

He directed his gaze forward, scanning the fields and outlying buildings surrounding the airport. "Hope you're ready to retire."

"What do you mean?"

"Shit, after we bag Konstantin and Agustin today, who else will there be to kill?"

The Handler, I thought, watching the fields and scrub brush disappear as the road entered the woods.

"You raise an excellent point."

"Know what I'm real excited about?"

"What's that?"

He patted the object resting between his feet. "This satchel charge right here. Been waiting a long time to use one of these on the objective. Can't wait to blow those fuckers sky-high."

This guy was the commander? He sounded like an enthusiastic rookie, which was no small feat given the experience he must have accumulated in his path up the ranks.

"How long you been in the Outfit, Orlando?"

"About ten years. Where'd you come from, before this?"

"Rangers, once upon a time."

"A Ranger? Goddamn, son, how'd you end up doing intelligence? Anyone got something to say about killing, it ought to be you."

Before I could reply, the point vehicle made another radio call.

"*Checkpoint Two.*"

"Leopard Six copies," Orlando transmitted back. We had just under three miles to negotiate a two-lane road past outlying villages and forest before reaching Yakutsk proper.

I said, "I haven't seen any oncoming traffic in a while. Maybe we should—"

There was a screeching *whoosh* ahead of us, and before my mind could register what that sound meant, the streaky haze of a rocket glided out of the trees to our left, toward the lead truck, and detonated.

The explosion sent the vehicle leaping skyward before smashing down and rolling onto its side, the underbelly blocking the width of the road.

Orlando called out over the radio, "Ambush left, ambush left—"I pressed my muzzle to my window and opened fire.

My bullets shattered the glass, and I sent my next burst to the spot where I'd seen the rocket emerge.

The driver floored the accelerator, swerving right and trying to ram the disabled vehicle out of the way. We had to speed through the kill zone before it escalated, but our bumper struck the edge of the downed truck and the tires began spinning.

The driver said, "We can't get through—"

Then his words ended in a second explosion behind us.

"Rear vehicle is down."

Orlando transmitted calmly, "Reverse out of kill zone. Road is blocked to our front."

Gunshots sounded to our left, the hissing metal pops of bullets impacting our vehicle. The Outfit shooters responded with a huge volley of gunfire blasted at known or possible enemy positions. I dumped the rest of my magazine into the forest, spraying wildly to return fire at an enemy I couldn't see.

I reloaded as the next transmission sounded over our radio.

"Road is blocked to the rear."

Orlando keyed his mic in response.

"Assault. Assault. Assault."

At that point, the order was more for confirmation of action than anything else— we were trapped in the kill zone of a near ambush. Assaulting was the *only* thing to do, and as I exited our truck on the side opposite the enemy fire, I saw that the Outfit shooters were doing it exceedingly well.

A single glance down the row of vehicles revealed the Outfit shooters operating in pairs, with one man charging into the woods for every partner laying down suppressive fire behind the cover of the engine block.

"First bound's on me!" I shouted to Orlando, following the wave of shooters bounding into the forest without waiting for an objection.

"Asshole!" he shouted behind me, the last sound I heard before he began firing.

I charged on line with the row of men, dropping to a knee behind the nearest tree trunk I could locate. I opened fire as soon as my muzzle cleared cover, shooting long bursts from right to left. Aiming could come later, once we had a foothold in the trees and began maneuvering forward. For now, the priority for the first wave of shooters was to lay down a massive volume of fire, allowing the second wave to move on line with us without giving the enemy a break.

It wasn't an exact science, but enough so that by my second burst I heard the gunfire go silent behind me. Within ten seconds I'd fired my final shots, and Orlando was crashing to a kneeling position at my right flank.

He began shooting immediately, my cue to get my ass moving.

I reloaded hastily as I rose, advancing forward for a three-to-five-second rush. The same process was occurring down the ranks, the first wave moving forward by a single bound.

But the distance of a bound was determined by terrain, and we didn't get very far. The forest was a tangled knot of brush and trees, all brown with the onset of winter save the evergreens dotted throughout. There were flashes of another color too—a mottled olive and tan of camouflage, appearing in fleeting wisps like a mirage.

These were our enemy, all we could see of them, and before we could move a downed vehicle, aid the wounded, or recover our dead, we had to either kill them down to a man or force any survivors to retreat.

They couldn't see us much better than we could see them, but they didn't have to; they'd surveyed the ambush site ahead of time, and established their positions to achieve interlocking fields of fire. As long as each man knew his left and right limit of fire—and they did, I was certain—they only had to wait for the rocket gunners to take out the lead and trail vehicles before opening fire.

I dropped to a knee behind another tree trunk, opening fire alongside the now-jagged row of shooters spanning the forest to my left. This time I was searching for targets, and when my eyes locked onto a flicker of movement, I drilled a half dozen rounds in the hope that one would hit. When there was no target to be found, I drove my aim to the nearest likely enemy position—namely, any tree trunk big enough to take cover behind—and salted it with two or three rounds to prevent a possible shooter from appearing. My shots needed to be slower and more precise now: I was on my third magazine, had only four remaining, and there was no telling how long this fight would last.

Sudden gunfire to my right signaled that Orlando had arrived alongside me. I put my weapon on safe as I stood and advanced alongside the first wave.

The snarl of brush got thicker as we proceeded. Progress was measured in inches and feet, clawed for against the forces of nature and incoming bullets. All we could do to assault was stay low, alternate movement with the man next to us, and return enough controlled fire to keep our enemy's heads down.

The thickness of the woods around us was, to some extent, an equalizer; neither side could throw smoke grenades to conceal movement or frags to kill. The grenades would simply get caught in the trees and explode overhead. So both forces were restricted to bullets, a tremendous disadvantage to the force who hadn't choreographed this battle action in advance.

Dropping into position to aim around the right side of a tree trunk, I heard an incoming round shear into the tree. A flurry of shredded bark rained down as I zeroed in on a muzzle flash—the most fleeting spark of fire amid the trees, as good as a bullseye and very often the only sign of enemy I could make out when a fight took to the woods.

I was firing as the flash faded, taking two well-aimed shots that resulted in a sprawl of dark movement. I sensed that I'd scored a hit, so I chased the two shots with five more to ensure the kill before my bolt locked to the rear.

Ducking behind my tree, I ripped the empty magazine out of my weapon, then grabbed another by feel and reloaded. I had just smacked the bolt catch with the heel of my palm when I heard a sudden cry to my right.

If the bursts of gunfire around me had been timed slightly different, I wouldn't have heard it at all—it was a momentary scream, reaching my ear in one of the fractional near-silences of combat where the only noises were the echoes of shots fired.

I looked back to see Orlando lurching through the trees just before he went down.

Dropping to the prone, I peered beneath the brush to try and assess his condition. He was only ten feet distant, and this should have been a momentary evaluation—confirm he was dead, and continue fighting. Come back for him when the battle was over.

And while he wasn't moving, I could see his left leg bleeding heavily, shot multiple times. There were no visible wounds above the waist. He'd caught a rifle burst to the leg, which wasn't fatal—not immediately, anyway. But even from a distance, I could see the near-black coagulation of arterial blood. At least one round had severed his femoral artery. If he were conscious, he would have been applying a tourniquet already, but the concussion of the fall or shock from pain and blood loss must have knocked him out.

The proper tactical move was to finish the battle before treating the wounded, but I could see at a glance this man was going to bleed out in the next sixty seconds.

All the Outfit shooters were still in the fight, and since the first truck had been incinerated, I was now at the far right flank. No one else saw Orlando go down, and if I didn't save his life, the Outfit would lose its commander on top of the other shooters who had already died today.

I crawled through the brush toward him, my focus narrowing to the space between us at the exclusion of all else. If I hesitated or got caught in the brush, it could mean extra seconds that would kill him as surely as a bullet to the head. So I chose each shifting movement of my arms and legs to drive me forward as efficiently as possible, trying to stay low. A snapping hiss sheared a branch in front of me—bullet at full velocity—and I saw a dull puff of dirt in the ground to my right—ricochet. Whoever had shot Orlando in the leg had a bead on the last movement he'd seen, and was taking potshots in the hope of scoring another hit.

And I didn't care. If he hit me, so be it. Every armchair philosopher who had never been to war would call an act like this valor. It wasn't. Because the truth known to every man or woman who had fought in ground combat was that there were things worse than death, and letting a fellow warrior die out of a desire for self-preservation was one of them. Orlando and I had first met hours earlier, but we were brothers in war, and I'd give my life trying to save him just as surely as he would for me.

I reached his body untouched, my eyes darting across the front of his equipment. This son of a bitch, I thought. Probably every Outfit shooter on the line had at *least* one spare tourniquet prominently displayed on the front of his kit. I'd secured two spare tourniquets on my own, using rubber bands for easy removal. But Orlando was the commander, so preoccupied with the big picture that he'd neglected that recommended precautionary measure—and I had no intention of wasting time to access his medical pouch.

I ripped one of my spare tourniquets free instead, its canvas loop falling open as it broke the rubber bands. I'd already prepped the tourniquet at maximum length, and given the size of Orlando's tree-trunk legs, this was a wise precaution.

Hurriedly routing the wide loop over his left boot, I slid the tourniquet up his leg, past the wound, and all the way up to his groin. I didn't care about saving as much of his leg as possible, only stopping the arterial bleed, and the surest place to achieve that was all the way up his thigh, where the leg was at its narrowest point. Situating the tourniquet in the narrowest pocket of his leg and upper groin, I grabbed the free tab of the strap and pulled out as much slack as possible.

Once the tourniquet was as tight as I could initially get it, I took hold of a six-inch metal stick known as the windlass. Twisting this stick further tightened an integrated strap, and I spun it in four increasingly difficult rotations. If he were awake, this would have been unbearably painful for him. Grunting with the effort, I forced an additional half-turn before the windlass would move no further. Flipping a triangular buckle over one end, I locked the stick into place.

Then I looked to his wound, and saw the bleeding stop completely. I'd successfully controlled his hemorrhage. Shallowly panting in utter relief, I moved to my next order of business: establishing communications.

As ground force commander, Orlando carried two radios with a hand mic on each shoulder. I didn't have to guess which was which. The non-firing shoulder was reserved for the tactical frequency that would reach his own subordinate leadership; the firing shoulder, Orlando's right, was reserved for a satellite relay to reach higher command. The former could be accessed in between gunfire. The latter meant that there was a sufficient gap in the fight to report to people who could do little at this point but monitor and report.

I grabbed the mic for his tactical frequency first, and transmitted.

"Leopard Six down, I say again Leopard Six is down. Suicide co-located, I'll relay situation to higher on command freq. Second-in-command, take charge of assault."

"*Suicide, Suicide. Leopard Five copies, I'm on it.*"

Satisfied, I released my grip on the mic button. "Five" was the indicator for Orlando's immediate subordinate. Grabbing the mic on Orlando's opposite shoulder, I prepared to transmit over the command frequency.

I was sure that Orlando had already reported the ambush, but I couldn't take it for granted. Even if he had, they'd be eagerly awaiting updates. At the risk of redundancy, I transmitted everything I had to report.

"Halo One, be advised Leopard element ambushed on Route Red vicinity Checkpoint Two. Unknown KIA and WIA, will advise. Two vehicles destroyed. Leopard Six is down, assault in progress, break." I released the transmit button and took a breath. "Mission abort. I say again, mission abort. How copy?"

There was a long pause now—no one wanted to be the guy at Halo One who agreed to abort the attempt.

"State your callsign."

What the fuck? What did it matter?

"This is Suicide. Leopard Six is WIA."

Another pause.

"Suicide, are you certain you cannot consolidate forces and proceed to the objective?"

This was possibly the most asinine thing I'd ever heard spoken on the net. And I knew exactly why—some pencil-necked dickhead in a climate-controlled tactical operations center knew that the Handler was listening in, and that someone else was at that moment producing a transcript of our every word.

I keyed my mic. "There is no fuckin' objective, you dick idiot. We got ratted out. And that didn't happen from anyone at the pointy end of the spear, so why don't you look around your own ranks for a traitor."

"Suicide, say again your last."

He heard me fine, I knew. The connection was crystal clear.

"You heard what I said. Leopard element is moving to the airfield for immediate exfil. Will need advanced follow-on medical treatment and blood transfusion for minimum one probable below-the-knee amputee, callsign Leopard Six." That would cue someone to identify his blood type and ensure enough units were on hand to keep him alive. "Estimate eight KIA. Unknown wounded."

"Halo One copies all."

I released my grip on the mic and grabbed my rifle, preparing to rejoin the assault.

Only then did I notice an eerie event that had transpired while I was focused on the radio: all gunshots had stopped.

This meant one of two things. Either the Outfit had prevailed over our ambushers, or the ambushers had wiped out the Outfit shooters. And if that was the case, I was about to have a very interesting conclusion to my day, left to single-handedly figure out Orlando's transport while the temperature plummeted below freezing shortly before nightfall.

But a moment later, I heard the distant cries to my front.

"LOA! LOA!"

The command was echoed down the line, the three-letter syllable giving me a palpable blast of relief. LOA: Limit of Advance. Orlando's second-in-command had determined that the ambush force had been killed or forced to retreat, so the assault need not continue.

The Outfit shooters would be hastily reloading, searching enemy bodies, and treating their wounded teammates before moving back to the trucks. My heart soared when I heard the sporadic *clack clack* of double tap gunshots, a sure sign that the Outfit shooters were administering twin headshots to fallen enemies.

My relief faded when I looked back to Orlando.

The arterial bleeding had stopped, to be sure, and even the venous hemorrhage from what remained of his left leg appeared to be minimal. But I was nonetheless confronted with a discomforting truth.

This bastard was going to be too difficult to carry through the brush single-handedly.

I yelled one word at the top of my lungs.

"SUPPORT!"

There were times when a shout was infinitely more effective than a radio transmission, and this was one of them. Devoid of reference points in the woods, I'd rely on a far simpler method beacon: my voice.

"SUPPORT!"

My cries achieved the desired effect. I heard crashing through the brush toward me, and a pair of sweaty Outfit shooters materialized. They were panting, faces flushed with exertion, lowering their weapons at the sight of me with their fallen commander.

"The bleeding is managed," I said, "but I need help getting him back to the trucks."

Before they could answer, I heard a tinny voice transmitting over the tactical frequency.

"Fire in the hole, fire in the hole, fire in the—"

An ear-piercing explosion from the road made all three of us flinch, the shockwave of sound resonating over us and echoing over the hills. Then a vehicle engine revved, and a great crash was followed by the screech of twisted metal before the transmission continued.

"We blew the trail vehicle with the satchel charge and rammed it off the road. Road back to the airport is clear."

"This is Leopard Five. Exfil, exfil, exfil. Confirm in sequence."

"Leopard One, copy."

"Leopard Two, copy."

"Leopard Three—"

As the Outfit team leaders checked in, the two shooters descended on Orlando's body.

"We got him, sir."

Before they lifted him, I stripped the command radio off Orlando's kit, shoving it into a cargo pocket and clipping his hand mic to my shoulder. I'd have to keep the spiraling cord connecting the two from snagging in the abundant brush between us and the trucks, but that was the least of my worries at present.

We'd lost two trucks' worth of Outfit shooters—eight men killed in the time it took for the rockets to impact. Now we had to get everyone aboard the remaining vehicles, haul ass back to the Magan Airport, and board the departure aircraft to blast off on our way back home before there were any more casualties.

I broke brush back to the trucks, hearing the fragments of radio transmissions over the tactical net as I moved.

"Four-One is ambulatory, gunshot wound to the right arm..."

"Be advised, Leopard One-Five is critical, sucking chest wound..."

"Two-Six is KIA..."

I transmitted over the command frequency. The pilots had been monitoring all our radio traffic, but the least I could do was prepare them for the chaos that was about to board their aircraft.

"Cobra Six-One, this is Suicide."

"Cobra Six-One copies, send it."

Goddamn, I thought, his voice sounded calm. It was easy to judge aviators, who were more often than not removed from the immediate risk of death or injury via close-range gunfire.

But those who relied on aircraft for survival knew the truth.

And that truth was this: the pilots and, when applicable, their aircrews were every ounce the warriors of their ground-fighting counterparts. In many ways, my aerial counterparts had it worse. They were operating infinitely complex machines in an environment that most shooters couldn't begin to fathom, and doing so when the lives of their teammates, much less their passengers and themselves, were at constant risk from the slightest human error.

I transmitted back, "Leopard element en route to your location for immediate exfil. Estimated nine KIA, minimum three WIA, we are mission abort at this time, how copy?"

The pilot responded with all the emotional investment of a fast food clerk—a professional disguise that required immense discipline, I knew, as he was well aware that his voice imparted confidence or lack thereof to those who relied upon him.

"Cobra Six-One copies all, standing by at cargo terminal, engines running. You give the go-ahead that last man is onboard, and we are full speed down the runway before the ramp is closed. Just get back to the airfield and we'll take care of the rest. How copy?"

Jesus, these aviators could impart confidence through every word. "Leopard element copies all, will be at your location in ten mikes."

Ten minutes may have been a tad optimistic given the time it would take us to negotiate the woods and the two-plus miles back to their location, but I'd rather have the pilots prepared sooner rather than later.

The rest of our exfil took care of itself. The professionalism of these Outfit shooters was extraordinary: they treated the maneuver no differently than if they were well-rested and on a routine training exercise at the Complex.

The truth, of course, was much different.

These men had traveled five time zones under the auspices of a no-notice readiness exercise, landing on the opposite side of the globe to learn

that this was not only a real-world mission, but the most important of their
—and their mercenary unit's—existence. On infil they'd been ambushed,
seamlessly crushed the opposition, and reversed course on a pinhead-spin
pivot without so much as a raised eyebrow.

This realization made me want to cry and scream and collapse at once;
and even as the acknowledgment of total mission failure resonated in my
being, I felt a deep undying love for the shooters around me. I didn't care
about my history or theirs. These were my brothers, and I'd now and
forever do everything in my power to protect them.

We reached the trucks, finding that the drivers had already reversed
course and were preparing for movement along the recently opened path
back to Magan Airport. We just needed to load our casualties and board
ourselves—even the fatally wounded shooters from the first and last trucks
had been recovered by the time we arrived—and all this occurred with
remarkable efficiency.

I followed the two men transporting Orlando into a panel van alongside
a medic who began administering far better treatment than I had. I had
barely registered the accountability of all personnel over the tactical
frequency when the convoy lurched forward, heading back westward
toward Magan.

Orlando's eyes fluttered open.

"How'd they clear the road?" he asked weakly.

"Blew the rear vehicle with your satchel charge."

"Son of a bitch," he groaned, flipping me the bird. "I really wanted to
use that."

Christ, what a nightmare. But it could have been much worse—the
majority of Outfit shooters were present here, and the ambush a delaying
rather than extermination maneuver on behalf of our enemies. Had they
been a little more patient, they could have let us enter the target building
before demolishing the entire structure.

This thought had scarcely crossed my mind when the phone in my
pocket began buzzing.

I withdrew it and held the display to my face, seeing Susan's name.

"Yeah," I said breathlessly, prepared to explain the entire situation in
minimal terms.

Her voice was choked with emotion. "Roma just got word of a surface-to-air missile being moved into position outside Magan. Radio chatter indicates it will be in position in five minutes. I don't know if this is real or not, but—"

"Got it," I barked, hanging up on her.

I mashed the key to the command frequency.

"Cobra Six-One, conduct emergency launch. There's a SAM launcher moving into position, ETA four minutes."

"Copy, Cobra Six-One is out of here."

I released the button and switched hands to transmit over the tactical net.

"Leopard Five, Leopard Five, this is Suicide. Prepare for alternate exfil contingency. We've got a surface-to-air threat."

"Copy, flexing to alternate exfil."

I clambered into the passenger seat as our convoy lurched out of the woods and back into the scattered fields and scrub brush surrounding the airport. Scanning the sky through the windshield, I searched for our departing plane.

It only took me a moment to locate it.

The silhouette of the transport jet broke away from the horizon, ascending into a clear blue sky. I watched it level off over the trees, staying low with the engines at full throttle. Soon the pilots would be beyond the lateral range of most man-portable missiles, and then they could ascend. As the plane continued thundering away, my eye was drawn to another feature penetrating the sky.

From the rolling forests north of the airport, a hazy streak of gray smoke appeared and streaked in a bouncing, jerky path low over the treetops.

"Missile inbound!" I transmitted to the pilots.

They didn't answer to confirm they heard me—but they didn't have to.

I saw them deploy their defensive countermeasures at once—streaks of sparkling fire shot out from the plane's flanks and left a great flaming trail in its wake. It looked as if the plane was on fire, but these were pyrotechnics designed to divert heat-seeking missiles.

I watched the gray smoke flying low, snaking over the ground as the plane carved a great swath of flame before firing two smoking, glowing orbs that lazily descended on either side. Then the jet banked in a hard right turn, changing course to distance itself from the fireworks display now lighting up the otherwise placid sky.

The missile's gray smoke trail was now arcing upward, ascending toward the flares and the aircraft itself.

I couldn't breathe, couldn't move, felt my chest constrict as I waited for the inevitable explosion—the only question was *where* the missile would detonate. It flew through the sparkling clusters of flares at an impossibly fast rate, and for one moment of sheer relief I felt certain the plane had effectively evaded.

But then something strange happened.

As if by some unseen force, the missile carved its way out of the stream of fire, swung at a sideways arc, and struck the transport plane in an aerial explosion of yellow-orange light that quickly darkened to black.

The sound hit us a beat later: a hollow, thumping bass drum of a concussion that seemed to erupt and echo to silence in the same breath.

Then the plane emerged from the smoldering black cloud—what was left of it, anyway—and fell to earth in smoking shards of metal. One wing fell free from the remains of the fuselage, tumbling end over end toward the forest below.

My feet felt frozen on the truck floor; I was riveted against the seat, but my hand seemed to raise the radio mic to my face of its own accord.

When I spoke, my voice sounded like it belonged to another person entirely. It was too cold, too hollow with disbelief to be my own.

"Halo One, be advised." I released the button and took a breath. "Cobra Six-One is down over Magan."

VANQUISHED

In absentia lucis, tenebrae vincunt

-In the absence of light, darkness prevails

10

The Mist Palace

I was back at the Mist Palace.

It always came back to this place, this foggy compound that I couldn't seem to escape in mind or spirit. Lying on my bed, eyes unfocused as I watched the ceiling in a room lit by a single lamp. It was nighttime now, almost a week after the catastrophic mission failure in Russia. The final tally was nine Outfit shooters and two pilots killed in action, the greatest single loss of life in the unit's history. Twelve men were wounded, three critically. Orlando would probably lose his left leg below the knee. I still wore the boar tusk pendant.

We'd managed to execute our alternate exfil contingency, eventually reaching Anchorage before dispersing for good. To his credit, the Handler had honored his word and relocated Susan and Roma to Colorado. Nothing awaited them in Russia except death at Konstantin's hands. The Outfit returned to its remote desert headquarters to bury its dead and resume readiness training.

And this morning, I had returned to the Mist Palace.

Why the Handler flew me here, I didn't know. He hadn't spoken to me since my arrival, and hadn't spoken to anyone as far as I knew. If the rumors were to be believed, he'd been spending an increasing amount of time in solitude, alone in his garden. Parvaneh's loss had broken him, and the events that transpired in Russia would drive him further into madness for two reasons. First, the mission was a failure in every sense of the word. Second, it was a sellout of catastrophic proportions: someone had leaked operational information to Konstantin and Agustin, and due to the extensive compartmentalization of this mission, that someone must have been one of his top staff. His Organization was rotting from the inside out; it was corrupt and fetid to its core. It could either implode or be kept in check by wanton killing, but the Handler faced a union of internal and external opposers he couldn't ultimately defeat. No one could.

I rose from the bed, retrieving my night vision device from the cabinet beside the door. Then I extinguished my lamp and returned to the door, testing the handle and finding it unlocked. This was the strangest thing since my return: they'd stopped locking my door from the outside, a courtesy reserved for permanent members of the Mist Palace staff. That reduction in security could only have come from the Handler himself. I felt the same nagging question I'd asked myself when he met with me in his office, alone and unsupervised.

Did he want me to kill him?

I opened my door a crack, breathing in the misty night air that felt nearly tropical after my return from Siberia. Glancing outside into the darkness, I gave a scan under my night vision and listened carefully for any signs of movement. Even though they'd stopped locking my door, the Mist Palace curfew still applied. Any guard could shoot me on sight.

But I saw and heard no one.

Slipping outside my door, I closed it behind me and moved toward the dark grove of trees to my left. I disappeared into their concealment within seconds, and now peered downward through my night vision to locate the next landmark of this route—the low, flat stones that all looked flush with the ground. But one wasn't.

Dropping to all fours, I found the one I was looking for, and, beneath it, the hollowed-out slick of dirt concealed so perfectly that I wondered if Parvaneh had arranged it that way to preserve her childhood secret.

I crawled beneath the rock without hesitation, the stone's underside scraping against my back. Pulling myself forward across a short, rocky cavern, I felt for the hole beneath me.

There it was, the final hollow void before the passage began in earnest. Gripping the sides of the entrance, I slid my legs over the edge and lowered myself into the tunnel.

I passed through the tunnel slowly, methodically, feeling an irrational pulse of fear that I would get caught. That someone else knew about the tunnel and was lying in wait for me.

Wooden beams braced the rocky subterranean walls stretching forward into darkness. The mining community once overhead had been built during the Cariboo Gold Rush in the mid-1800s, according to Sage. This passage had existed for almost two hundred years, and any trees felled in its construction had long since been replaced with untouched forest.

And as I passed down the mining tunnel's ancient corridor, I faced the most critical moment of my life. Because I could certainly kill the Handler.

Except Konstantin and Agustin were still out there.

If I pursued them, I could die in the process and all three could survive. And whether or not I killed the Handler, someone worse would always want the throne. The only way to eliminate the whole evil mess was to destroy all three men and the Organization itself at its core, and that was regrettably beyond my, or anyone's, abilities.

I had to do something; the question was what.

I thought of Parvaneh dying, then Karma. This entire swarming mess of revenge had led me back to where I began: the Handler alive, and everyone I loved dead.

By the time I reached the rockfall that marked the end of the tunnel, my decision was made.

Finding a gap in the rocks before me, I began climbing upward to ground level. Pulling myself along the rough surfaces of a narrow cavern scarcely wide enough for an adult, I reached my exit point. A final slick of cold mud led to the surface, the opening nothing more than a simple hole in the earth overhung by a flat rock concealing it from view.

I emerged into dense underbrush, then slowly rose and appraised my surroundings.

Beyond the grove of trees in which I stood, I saw the garden exactly as it had been on my previous two visits—once upon my return from Rio, and once when I'd followed Parvaneh. Night vision was no longer necessary, save to periodically scan for obstacles. The rest of the garden was peacefully lit with pastel ground lighting, and I could hear a tall fountain cascading softly in a distant pond. The footbridge arced as it connected stretches of path leading to my right, where it ended in steps ascending a small hill.

Atop the hill stood the garden's single structure, a bamboo pavilion.

The sight of it nearly cowed me into submission, into retreat. It was virtually a symbol of the Handler's omnipotence. The last time I'd confronted him there, I'd just returned from Rio to find Ian captured. And after Parvaneh had fled the garden, I'd found out what true omnipotence was. It began with the Handler's words: *David brought a gun in my immediate proximity for one reason alone: because I wanted him to.* Then he pointed the pistol at me and pulled the trigger—it made a hollow click, its firing pin having been removed when I was unconscious from my wounds. After that, a half-dozen shooters emerged from the bushes around the hill, his failsafe protection carefully hidden until it no longer had to be.

Now there was a single figure in the pavilion, seated on a bench and staring into the darkness ringing the hill.

The Handler.

His lanky figure was motionless as he sat lost in thought.

This couldn't be true, my mind screamed. There's a catch, it's a trap, and the moment you're spotted some unseen bodyguard is going to blow you away. There were no excuses for what I was doing, no explanations to offer. Attempting to approach the Handler alone was a death sentence, pure and simple.

It was now or never.

I painstakingly made my way out of the underbrush, slipping between trees to reach the footpath. Then I followed it toward the pavilion, the hill blocking my view of the Handler as I approached him. I warily looked over my shoulder to find the serene garden surroundings as placid as ever. This was really happening, I realized. He was by himself, completely vulnerable to attack.

That's what you thought last time.

But I closed with the steps regardless, an almost gravitational force drawing me upward. I ascended almost silently, every footfall a hushed whisper of stealth.

And as I reached the top of the stairs, the pavilion's interior came into full view and I saw that the Handler was well and truly alone.

He was still seated, eyes fixed in the distance.

I took a final step, standing on the pavilion floor no more than ten feet from the Handler's defenseless form.

"Don't call out," I said.

He didn't react, didn't turn to me or even blink at the sound of my voice. By all appearances, the Handler hadn't heard me at all.

I swallowed. "If I were here to kill you, you'd be dead already."

Only then did he speak, his voice a low, disinterested growl.

"That prospect, David, has been bothering me less as of late."

Maybe he didn't want me to kill him after all; perhaps he just didn't care anymore.

"The mission compromise in Russia wasn't due to the Outfit, or the agents. You've got a leak at a very high level inside your Organization."

"Of that, I am well aware."

"It's probably one of your vicars, and if not, it's someone so high up that they've got access to the top compartmentalized proceedings."

"In the history of the Organization, the vicars have never betrayed the Handler. Yet now, I cannot rule them free from suspicion. So you see the inherent problem."

"Yes." I nodded. "It's not an internal conspiracy, like it was with Sage. This time it's an alliance between one of your top people and your external opposers—Konstantin and Agustin. This is the most dangerous possible course of events. And you can't kill your way out of it."

"On that point, David, you are mistaken."

"But you don't know who the leak is—"

"Which is precisely why death is the answer. As it always is."

"I don't follow. How do you plan on finding the traitor?"

"I already have." He looked toward me then, his amber eyes dull with disinterest. "So have you."

"I said it could be any of the vicars. Or their top people. And none of them would betray you without being able to do so successfully. Sage could fake a polygraph. And you screen for people who will take secrets to the grave, torture or not."

"Which is why, young David"—he turned his attention to his left hand, inspecting each fingertip like a spider ticking off its legs one at a time—"I kill them all. The three vicars and their top staff. Fifteen souls snuffed out as they should be. I may even throw Fiona's body into the fire. Then I promote replacements from within."

My chest began tingling. How could I talk him out of this? "Konstantin and Agustin would love if you did that. Killing your top brass would weaken your position, endanger your throne even further, and the external opposition would seize upon that. Whoever you promote in their place would be less capable, and they'd be looking for the first opportunity to defect before you killed them, too."

"They will be kept in check through fear."

"If that were certain, you wouldn't be in this position. Everyone's already afraid. But this time, their fear is that you're coming unraveled."

"You should know by now, David, that control is my specialty."

"Not anymore. And I'm not the only one who can see the fissure. It's not just your Organization losing control in the world. It's you losing control over your own mind."

He said nothing, but his head cocked toward me in a birdlike twitch that made my breath catch. But I went on.

"Surely you've seen the way people are looking at you. You're spending more time here in the garden, alone in thought. Less with the people who are looking to you for leadership at a critical time for your Organization."

"You probably love this. You've wanted me dead for some time. Perhaps I should send your body to the flames."

"If I wanted you to fail, why would I be talking to you?"

"Why indeed, David. To taunt me, to gauge the reflexes of my mind, to point out things I already know, to stand face to face with the king? For what purpose, to what end?"

"To speak with you alone. There are exactly two people I can rule out from suspicion, and two people alone: you and me. No one can know this conversation occurred, and this was the only way I could speak with you in total secrecy."

"Speak with me." He lifted one hand, flexing the long fingers again, examining first the back and then his palm. "Why would you want me to succeed now, after opposing me for so long?"

"You know the reason."

"Enlighten me. Because regardless of your intentions here tonight, I do not believe that you no longer want me dead."

He was talking me into a corner, forcing me to confront dark emotions that I wanted desperately to leave unexamined during this meeting. The last thing I wanted was to get emotional now; the Handler was in a brutally unstable place, and if I left the garden without killing him I'd bear the consequences of that.

"Yes, I want you dead. You killed everyone I cared about and all but deposited their skulls into my lap. My one surviving friend, Ian, was turned into a slave for your Intelligence Directorate and only freed when I saved your life by stopping Sage's assassination attempt. My reward was being sent to die in Argentina, and having to find a way out. Explain to me why I wouldn't want to kill you."

"And yet, here you are."

"That's right." I swallowed. "Because something worse is out there—Konstantin and Agustin. Your life is a matter of revenge. Their lives are a matter of revenge *and* stopping a greater evil that will breathe life into the worst causes the human race has been capable of producing. Terrorism chief among them."

"There are realities in this world of ours, David. And in some cases, having a degree of influence is better than no influence at all."

"Oh, I know you've got your connections with international terror. But they're nothing compared to the scale of what Konstantin and Agustin will build. And I'm not interested in wondering if the next 9/11 will occur because I didn't do everything in my power to stop them."

"How noble of you, David Rivers."

"We both know I'm far from noble. But it's a savage fight to keep these powers at bay, and one thing you cannot accuse me of being is unwilling to put my own life on the line to wage that fight. Including now."

"I will make the determination of what occurs in the fight against my enemies. I have the ultimate perspective on global affairs, and despite what you think, I am of perfectly sound mind."

"You haven't been of sound mind since Parvaneh died."

He was up in a flash, legs spinning over the bench as he leapt to his feet with animalistic speed. Before I could react, his tall frame was fully erect, charging, one hand jabbing to grab my shirt and the other reaching for something on his belt.

My back slammed against a support beam of the pavilion, the Handler pinning me against it with a forearm across my chest. A knife blade was against my throat, its wafer-thin blade so close that it would break skin if I spoke.

He addressed me calmly, almost a whisper.

"I do not believe I care to hear her name leave your mouth ever again."

The veins of his forehead were engorged, his face a dark blister red. I'd never seen anyone so angry as this, eyelids open wide enough that his amber pupils were fully encircled by the whites of his eyes.

As I spoke, the movement of my throat muscles split the skin neatly across the blade.

"Trying to get Konstantin and Agustin in one stroke was too ambitious, given the leak that we're both now aware of."

I could feel the blood beginning to seep out, spreading from my throat onto the blade's metallic surface. The effort burned, the shallow cut aflame as I spoke. But I couldn't stop now.

"Since we can't remove the leak without decapitating your top leadership and weakening the Organization, we should hit your external opposition first. And we do so in a way that sends a message to everyone who opposes you."

This comment seemed to enrage the Handler further, his voice turning to a frail rasp of hatred. "Any plan you propose will require the involvement of others who could inform my opponents. Why did you come here?"

But he pulled the blade back a fraction of an inch, allowing me to reply without the metal cutting further into my throat.

"There is one plan that we can keep between us. And all it requires of you is to do one thing, very publicly and very convincingly."

"What is that, David?"

I watched him closely, seeing a degree of fury leaving his face, fading to the onset of curiosity. Wonder, even, though I didn't think the Handler was capable of such a reaction.

With the warm blood blossoming evenly around the shallow wound in my throat, I swallowed before replying.

"I need you to fire me."

11

The Handler's courtroom seemed absurdly luxurious after my stint in Russia. I'd stood judgment here twice before, making this my third—and final—time. My chair was at the center of the scarlet carpet, situated before the three chief vicars' looming gaze.

Omari, the portly, mustached Vicar of Finance.

Watts, the silver-haired Vicar of Defense.

And Yosef, the dwarf in a black yarmulke, Vicar of Intelligence.

They were the Handler's top three advisors, and both my gut and the circumstances of the mission compromise in Russia told me that one of them was directly serving Konstantin and Agustin.

The elevated seating area at their side was reserved for the Handler, who seemed distracted by some troubling thought as the proceedings began.

Fiona stood behind a podium. She was young, with freckled cheeks and hair in a short bob cut, eyes looking uneasy through her large framed glasses—the polar opposite of Ishway, the Handler's personal assistant that Fiona had replaced. As was the case when I first met her, she came across as an academic whiz kid, some intellectual prodigy whose considerable talents were required to track the Handler's complicated affairs.

Fiona addressed the court in a solemn tone. "This open assembly is to

determine the fate of David Rivers following the mission failure in Russia."
She looked to the Handler. "Sir, would you like to—"

He waved a disinterested hand, and Fiona quickly addressed Omari.

"The assembly will continue with the counsel of the Chief Vicar of
Finance. Vicar Omari, speak the truth."

Omari pushed back his chair, speaking in his Kenyan accent before he'd
finished rising to his full height. "There is only one solution to the problem
of David Rivers. It is the same that I advocated upon his return from the
deep cover assignment that revealed Sage a traitor, and a course of action I
have known in my heart to be proper ever since."

He turned his head to face me, locking eyes with me as he continued
speaking with the same detached resolve. "Kill him. We have wasted far too
much time debating the fate of a common murderer, a thug who galivants
through the Mist Palace as if he has earned a place here. He has tried to kill
our leader, the very fact of which should be an immediate and irrevocable
death sentence that David has avoided for far too long."

I watched him fixedly, my eyes communicating my every thought.

*Careful, Omari. You just found a place on my hit list, and things don't end well
for the vast majority of people who achieve that distinction. One day soon, I'm
going to show you exactly what a "common murderer" like myself can accomplish.*

But I said nothing, and Omari concluded, "I have withheld nothing
from the assembly," before sitting.

Yosef was next, his diminutive frame rising. He cleared his throat before
speaking in his raspy, Israeli-accented voice.

"David's friend Ian has remained under passive surveillance since
departing the Mist Palace. We should recapture him at once, and restore
him to my service in the Intelligence Directorate. Ian's previous perfor-
mance was exemplary, as was David's, Your Grace, when Ian's life was held
as collateral. With Ian alive and under my control, I will be able to employ
David in the role he knows best: assassin. He will achieve the deaths of our
enemies until he meets the fate of all assassins and falls in the course of his
duties." He looked to the Handler. "Your Grace, I have withheld nothing
from the assembly."

Then it was Chief Vicar of Defense Watts's turn. He rose casually,
speaking in an affable Boston twang, and I wondered why my mind began

screaming that he was the one who'd gotten so many Outfit people killed in Russia.

"Sir, I have no doubt that David would perform well as an entry-level operator in the Outfit. He's proven that much in his previous assignments. And while he's no more suited for leadership than he ever was, I'd tell you to send him back to your private army—except for one fact we can't ignore any longer.

"He still wants you dead. Except now he's been off the leash here at the Mist Palace, has seen enough of our inner workings to do some serious damage in the event he meets other assassins or, God forbid, becomes a turncoat for the opposition.

"My recommendation is simple. David stays here at the Mist Palace, forever. He reverts to visitor-level security protocol, restricted to his room unless escorted by a security detail. How he finds gainful employment isn't of concern to me, as long as he never leaves this compound again. I have withheld nothing from the assembly, sir."

He sat back down, and Fiona made her final announcement according to the procedures of the court.

"The chief vicars have spoken. Sir, do you require any additional counsel before reaching your final decision?"

"I do not." The Handler turned contemptuous eyes toward his vicars. "David has myriad issues with his psyche, to be sure. But he was risking his life to avenge my daughter in Russia while you three sat here safe in the palace I have provided for you. One of you"—his voice lowered an octave—"has already betrayed me. Or your highest staff has, which makes you complicit by virtue of ignorance. And when I find out who that is, you will enter a state of existence far worse than death. My personal medical staff will be charged with keeping your mind alive to witness the horrors that will occur to your body over twelve months of degradation, starvation, and torture. I will visit you daily to watch your spirit depart long before you die. Think on this fate, because none of you will be allowed to leave the Mist Palace until I discover the betrayer among us."

Jesus, I thought. The vicars were trying to project confidence, but it was difficult not to cow before words like that. Though if any of them was obviously the betrayer, I couldn't ascertain it from their expressions.

He continued, "David Rivers, you have failed me. But yours was not a failure of disloyalty. I hereby banish you from the Mist Palace for all time. You will return to the Outfit at the lowest possible rank. There you will serve me until death, with no option of retirement."

"I understand."

"No," he said, "clearly you do not. I have tolerated far too much of your disrespect in the hopes that you would prove to be the warrior that you clearly are not. Now if you do not show me the respect that I am due, I will execute you here and now. You have been sentenced to a lifetime of servitude in the Outfit. Now speak the words, or your sentence shall be one of death."

"I hear and I obey."

"Get the fuck out of here, now and forever." Two guards descended on me, and I caught one final glimpse of the Handler turning his stony gaze toward the three vicars. "I wish to have words alone with my highest council."

12

The Complex
Two-hour Flight from San Antonio International Airport

The Gulfstream's clamshell staircase unfolded before me.

I gave a final rearward glance at the cargo aboard the jet. In addition to my bags, there was a delivery of boxes that I was responsible for escorting to the Complex. Most were marked with seals indicating sensitive, compartmentalized intelligence within, along with cryptic callsigns who were allowed to open each one at the destination. The packages were of varying sizes, but the most notable was a long wooden crate that, judging from the porters who'd struggled to load it onto the plane, was of immense weight.

Taking a resolute breath, I looked forward and descended the plane steps to take in a view I hadn't seen in some time.

The plane had taxied into the Complex hangar, and I looked at the dusty white walls around me. I hadn't seen them since my return from Somalia, when I'd disembarked the plane with the case I'd recovered hand-cuffed to my wrist. Sergio, Viggs, and Cancer had been waiting at the bottom of the stairs.

Now Viggs was dead, while Cancer and Sergio were in hiding somewhere in Argentina, along with Reilly.

And instead of familiar faces, a detail of four men beside a waiting pickup greeted me. A fifth man was at the bottom of the steps, and he called out to me over the idling Gulfstream engines.

"Good flight?"

"Yeah," I said, stepping onto the hangar's concrete floor and glancing at the high ceiling of crisscrossing metal beams. Suspended from one of the girders was the giant American flag I remembered. "Come on, these guys will unload your bags along with the delivery." He jerked his head to indicate the four waiting men, then pointed a finger at the opposite pickup. "I have to get you to the headquarters building. Orlando is waiting to see you."

We boarded a pickup, and he drove me through the security infrastructure I remembered well from my previous stay at the Complex. Our truck was in a "lock-out chamber," encapsulated by locking gates to the front and rear, while two Outfit guards scanned the vehicle's underside with pole-mounted mirrors and a third walked a bomb-sniffing dog around the outside. Only then did the front gate open, and my driver pulled forward.

The dark brown perimeter fence shielded the main Complex facilities from outside view, and when we passed inside it, I could see the areas where I'd trained in preparation for Somalia.

I glanced at the high metal roofs of multi-level structures designed for practicing urban combat, their internal and external walls ballistically rated for live-fire drills. Tall dirt berms marked outdoor shooting ranges that lined the periphery, facing out from the bone-white walls of the main Complex buildings.

We pulled to a stop alongside the headquarters building, where two men waited outside the entrance. One was a man I'd never seen before, quickly taking notes on a green field notebook as the speaker beside him dictated.

The speaker leaned against a crutch with one hand while the other pulled a cigar away from his mouth, a great billow of pale gray smoke dissipating to reveal his face. It was Orlando, looking significantly better than the last time I'd seen him. His left leg was in a massive cast from the knee down, his considerable weight now supported by two crutches.

"Orlando," I said, stepping out of the pickup and slamming the door. "How are you holding up?"

The pickup rolled away behind me, and Orlando released one crutch to accept my outstretched hand and pump it in a quick shake.

"This little scratch?" He thumped the end of a crutch in the dirt. "Forget it's there, most of the time. Glad to be back?"

"No place I'd rather be."

"Good. I wanted to personally welcome you back to the Outfit. Jerry here will take you to your team leader and make sure you have everything you need."

I noticed his assistant watching me oddly while scrawling another note in his book.

"Thank you, but first I need to speak to you alone."

"No, you don't." Orlando drew another puff and breathed the stream of smoke over his shoulder. "Your days of high-level mission access are over. You saved my life, sure. But now you're back to Outfit protocol, which means you earn your place here every day just like the rest of us. You'll report to your team leader, conduct initial counseling, and then get your white ass to work."

I lowered my voice for emphasis.

"Orlando, I need to speak to you. Alone."

He could see that there was something gravely important to me, but had no idea what it could possibly be.

"All right. Jerry, fuck off for a few minutes."

His assistant reluctantly entered the building, and Orlando chomped at his cigar without taking a drag.

"What is it, goddamnit?"

"We need to go someplace private. Inside."

"Oh, for Christ's sake, David." He took a final puff from his cigar, tossing the butt into a trashcan as he exhaled. "A little help with the door, princess."

I opened the door for him, and he maneuvered himself on his crutches down a short corridor to the command conference room.

Orlando went inside, and I followed him into a room set up like many such command conference rooms in the military. There was a central table lined with chairs, a coffee pot that was currently full and probably rarely left empty for long, and two interior doors: an open one leading into Orlando's office, and a closed one probably belonging to his senior counterpart. The light appeared to be off.

I closed the door behind us, and turned to see that Orlando didn't appreciate the gesture at all.

"Don't get comfortable, we won't be here long. I don't care about our shared history in Russia. We have standards here, and at no time did I mention an open-door policy. Any future interaction between us will occur through proper military channels. Now you've got thirty seconds to tell me what exactly you..."

His voice trailed off, eyes dropping to see me removing an ivory envelope from my jacket.

I handed it to him, and he looked at the blank white backside in confusion.

"I told you it was important."

He turned the envelope over in his hands, then froze. I watched his expression—clearly he didn't believe what he was looking at.

The envelope flap was secured with the pressed glob of red wax bearing the Handler's seal.

He locked eyes with me, bewildered.

"This..."

"It's real," I said.

Ignoring me for now, he cracked the Handler's personal wax seal and tore the envelope open. Then he removed the single page containing precious little text, all of it written in the Handler's neat script. His signature was scrawled across the bottom, the entire message composed with the massive fountain pen that he used to sign strategic directives into existence. Normally the orders were typed, though in this case the Handler hadn't wanted any digital record of the contents.

Orlando read the page quickly, his eyes darting across the script from top to bottom. But as he did so, the color began fading from his face. By the time he finished, his expression was bordering on horror.

Finally he lowered the letter and looked at me with wide eyes and a gaping mouth. I felt the back of my neck burning. I knew he wouldn't like this, expected that in all likelihood he'd look for any way to refuse the order. But the letter had been explicitly written to leave no way out, no alternative other than complete and total submission. And it hurt me deeply to see Orlando now, to watch a man I greatly respected reduced to a state of loathing after reading the summary of a mission that I alone had conceived and set into being.

"Well?" I asked, unable to bear the silence between us any longer.

He closed his mouth, then opened it again, his eyes never moving from mine.

"My God, David... what have you done?"

13

_____

29,000 Feet Above Ground Level
Norilsk, Russia

Even inside the plane's cabin, the cold was unbelievable.

I was outfitted beyond well enough to survive this—statistically, at least. My cold weather equipment would have allowed me to stand at the summit of Mount Everest without succumbing to hypothermia, and was supplemented with a bonus that mountaineers couldn't afford to haul uphill: an electrical heating unit that emitted warmth through coils ringing my core and limbs.

And despite all this, I felt like I was submerged in ice water.

My every breath sucked in flavorless air through the rubber mask encapsulating the lower half of my face, providing bottled oxygen at this altitude that would otherwise induce quickly fatal hypoxia.

In addition to the mask, helmet with night vision, and visor, and on top of the excessively bulky snowsuit, I wore a standard freefall rig complete with reserve parachute. Strapped to my side was a modified M1950 weapons case, a bulging four-foot-long nylon package strapped vertically from my armpit to ankle. When I'd parachuted into the Iraq invasion as a young Ranger, my M1950 was stuffed with a machinegun tripod and my M4 assault rifle. Those two items alone turned the weapons case into a nearly thirty-pound anchor for the low-altitude, static line combat jump.

But tonight my weapons case weighed over three times as much, totaling upward of a hundred pounds. While I was too restless to sit, I could stand only at an awkward half-kneel, letting the bottom of my cylindrical weapons case rest against the aircraft floor to take the weight off my side. There would be no jumping tonight; instead I'd waddle awkwardly off the plane and fall into the windstream outside, much as I had in Iraq.

The ramp began to lower, and I felt my breathing and pulse quicken with the alacrity of a dead sprint. Oh, how I dreaded what was about to occur. There was always a certain level of exhilaration reserved for the final moments before a mission infiltration, but never before had the stakes been so high. Never before had I been single-handedly responsible for so much, nor the consequences of failure more dire.

As the ramp slowly lowered to expose more of the night sky, bleached to a foggy green haze of innumerable stars through my night vision, I began to question this entire mission—the morality of what I was about to attempt, the effects it would achieve if successful, and the catastrophic fallout if I stumbled in any single aspect of its execution.

But it was too late to go back now. I'd conceived of this plan from start to finish, and was torn equally by the first two reactions I'd received from outside parties. The Handler, in his garden with a knife against my throat, had responded with an almost gleeful enthusiasm. He'd turned into a child, and an excited one at that, which was my first disturbing realization that perhaps this time, I was going too far.

The second had been Orlando, and his muttered response from a few days earlier was playing in my head as I awaited my leap into a void from which I could never return.

My God, David...what have you done?

Too late to change course now, I thought as I clumsily labored toward the edge of the ramp.

There, beneath the starscape of shimmering points of light unhindered by man and enhanced by my night vision, was the endless rolling tundra of northern Russia. Great swaths of it were obscured by the murky haze of a snowstorm rolling in from the east, approaching fast but not fast enough to interfere with my jump.

As for the rest of the landscape, my glance over the ramp's edge merely revealed what I already knew: it may as well have been the surface of the moon.

From this altitude there were few observable landmarks, and my visual scan was more out of curiosity mingled with terror than it was any determination of when to jump—or fall, as the case may be—from the ramp on which I now stood.

For that I'd be reliant on the aircraft's advanced navigation system, which took into account weather data and wind speed and direction in calculating activation of the green light beside me.

And this, I thought, was what it all came down to. Standing on the ramp, awaiting the literal and metaphorical jump into the unknown. My stomach was a twisted pit, heart thudding deep within the layers of cold weather equipment that just barely kept me alive at this polar altitude. Konstantin's boar tusk was there too, still pressed against my skin. But this moment was the essence of what separated me from those who pulled the strings in places like the Mist Palace—others planned and judged, praised or punished based on what they thought should have occurred in places and on missions that they'd never dare go themselves. Ultimately I stood in the ranks of those who willingly flung themselves into danger to accomplish great things, and bore the consequences, whether exhilarating, catastrophic, or fatal.

This time, however, the mission concept and the risk were mine alone.

The ramp light flicked from red to yellow—thirty seconds from exit. But just as I took a breath to steel myself for the endless half-minute wait, the light flicked from yellow to green.

Had the navigation system made a mistake? Was it an electrical error? There was no time to consider further. Our flight plan afforded no second chances to make the jump.

Stumbling forward a final two steps, my body tilted over the ramp's edge. With the weight of my equipment pulling me toward the earth, I tumbled face-first into the freezing polar air over northern Russia.

The jet wash sucked me away from the plane in a split second. I entered a deliriously violent tumble as the battering forces of air transitioned from the plane's exhaust to the high-altitude winds. My view through the night vision was a whirling cyclone, impossible to decipher—a blur of ground, flash of stars, wisp of cloud, ground stars cloud ground cloud stars—and I arched my back as hard as I could to stabilize.

But my whipping tumble wouldn't stop, or even slow. Instead it seemed to be accelerating in chaotic instability, forcing my thoughts to retreat into a hazy realm of consciousness that indicated I was about to pass out.

I felt one painful blow to my side from the top of my weapons case, then another. Foggily, I realized that one of the tie-down attachments must have broken under the gale-force jet wash.

Now the weapons case had turned into a hundred-pound battering ram against my rib, and no adjustment to my body position could overcome the instability it caused. The world was a sickening kaleidoscope of ground cloud stars cloud ground stars. I couldn't read my altimeter, couldn't estimate how many seconds had elapsed since I exited, and couldn't end the nightmarish 360-degree spin that pushed me to the brink of unconsciousness in any way—except one.

I pulled both hands inward to the right side of my chest, clutching a metal handle on my harness and yanking it outward.

My main parachute fired, its spring-loaded pilot chute blasting outward. My panicked thoughts congealed into a single hopeful, desperate plea that I'd be jerked upright, saved by a clean deployment to find myself gracefully suspended from a fully inflated parachute that sailed unflappably forward.

And while I found myself vertical, the rotation remained. Instead of a gyroscopic blitz, however, I could now see a discernible horizon, the stars and ground in a fixed, proper orientation as they spun past on a horizontal axis.

I placed both hands on my parachute risers, trying to force them apart as I looked up to appraise what had become of my canopy.

Over my head, the risers converged into a snarled knot of canopy billowing in the wind, half-fluttering and half-collapsed. At first glance, I knew it was hopeless.

Dropping my hands from the risers to my chest, I grabbed a fist-sized pillow of fabric and yanked it outward.

The parachute detached, disappearing in the sky as I fell straight down, releasing the cutaway pillow and bringing both hands to a metal loop on

the opposite side. Then I yanked the metal loop as if my life depended on it
—which, right now, it did.

My reserve parachute fired its spring-loaded pilot chute, then blasted
open a second later.

I looked skyward to see the four blissfully squared corners of a green
rectangle hovering above me; my last chance of surviving a terminal fall to
earth had worked, and my reserve parachute now sailed cleanly forward.
And the impossibly heavy weapons case was, thank God, still attached to
my left side. A single loop of tie-down that pulled the upper end tight to my
side had snapped and caused my flat spin, but the metal clip attaching the
case to my parachute harness was intact.

I frantically checked my altitude. The glowing disc on my left hand
indicated 24,300 feet above ground level; my uncontrollable spin had cost
me almost 5,000 feet, and that was all altitude I might not have to spare.

Flipping down a chest-mounted tablet, I saw the display glow to life
with a digital compass and GPS showing 27.8 miles to target. Taking control
of the steering toggles on my reserve chute, I spun a sharp turn until the
directional arrow aligned with my destination.

A hasty evaluation of the data revealed that I could still reach my
intended landing zone, but just barely. A change in the prevailing winds at
altitude would be enough to take me off course, and then things would
really get interesting.

Now came the long flight, and I could feel my core temperature dropping despite the myriad heating measures in my suit.

I'd just conducted a HAHO—high altitude, high opening jump. I was
far from target, I could cover that distance under parachute—stealthy, near-
silent, and difficult to discern under night vision or thermal imagery until I
was about to land.

And now, 24,000 feet above the arctic tundra, I was flying toward my
target.

The cold was crippling. When I lifted my hands above heart level to
operate the steering toggles, the blood draining from my fingertips quickly
resulted in both hands feeling as if they were submerged in ice. My night
vision lenses continually frosted over; I had to keep wiping them clean with
my glove.

I had a long flight ahead, relying on the chest-mounted tablet to guide my course until I had Konstantin's compound in sight through my night vision. That would be my first and only landmark of civilization. The nearest small towns were well over a hundred miles distant, leaving me with a view of sprawling tundra that appeared in washed-out green hues far below. It appeared endless—or would have, I supposed, if not for the encroaching storm.

The misty ether clouding my view was so nebulous as to be almost dismissible as an illusion: my lenses frosting over again, perhaps some moisture within the night vision device.

But I knew better.

Siberia's short summer was coming to an end. Micah had told me this area experienced only three months without snow, and the first winter snow would begin tonight. Despite pitching this plan to the Handler as soon as I'd thought of it, and despite him putting it into action without delay, I'd end up beating the first snowfall of the season by hours, not days.

This was an almost pointlessly ambitious plan, but its very inconceivability made it my only option. This entire thing *could* have been very simple, but, of course, the Handler still wanted Konstantin alive. That tiny detail made the entire mission exponentially more complicated, and if I failed to deliver, I may as well die on the objective. Which, if I was being honest, had a greater-than-passing chance of occurring anyway.

But if I wanted to avenge Parvaneh and, more importantly, stop Konstantin, this was the way, though it wouldn't solve everything. Even if I succeeded, Agustin would still be alive, as would the Handler, along with his vicars. If and when I made it out of this alive, I could worry about them.

In the end I had two options: watch everything fall apart while waiting for some future opportunity to vanquish all my enemies at once, or do what I could *right now*. And right now, I had only the power to target a single element in that trifecta of evil, so I made the only play I could. Doing so required compromising my secret path into the Handler's garden, thereby closing off that means of killing him forever. But a secret meeting with him, together with a sealed order granting me everything I required, was the only way to ensure total mission secrecy.

Then I saw Konstantin's compound.

I was in disbelief at first; I should have been far too high, the compound far too laterally distant for me to make out. I checked my GPS and directional indicator, then looked back up.

That was his compound, all right. Against a crawling rocky landscape of trees, scrub brush, and the occasional small body of water, the sole evidence of man appeared so bizarrely concentric, so symmetrical, that it stood out like a billboard even from this altitude. The unnatural shapes and corners of buildings and generators looked like a cluster of toys forgotten in the field.

I gauged my glide path. I didn't want to soar into the center of the compound and risk being spotted; my goal was to touch down at the periphery, near the row of generators whose distance from living accommodations would prevent me from being seen, and whose noise would shield the flutter of my parachute and the tumble of my boots making landfall. In the event of a random thermal sweep inside the compound perimeter, the generator's heat signature was my best bet of blending in. And most importantly, the vibrating earth around the generators was the one place I knew would be devoid of ground movement sensors.

The compound seemed to be racing toward me too quickly, and I feverishly scanned for the movement of human figures darting into position to capture me. I flared to land, soaring into the ground on the far side of a generator unit.

My boots struck hard, and I rolled onto my side to let the momentum flip me over until I'd crashed to a halt. If I wanted a soft landing, I could have lowered my heavy weapons case on its lowering line—but the risk of entanglement with some unseen ground obstacle was far too great.

The second I came to rest, I detached a parachute riser and pulled it toward me to deflate my canopy. When it was reasonably bundled and in no danger of re-inflating to announce my presence like a hot air balloon over the row of generators, I stripped off my outer gloves and ripped away a Velcro retention strap under my right armpit, then quickly expanded the adjustable shoulder sling and readied my suppressed Heckler & Koch MP7.

I scanned for targets, half-hoping for some hapless sentry strolling by whose night I could ruin before he announced the presence of an invader within their perimeter. But the generators' hum was undisturbed by man, my limited view free of guards.

I let the MP7 hang on its sling. Its compact size put it somewhere between a large pistol and a small submachine gun; at only four pounds, the MP7 was designed for personal defense, its forty-round magazine loaded with bullets designed to pierce body armor. And while I didn't think any intrepid guards would be enduring the discomfort of armored plates on their average night in the wilds of Siberia, I fully expected the outdoor sentries to be clad in untold layers of cold weather gear—and that had a strange way of making hollow-point bullets expand and tumble in unexpected ways. But any bullets capable of penetrating Kevlar with titanium backing, as mine did, would have no such difficulty finding their target.

Stripping off my parachute harness, I stepped out of the assembly. I removed my helmet, then switched my night vision onto a head harness and unfolded an aviator kit bag to stash everything in. Mostly everything, anyway—my bulky heated outer garments to survive the high-altitude flight were a spacesuit unto themselves, and along with the helmet and oxygen equipment, weren't getting stuffed into anything.

But I didn't need to completely conceal the evidence of my incursion, only stash it well enough to pass initial scrutiny. Once my canopy was in the kit bag and at no risk of re-inflating with wind, I shoved, kicked, and otherwise prodded the mess of equipment into the three-foot space for air circulation beneath the nearest generator.

I checked my watch. Only one item left to dispose of: the modified M1950 weapons case that had been strapped to my side during the jump. Hoisting the four-foot nylon tube over my shoulder, I moved as quickly as its hundred-pound weight would allow—down the row of generators, away from my parachute equipment. Once anyone realized I'd entered their compound, they'd scour for evidence of how I did it. My parachute would quickly be found, and that was fine.

As long as my weapons case wasn't.

To stash it, I chose a generator far down the row, encased in an outer box to protect it from the elements. Turning the handle to an access panel, I swung the insulated door open and was met with a blast of stinking heat and exhaust. But what bothered me most was the noise: a sudden and irreconcilable increase in the volume of the generator's groan. Anyone within thirty feet would hear it.

The damage was done now, so I shoved the weapons case into the dark space beyond the access panel, repositioning it to fit all the way in the darkened gap. Once it was gone, I sealed the panel back in place.

Then I ran down the row of generators, separating myself from the noise I'd made and finding another elevated ground unit. This time I wasn't planning on stashing my parachute beneath it; instead, I would stash myself. Sliding under the unit, I positioned myself in the prone, MP7 accessible, and edged forward to peer out with my night vision. If anyone came to investigate the noise and found what I'd hidden, I'd have to take the enormous risk of trying to kill them silently before they raised the alarm.

I heard movement before I had time to react, and two sets of boots strode past less than an arm's length from my face. Holy shit, I wasn't expecting them to come from *behind* me. My pulse was hammering against the permafrost beneath me, my body heat draining into the earth—gone was the mega-insulated, self-heated shell I'd jumped with. Now I was down to basic cold weather gear that I could actually maneuver in, and I'd very likely be taking my shots at these guards with hands that shook from the cold.

The men came to a stop near the generator unit I'd opened. Christ, this was going to be bad. One man would be child's play; two risked one darting off before I could tag them both, and then I'd be in one hell of a pickle. Nowhere to go, a few MP7 reloads to my name, and Konstantin's compound my final resting place. *Game over, David Rivers—you're spending eternity in Siberia.*

Edging forward with the MP7, I slipped my head out to see them. A blinding flash of light caused me to retract it just as quickly. They were sweeping flashlights around the row while conversing in Russian. Fair enough, I thought. I braced myself for a hasty, concealed shot; when I heard the generator's volume shoot up from them opening the door, I'd pop out like the whack-a-mole from hell and burn them both down.

Hopefully.

The lights suddenly extinguished, but the conversational tone of their voices continued as they moved out in a different direction.

I closed my eyes, breathing a silent declaration of gratitude for my luck.

After exiting an aircraft 29,000 feet over the earth nearly thirty miles away, I'd crossed the night sky, beaten the storm, and successfully infiltrated the compound undetected.

Now it was on to phase two: find Konstantin, and make him pay.

* * *

The near-miss with the two guards had given me confidence in one regard: I could move out in the direction they had approached from without fear of ground sensors. Thermals, surveillance cameras, and visual observation, yes—but not ground sensors, and that was something.

I crept stealthily through the compound, tucking myself into the deepest green shadows that my night vision revealed. The movement warmed me somewhat; I really could've used some more cold weather gear, but stealth and maneuverability were the priority, not comfort.

The benefit of the cold was that no one was condemned to be outside in such weather, save a few sentries. These people generally thought their compound impenetrable, and they were about to pay for that.

A whipping chill blew over me. I was grateful for the noise concealing my movement, but the storm was moving in fast. There was no time for a slow, methodical approach—locating Konstantin was an all-or-nothing proposition, just like this whole mission.

I made my way between low buildings toward the elegantly constructed log cabin at its center. It didn't take long to locate—the architecture stood in contrast to everything else within the compound perimeter, and if I needed any clues on where to find the boss, the attached eight-car garage would guide me.

I moved toward the garage and, more specifically, the single door meant for people instead of vehicles. If there was one place in the building where no one would be at this hour, it was the garage.

The door had a deadbolt, but I tested the handle regardless. It was, of course, locked. But I, of course, was prepared.

A majority of what little equipment I carried was dedicated to breaching doors by various means. I carried bump keys, electronic lock pick guns, and even small explosive charges in the event all else failed.

My first course of action, however, was the simplest.

I found my set of bump keys, locating one that looked like it would fit into the keyhole.

The bump keys were nothing special—just a set of keys in various sizes with symmetrical, filed-down teeth that allowed them to enter a variety of keyholes. A standard set of ten keys and a bit of working knowledge enabled you to defeat the vast majority of commercial pin tumbler locks, and I'd practiced little else on my most recent flight from North America.

I inserted the bump key, pulled it out one click, and then withdrew a bump hammer—a pocket-sized rubber mallet with a flexible handle.

Giving the key a slight turn and holding it in place, I tapped the back of it with the bump hammer. Nothing. I pulled the key back out one click, then repeated the process while keeping slight pressure on the key as if trying to turn it. The key plunged back in, but remained as vertical as when I'd inserted it. I withdrew it one click, trying again.

The principle was simple. Bumping the key into the keyhole caused a momentary jolt among the key pins and driver pins of a standard pin tumbler lock; if done correctly, they would eventually align in the unlocked configuration. That alignment lasted only for the blink of an eye, but if you maintained continuous fingertip pressure on the key, that moment was enough.

A final tap with my bump hammer caused the key to flip a quarter turn under my fingertips.

I rotated the key the rest of the way, then pocketed my bump hammer and let myself inside.

Closing and locking the door behind me, I examined the dark garage through my night vision. Forget stealing a vehicle from the outdoor motorpool, I thought. I'd take one of these instead.

The eight vehicles ranged from luxury SUVs with visible rifle racks to what looked like modified dune buggies, all lined up with their bumpers facing their respective garage door.

But the one that caught my attention was a Hilux pickup like the white ones parked outside, modified into a monster-truck variation that could cross the arctic terrain with ease if not comfort. I approached it to test the driver side door handle.

It popped open, and I partially climbed into the cabin to confirm the key fob was affixed to a permanent mount beside the dash. Not a lot of car thieves in this part of Siberia, I supposed, exiting the truck and gently pushing the door shut. This truck had just become my getaway vehicle...if I made it that far.

Recovering a small fixed-blade knife from my kit, I took a few moments, to spear the tires of every other vehicle in the garage. It took a fair amount of strength to puncture the winter tires' thick rubber, but the garage was soon filled with the soft, hissing exhale of air. These weren't the only vehicles in the compound, but I couldn't risk the exposure of seeking out every truck on the premises. I was immensely lucky to have made it this far, and proceeded on to the next phase of my plan.

I entered the house.

* * *

The corridors were silent as I slipped through, listening for the slightest sound of movement. Locating the bedroom was second in importance only to remembering the route back to the garage.

Recessed floor lighting provided enough ambient light for the view to be crystal through my night vision, and I discerned the master bedroom by virtue of a massive slab of pine that stood out from every other interior door I'd seen.

I tested the handle—locked, of course. The door had a keyhole for a deadbolt, and I suspected that a few bodyguards somewhere in this building held the key. As much as I would have liked to slay one of them and take it, the safer option was to use the bump key again, so that's what I did.

This was still a riskier proposition than doing so outside. Bumping a lock required a tap that made noise; depending on Konstantin's location in the room, he could conceivably hear it and come to investigate—or simply trigger an alarm.

Then the night would get very interesting, very fast.

I selected a bump key and inserted it, using the very gentlest of taps with the rubber surface of my bump hammer. The noise seemed deafening to me, but I heard no footsteps, no curious parties coming to investigate.

After only four taps the key flipped in the bolt.

Turning it the rest of the way, I felt the deadbolt slide open. Then I pocketed my keys and hammer, trading them for an air pistol loaded with tranquilizer darts that would instantly deliver a potent surgical anesthetic. One direct hit should induce near-immediate unconsciousness; two or

136

more would risk death by overdose, and if Konstantin died, this would all end poorly for me.

I turned the door handle and pushed it open.

I was ready to fire at once, the pistol tucked into a hip fire position, but I soon saw that wouldn't be necessary.

A short corridor extended before me, appearing to open into a much larger space. The corridor walls rippled with the orange glow of a fire beyond, and I slipped inside and closed the door behind me before flipping my night vision upward on its mount.

I latched the deadbolt back into place behind me. As I continued down the corridor, I could hear the loud crackle of flames and the popping sounds of hardwood burning. No wonder Konstantin hadn't heard me bumping the lock—the fire must have been enormous.

The view of the room beyond gradually slid into view.

And for all the modern construction here in the compound, Konstantin's bedchamber looked medieval.

The roaring fire blazed in an immense hearth, its flickering glow illuminating high walls of inlaid stone beset with the heads of beasts—giant brown bears with their fangs exposed, moose and elk with enormous racks, a row of three tigers.

But most of all, there were boars.

Snarling pig heads bared their tusks in every direction, impossibly broad shoulders against the wall tapering to the snout, shaggy ears flared. The marble substitutes for the boars' eyes caught more light from the fire than those of any other animal; they seemed to reflect the flame from all around, a hundred sparkling red eyes watching me enter.

Suddenly I heard two voices murmuring from around the corner, where I presumed the bed to be located.

This caused a shock of alarm to run through me for two reasons. The first was no different than when I encountered two sentries outside: to silently take one person by surprise was difficult enough. Two was near impossible.

The second reason was a moral one.

In large part, my plan hinged on this place operating as Micah said it did: the Slavic model, whereby wives and children were left in civilized locales while the men rotated in and out of headquarters, thus ensuring that even if leaders were assassinated in other Russian cities, their organization would survive intact. This compound was the beating heart of the Far North Coalition, and no one had ever penetrated its defenses...until now.

But if Konstantin was conversing in his bedroom at this hour, I could reasonably ascertain that the other party wasn't there to fold his laundry. I knew he had a wife in Yakutsk, and Susan alluded to him employing prostitutes outside of his marriage. Was an innocent woman here?

I suppressed the thought. *One step at a time, hero.* All those ethical considerations would be wasted thoughts in the event I got killed in the next ninety seconds, which had a not-unlikely chance of occurring.

And as I approached the corner, the fire's heat increasing and the animal eyes glaring down at me, I recognized both voices. One was Konstantin's; the other, while certainly not a wife, could pose a problem, to say the least.

I spun around the corner, leveling my tranquilizer pistol toward the voices.

Just as I expected, the bed was there—a giant sprawling affair heaped with blankets and animal furs.

Konstantin was there too, sitting up on a pillow propped against an intricately carved wooden headboard stretching ten feet overhead. The fire cast a shadow across him; I realized it was mine. He looked up at once, just in time to see me leveling the air pistol at him.

Without a sound, he lunged sideways toward his nightstand—whether for a gun or a panic button, I couldn't be sure.

I fired first at him. The air pistol made a soft *pfft*, and the dart sailing across the space between us pierced his chest just below the collarbone.

I barely had time to register the hit when his body was blocked by the other person sharing the bed with him.

It was the bearded giant who killed Micah on my first visit to the compound. There was no time to transition to my MP7, so I turned the sights of my air pistol toward him instead.

But the giant was gone in a flash, pushing himself over Konstantin's body with impossible grace and agility for a man his size. I tracked him with the sights, firing three times in rapid succession as he reached for the same nightstand that his lover had.

The first dart struck the headboard, making a sharp *pock* that I could hear over the crackling flames behind me. But the other two landed silently, one in his tattooed shoulder and the other in his rib.

I chased the shots across the room, charging toward the bed to fling his now-unconscious body away from whatever they'd both been reaching for. He was already slumping into a heap of dead weight, his arm knocking into the base of a lamp on the nightstand.

I was too late.

At that second, the panic alarm sounded.

I could hear the shrill, piercing wail emanating from inside and outside the bedchamber. The room's overhead lights came on automatically, flinging my surroundings into a blinding glow. I had seconds before bodyguards arrived, and in this case I couldn't rely on the evolutionary instinct of fight or flight.

Because I would have to do both.

I emptied the tranquilizer pistol into the giant as I raced to the bed, then let it fall from my hand. By the time I stopped at the giant's body, his side and back were a pincushion of darts and he was slipping into a soon-to-be-fatal coma. I tried to push his body off Konstantin. But God help me, adrenaline and all, he was simply too damn heavy. I changed tack and used both hands to pull him instead, letting gravity take over as he cleared the edge of the bed and crashed to the floor.

Stepping on his chest to retrieve Konstantin, I had a much easier time—he weighed less than I did, and my current adrenal levels were more than sufficient to allow me to jerk him out of the bed. I hoisted him over my shoulders in a fireman's carry, freeing my right hand to operate the MP7. Then I pulled the buttstock against my shoulder as I wheeled toward the door, certain I would find an army of intruders bursting in.

But none came—at least, not yet.

I crossed the room as the siren continued, thinking this was just like assassinating Saamir— trying to run amid the shrieking fire alarm, trying to fight my way out. But I didn't have nearly as far to go here; not to my immediate destination, at least.

Spinning around the corner, I saw the door where I'd entered. The deadbolt was turning, a strip of light appearing as the door was flung open.

I leveled my suppressor at the door and squeezed the trigger.

It wasn't my most accurate fully automatic burst, but sufficient to rip two dozen rounds through the barrel in the time it took me to feel the weapon's recoil.

The door flung all the way open, assisted by the responding guard's collapsing body. A second man was behind him, struggling to maintain control of his submachine gun—he'd been hit too, some of the armor-piercing rounds having penetrated the door *and* his friend's torso before striking him. My God, this gun was nothing if not amazing. I depressed the trigger again, lighting him up with a short burst that sent him falling to the ground.

To my shock he was still alive and groaning, but out of the fight, and so I stepped onto his dead partner's back and kicked him in the face on my way past.

The lights were on in the building, simplifying my navigation as I hurriedly followed my path back toward the garage.

Moving past a hallway with Konstantin slung over my back, I saw movement and turned to aim. A responding guard less than ten feet away skidded to a halt at the sight of me.

His face contorted into a priceless expression of shock.

I loved watching people scramble when they couldn't believe what was happening. Sure, these people were equipped and theoretically prepared to deal with a variety of contingencies. And when pressed, they could—but it didn't completely mitigate the sheer disbelief that, after years or decades of uneventfully standing guard, a rogue agent was absconding with their boss.

We aimed at each other near-simultaneously. The difference between us was his momentary hesitation as he realized that he was in very real danger of shooting his boss, and where would that leave his pension?

I let him have it with an automatic burst. Only a half-dozen rounds or so fired before my bolt locked to the rear.

Shit. Forty-round box mags fly when you're having fun.

The man stumbled backward, struck by at least a few of my shots but certainly not incapacitated. These weren't the most powerful bullets in the world, but automatic weapons suitable for one-handed operation couldn't be cannons. I darted out of sight anyway, confident that the guard was bleeding out too quickly to pursue.

I was at a run now, adrenaline propelling me forward at a fast clip despite Konstantin's body over my shoulders.

Finally, I reached the garage.

The sight of Konstantin's truck brought with it an immense rush of relief. This feeling crescendoed as I opened the passenger door. Straining to plant a boot atop the running board, I roughly shouldered him inside, then slammed the door, preparing to move.

But the door wouldn't close.

I pulled it farther open and slammed it again, but it bounced softly back at me. Fuck it, I thought, Konstantin could deal with the cold air— then I realized his leg had slipped into the doorframe. I lifted his foot and shoved it inside, and the door snapped into place with ease.

Using my newly liberated hand to reload the MP7, I ran around the hood to the driver side. As I did so, I realized I should have merely skipped the reload and climbed over Konstantin to gain some protection from the truck's exterior. It was too late now, and as I cleared the driver side bumper on my way to the door, I saw shadows in the doorway behind me.

I didn't look, didn't distinguish targets, didn't even aim.

Instead I raised the MP7 in the direction of the light, had the safety flicked off in the time it took me to lift the weapon, and squeezed the trigger.

The armor-piercing rounds flew past the suppressor as I ripped a long burst, releasing the trigger only when I could no longer fight the barrel's rise from recoil. I depressed the trigger again, sending another burst into the shadows.

Then I flung open the driver door, hoisting myself inside. Had I hit anyone? Everyone? I didn't care, and right now it didn't matter. I hit the push button start, threw the transmission to drive, and floored the accelerator.

For a split second, nothing happened.

Then the stereo came to life: a loud, booming concerto of Russian opera singing.

As I desperately glanced down to make sure I'd placed the truck into drive and not neutral, the engine caught up with my pedal input, and the massive truck lurched forward with a velocity that threw my skull against the headrest.

The truck crashed through the garage door and into the black night. I impulsively tapped the brakes, fearing I'd crash into an adjacent building and face the very embarrassing circumstance of having inadvertently sabotaged my otherwise flawless prisoner snatch.

But I had plenty of room to maneuver out here. I cut the huge truck's wheels to the right, aiming between structures as I struggled to orient myself.

I was almost free now, headed away and wondering how to turn on the headlights in this thing. Didn't matter, that's what night vision was for. I flipped the device down over my eyes, turning the compound into a green landscape and providing the clarity to realize that, oh shit, I was headed the wrong way.

I wheeled the truck left between buildings, wanting to turn off the radio so I could think. But just then a man came running out from a building and tried to flag me down. He had no idea what was happening, saw Konstantin's truck and heard the music, and by way of updating him on the current circumstances of the Far North Coalition, I whipped the steering wheel sideways to run him over.

The front bumper hit his torso dead-on, and the truck was so big I barely felt the *thump*. I was laughing now, driving recklessly toward my exit point from the compound and almost hoping someone else would step outside.

Spinning a final drifting turn around my reference point, the twin obelisks facing north, I got my wish.

It wasn't one man, but three! My heart leapt with joy, until I realized they were armed and seemed to be at least somewhat cognizant that the monster truck bearing down on them wasn't being driven by their beloved Konstantin.

One did the honorable thing and leapt out of my way, but the other two raised their weapons—and in the time it took them to aim, I was driving the engine block through their bodies at close to 50mph.

Then, to the tune of Russian opera blasting in the cabin, I was speeding through the obelisks on a known azimuth. The truck blasted free of the compound and into the Siberian night.

I began juking the truck left and right, carving an erratic pattern northward. This was the moment of truth—they had me in the sights of their remotely operated long-range machineguns now, the truck's thermal signature lit up like a hot coal on the screens of every operations center technician.

At the push of a button, they could fire a single burst and turn my vehicle into a flaming yard sale with me inside—and I was afraid they might. Maybe the operations center hadn't yet realized that Konstantin was gone, or maybe they did and would prefer to incinerate their leader rather than allow him to fall into enemy interrogation. That much I could live with—if I died in that way, then at least Konstantin was going with me.

I swerved the steering wheel like a drunkard, not to stop them from shooting—I couldn't do anything to prevent that—but to keep them from achieving a precision shot against a wheel that would disable my vehicle. That in itself was risky for them; the slightest miss could kill their leader, and they would rightly assume that my first course of action if my vehicle stopped would be to execute Konstantin. But right now, scoring a mobility kill against my truck was the only move they had.

Almost the only move, I realized a second later.

A geyser of dirt exploded in front of my bumper, and I swerved away in the time it took the machinegun's blast to reach my ears. Another round impacted, this one only slightly closer—they were firing warning shots, demonstrating they would kill me if I didn't stop. Deciding to put that threat to the test, I continued jerking the wheel in a zigzag path. The truck's bouncing cab felt like being inside a rock polisher, with every hard bump sending me momentarily airborne from my seat. But the continued warning shots to my front assured me they were too scared about killing their leader with an errant bullet.

"What's the matter, you pussies?" I shouted, my voice a lunatic's scream echoing to an audience of one. Konstantin was still unconscious. Within minutes, I'd be beyond machinegun range, thermal visibility, and ground sensor detection.

But the landscape beyond the field was growing more wooded, and I tried to distinguish a half-efficient driving line under the murky green hues of my night vision. Without looking, I used one hand to fumble for the radio volume knob, ending Konstantin's music for good.

Suddenly the landscape illuminated brightly, as if my optic had increased three hundred percent in effectiveness. It was almost too bright, I thought, and then, with a deflating sense of dread, I realized it was.

The blazing headlights of multiple vehicles were illuminating me from behind, lighting my path as they homed in on me.

Shit, I thought, guess we're all going "white light."

I pulled the helmet and night vision from my head, throwing it atop Konstantin as I fumbled with the steering wheel stalks to find my own headlights. The left turn signal activated, and I shut it off and tried the opposite side. Wipers began flicking across my windshield.

Finally the headlights on my front bumper activated, and the entire world before me turned to daylight. That's better, I thought, checking my mirrors to see at least five trucks behind me, one or two of them driving like ducks in a row on my trail, the others spreading to the flanks and trying to find a way to cut me off.

We all had equal power, I knew—I may have even had a bit more, because if anyone's truck got the extra horsepower in that compound, it was the man slumped unconscious in the seat next to me. But I'd lost some time with the erratic driving required to keep the machineguns from blowing one of my wheels, and my pursuers were closing fast in a straight line behind me. If they caught up, I had only one choice.

I looked over at Konstantin.

The truck's bouncing movements had caused his body to fall into an odd sideways fetal position, his legs in the footwell, head and shoulders resting on the seat beside me. He looked like a sleeping child, contorted into positions that no adult of fixed bone density could maintain.

I checked my mirrors, seeing that the trucks directly behind me remained the same distance away. But two that had spread to the left flank must have found some more expeditious path to travel, and they had closed about half the distance.

Things were getting dicey fast, and I surprised myself with an absurdly maniacal laugh that sprang out of nowhere.

What was so funny?

What *wasn't* so funny, I thought. Before becoming a mercenary I'd almost killed myself. Now my job attempted that for me. Moments like this —or, perhaps, the repeated exposure to them—bred a brand of gallows humor exclusive to people who lived this life. After all the awkward and nonsensical attempts to conform myself into regular society, I was certain that I *was* the way I was because of war. Jesus, man, anyone who hadn't been hardened by combat would be reduced to a paralyzed state of fear by my current situation, including my eighteen-year-old pre-Army self.

Now, after my ever-growing list of near misses with death, I was almost reveling in this. Beneath the adrenaline and the intensity of trying to stay alive, of trying to keep Konstantin alive for the time being, was an irrational undercurrent of joy reserved for taunting death. It was addictive, as well it should be: why else would anyone repeatedly go to war? The duty and country aspect only got one so far into the experience—for me, it had evaporated shortly into my first combat deployment. It had lasted until I saw my first enemy dying before me, fatally wounded by the first bullets I'd ever fired outside of a training range, and I recognized in his stare a man no different than I was. A warrior who, ideology aside, I had more in common with than the politicians who'd sent me there.

Even as a teenager, I philosophically recognized this truth. Upon returning to the States, I *knew* I was different, no longer felt connected to society or life outside war. Everything was the same, except me. Did I resign as a warrior? Hell no! Even now, with the myriad psychological issues I'd accumulated on subsequent missions like a global Easter egg hunt for insanity, I wouldn't change anything. I'd continued along this path for a reason, and not because it wasn't fun. Because once combat was experienced, *nothing else in life* was fun. Devoid of war, the human experience felt like a gaping maw of emptiness.

Besides, I could have stepped off the hamster wheel at any time. I'd wanted combat when I joined the Army, demanded an Infantry contract, volunteered for the Rangers, gone to combat in Afghanistan and Iraq before going to West Point. There, I could have chosen any number of noncombat specialties, but I chose Infantry again. When they forced me out of military service, the prospect of combat now forever unattainable, I'd immediately lapsed into an unrecoverable suicidal depression.

No wonder my chance recruitment into the mercenary ranks had saved me. My life and psyche in the regular world were shit compared to my peers who'd never gone to war. And who cared? Would I change anything if I could go back and do it all over again? No. I'd earned my scars, physical and psychological, and I was beginning to feel a strange sense of pride about them.

With a sudden rush of what could be bizarrely described as self-acceptance, I looked out the driver side window and felt any positivity drain from my soul.

Two trucks were rapidly closing on me, having found a stretch of smoother ground. No matter—a spray of MP7 fire should make the drivers think twice about getting closer. I pawed at the doorsill beside me to roll down the window, and found there was no way to.

Of course, you idiot. These are arctic-modified trucks.

I considered shooting out the window with the few bullets remaining in my MP7 magazine, but decided the effort would cost me too much in terms of keeping my vehicle from hitting an obstacle and flipping over. Besides, I had no hope of reloading while piloting this vehicle at its fastest possible speed.

No sooner had this thought occurred when the nearest truck behind me opened fire.

I ducked reflexively, hearing the rapid-fire pops of controlled gunshots erupting. My sideview mirror revealed two shooters in the bed of the truck, trying to hold on as they took reasonably precise shots over the top of the cab.

When no bullets penetrated the glass, I realized they weren't shooting at me—why would they? Fearing an errant bullet would strike their lord, they were firing at my tires in an attempt to disable my vehicle.

If they succeeded, they were in for sour news. Because the MP7 was still secure on its sling, the moment my escape was hindered I'd plant its suppressor in Konstantin's ear and let him have a burst of armor-piercing rounds that would vaporize his brain, pass through the seat below him, and rip past the undercarriage of the truck on their way out.

It wouldn't be a bad way to go as far as I was concerned. Having completed my most audacious—and insanely suicidal—mission attempt to date, I'd managed to snatch their leader from his bed, shoot an unknown number of people in the compound, and turn three others into arctic road-kill. Weighed against those accomplishments, executing Konstantin at point-blank range and going out in a blaze of gunfire didn't seem such a bad option.

But since my truck hadn't been disabled just yet, I did the only thing I could: swung left until I nearly struck the nearest pursuing vehicle, forcing it to swerve out of the way. I couldn't afford to crash into it, or even brake and let it rear-end me to send its shooters airborne with the impact. At this point, the only thing I had going for me was momentum, and any compromise of speed would allow the other trucks to draw even nearer than they already were.

But it wasn't enough.

The trucks to my right began gaining ground, and those to the left were closing in and taking potshots at my tires. The others behind me were fanning out to bridge the gap. It was a matter of time before my truck was disabled. They were too close now; there was nothing else I could do. I was seconds away from having my tires shot out or being rammed into an unrecoverable spin and then boxed in.

Steering with my left hand, I used my right to hoist the MP7. One more glance at my mirrors confirmed the obvious—I wasn't making it out of here. Amid the bouncing cabin, I tried to aim the MP7 toward Konstantin's head.

But I couldn't angle my weapon over the console; the sling was too tight.

I loosened the sling to pull the MP7 off my shoulders, then used one hand to press the suppressor into Konstantin's ear.

Suddenly the truck next to me exploded in a fireball, its chassis leaping into the air before tumbling end-over-end. I looked to my mirror, seeing the flaming wreckage coming to a halt just as a second truck blew up.

This one vanished in a momentary orange cloud of destruction, flipping sideways in an angry knot of smoke.

I scanned the ridge to my front, seeing a faint flash of light appear and vanish. Then a thin wisp of smoke streaked past my cab, striking the engine block of a third pursuing truck and turning it into scrap metal. The thunderclap of a rocket explosion echoed as the remaining trucks broke their pursuit, spinning wild U-turns in an attempt to escape the ambush I'd led them into.

And while I dared not slow to look back, their attempts to flee seemed futile.

The Outfit shooters on the ridge continued sending rockets toward the remaining vehicles, systematically destroying them. I heard explosions behind me, caught glimpses of the fireballs in my rearview mirror, and distantly wondered if any of the trucks would survive.

I tried to re-sling the MP7, but the darkness and the bouncing truck cab made that impossible. I tossed it onto the backseat instead, returning both hands to the wheel as I kept the accelerator floored.

I maneuvered the truck uphill and over the saddle separating the ridges.

The earth beyond dipped into a wide ravine, then stretched into the wide, flat bowl of terrain deemed acceptable by an airfield survey.

This was the mission completion we'd engineered for Yakutsk—Konstantin alive, safely extracted and delivered to the waiting aircraft. I'd narrowly beaten the odds; I should have been relieved.

But the improvised airstrip that came into view put me in a state of shock.

How could this be, I thought—I'd engineered this mission start to finish, and Konstantin's transfer from vehicle to aircraft was supposed to be a mirror image of the first attempt. So why was I seeing this?

The Outfit plane was there as planned, ramp lowered, idling with streaky hazes of heat wafting from its engines. A small perimeter of Outfit men were providing local security, though the bulk of their force had occupied the ridge to safeguard my escape. All that was according to plan.

But there was also a second plane in the field, one I'd never seen before. This other aircraft was smaller, some twin turboprop cargo plane equipped for short takeoff and landing. This shouldn't have mattered right now. I should have dismissed it and carried on, unconcerned.

But the pulsing light of an infrared strobe on the ground indicated the transfer point was not with the Outfit plane as planned; it was with this second aircraft.

Suddenly I regretted dumping my MP7 into the backseat. If I hadn't, I would have seriously considered blowing Konstantin's head off then and there. Because it should have just been myself and the Handler aware of this plan; it was the highest priority, and any changes could come only from the top levels.

And that's exactly what I feared.

It looked as if the vicars had gotten wind of the operation and made a slight alteration to plans—perhaps they couldn't stop my jump, but they could pen an adjustment that would save Konstantin from whatever the Handler had in store.

I momentarily debated my options. The Outfit wouldn't betray whoever was in charge on the airfield, so there was no point driving to their transport plane instead. Nor could I kill Konstantin now, at least without stopping to find my gun. I told myself not to overthink this. My gut instinct told me to drive to the strobe blinking near the ramp of the smaller plane, but for reasons unknown to me, my brain was screaming that there was something very, very wrong with doing so.

I cut the wheel right and headed for the smaller plane.

As I approached its open rear ramp, I saw only three men standing around the strobe light. I sped toward it, knowing the Outfit would smoke any more of Konstantin's would-be rescuers who appeared, but I still didn't want to push my luck.

As I braked to a halt next to the strobe, the three men descended on my truck.

Two of them ripped open the side door and yanked out Konstantin's unconscious body like a rag doll. Opening my own door, I barely had time to set foot outside the truck when the third man took hold of me, throwing me against the side and kicking my feet apart like a cop.

Then—bizarrely—he began frisking me.

"Relax, buddy, I'm unarmed."

He completed a hasty frisk, finding my knife and tossing it aside. Then he wheeled me away from the truck, forcing me a few steps toward the ramp of the plane. He kicked a boot to the back of my knee, and I fell into a kneeling position in the permafrost.

My pulse pounded in my ears—I'd just delivered on an impossible mission, conducted a one-man prisoner snatch in the middle of Siberia, and barely made it to the airfield only to find that the plan had changed.

And at the moment, the man standing behind me was forcing the barrel of a pistol into the base of my neck.

"Sir?" he shouted, his voice clear over the idling plane engines.

"What the fuck are you talking about?"

"SIR?" he yelled again, louder now.

I looked up toward the plane, where the other two men were dragging Konstantin up the ramp and into the cargo hold with all the ceremony of workers at a meat-packing plant.

Then I saw another man standing at the top of the ramp, glowing in the red lights of the aircraft's cargo hold.

He was very tall, very lean, one long arm braced on a piece of metal over his head and the other drifting languidly at his side. No weapon was visible; he didn't even appear to be wearing cold weather gear.

This couldn't be, I thought. It couldn't be *him*.

But then he spoke, and I knew without a doubt that I was looking at the Handler.

"Let him on!" His voice was the next closest thing to a roar, an inebriated slur of madness. "I'll have use for him in the future." A bizarre, chortling laugh. "The killing... has just... begun."

The pressure of the gun barrel disappeared from my neck, and the man hoisted me to my feet and, with a hand clenched to my arm, tried to escort me to the ramp.

I flung his arm off and jabbed an index finger in his face.

"Keep your hands off me, you dirty little motherfucker."

I turned before he could reply, and strode angrily up the aircraft ramp. The Handler didn't look at me as I walked past with the guard in tow; he didn't seem to be looking at anything. One arm was still holding onto a metal bracket overhead, and his torso was swinging gently in the residual wind from the idling turboprops. His sunken cheeks were unshaven, his eyes hollow pits that stared into oblivion.

"Is it done?" the Handler shouted without looking at me.

"It's done," I replied, uncertain what else to say.

He asked nothing else, gave no indication that he'd heard or understood.

Now I could see Racegun stepping into view, stopping beside his master to supervise my ascent up the ramp.

I shot him a look that said, *What the fuck?* He didn't return my eye contact. Instead he was scanning my body, watching my hands, his mind going through the constant cycle of assessing threats to his protectee. But Racegun's jaw was tense, his normally confident air gone entirely.

This entire scenario was his worst nightmare. His primary, probably the most threatened individual in the world who wasn't charged with running a country, was now aboard a small aircraft in Siberia, as far as he could get from the Mist Palace's many concentric rings of security.

I walked past Racegun and the Handler, directing my gaze to an even more surreal scene inside the red glow of the cabin.

There was a row of drop seats on either side of the plane, but the central fixture was an adjustable medical chair. It looked like something out of a dentist's office, with rests for the occupant's arms and legs, and it was flanked by a standing toolbox with multiple drawers. Both the chair and the box next to it appeared to be welded to the aircraft floor, and they faced sideways, centered directly in front of a central porthole window.

Two men lowered Konstantin into the chair and began belting him to it, strapping his arms, wrists, chest, and ankles into place. I didn't need to see inside the toolbox. The chair's view of the central window told me all I needed to know: for the Handler, destroying Konstantin's kingdom wasn't enough.

Instead, Konstantin would witness the destruction in its entirety while the Handler tortured him with what was surely an imaginative number of medieval instruments.

I looked all around me, unable to believe everything I was seeing. But the only detail I'd missed at first glance was a frail-looking man beside a wall of equipment contained in various labeled pouches. He deftly inserted a catheter into Konstantin's immobilized arm, then connected it to the IV tubing of a saline bag to begin an intravenous drip.

Of course, I thought. The man was a doctor. Why not. The Handler would do the damage, and the doctor would artificially prolong Konstantin's life so that more pain could be inflicted.

I grasped the true extent of this madness when the doctor pricked one of Konstantin's fingertips, smearing the blood across a paper strip. He was performing a field blood test, and I realized there was a cooler below his medical supplies. Its glass door was lined with bags of labeled blood—they didn't know Konstantin's blood type, so they'd brought samples of all of them. This man was charged with keeping Konstantin alive, up to and including airborne blood transfusions.

The plane began rolling forward, and I looked back to see the Handler advancing toward Konstantin, with Racegun remaining steadfastly at his side. The ramp was completing its ascent to lock into place, and the sound of the plane's engines increased as they reached full throttle.

I grabbed the frame of a drop seat to hold myself in place, seeing the others doing the same as the plane rumbled forward across the tundra. The

Handler was holding onto the seatback supporting Konstantin, who, quite ironically, was the only one belted in for takeoff.

And my braced position almost wasn't enough to keep me standing.

I knew from the airfield selection that our plane was capable of takeoff and landing from short spaces in harsh terrain. But when the pilots lifted off, they went near-vertical so quickly that I almost went flying backward into the ramp—we all did.

Since the Handler hadn't taken a seat, no one else would either. So we all gripped whatever we could, legs braced, trying not to get tossed to the back of the cabin.

As we thundered upward into the sky over Siberia, it occurred to me that if I'd failed to bring Konstantin back alive, I would be the one strapped to that chair.

I watched the Handler as we ascended. Both his arms were wrapped around the top of the medical chair as he leaned forward and kissed the top of Konstantin's bare scalp. Then he let his shoulders sag back, his head almost lolling with the momentum of our takeoff. His face was blissful, pleasant—he had his prize, the plaything against which he'd inflict all his considerable rage for the death of his daughter.

The trio of bodyguards were looking to Racegun, but Racegun's eyes had found the floor.

I felt the plane turn slightly, circling at the Handler's direction. No sane pilot would do this, but it helped when you were threatened with torture and death. Under such conditions, I supposed, even aircraft safety parameters became somewhat malleable.

The Handler straightened to a full standing position and then circled to the front of Konstantin's chair. He lowered himself to eye level and placed his hands on his knees.

Then, as if Konstantin could hear him, he shouted, *"WAKE UP!"*

The doctor scurried into action, removing the cap from a prepared syringe and administering the medication through the injection port on Konstantin's IV tubing.

When Konstantin didn't immediately awake, the Handler said loudly, "Hit him again."

"Sir, the meds can take a few seconds to take effect—"

"HIT HIM AGAIN!"

The doctor jumped, then produced a new syringe and removed a cap from the needle. He moved toward the chair once more but never got a chance to use the syringe.

Because at that moment, Konstantin awoke.

His eyelids fluttered open, head suddenly lifting off the padded rest behind him. For the briefest fraction of a second, he started to appraise his surroundings. But the Handler put an end to that.

Slapping Konstantin across the face with unbelievable force, the Handler reversed the motion to backhand on the return swing. Konstantin's head thrashed about with the blows, and before he could recover, the Handler grasped his bald scalp and jerked his head forward.

He pulled his own face into Konstantin's, their eyes separated by inches as the Handler addressed him, every word a shout.

"Welcome, Konstantin!" He swung an arm to the side, indicating the aircraft cabin. "You wanted to be king—how do you like your throne?"

The Handler produced a scalpel from the drawer, and in a darting motion flayed a strip of skin from Konstantin's cheek. The skin remained at the bottom of the vertical wound, hanging off Konstantin's face like a bloody leech. The Handler ripped it off and threw it over his shoulder.

"You want my crown? Well, take it!"

He donned a pair of welder's gloves, the thick material making his hands appear cartoonishly large in the cabin's dim red lights. Then he reached into the toolbox.

My God, I thought, what was he going to retrieve next?

The Handler, for his part, didn't disappoint.

When the welder's gloves reappeared from the drawer, they were holding a crown of sorts. It was a metal halo that would fit the scalp of an average man, but protruding from its diameter and extending in all directions was a sickening art experiment of metal filaments, each delicately suspending a single double-edged razor blade. The blades glinted and sparkled under the red lights; there must have been fifty of them spiraling the halo's diameter, forming an intricate, concentrically arranged snowflake pattern.

Konstantin was frantically trying to see what was happening. Once he realized what was about to occur, he did the smartest thing he could.

He kept his head perfectly still.

The Handler didn't seem to mind; he just lowered the halo of razors over Konstantin's bare scalp.

The blades sliced through his skin as easily as paper, and Konstantin's entire head from the temples down was covered by a veil of blood.

He began screaming at once—a shockingly loud, horrifying sound.

The Handler leaned into Konstantin's face, exceeding the screams in volume—but the Handler wasn't screaming.

He was laughing.

Boisterous, hysterical laughter.

Any other human would be capable of this state only if blacked out on substances, but the Handler was stone-cold sober, untouched by all substances but a deep, boiling rage that possessed his being, taking control of his mind and revealing the true depths of his depravity.

The Handler tossed the welding gloves aside and took an exaggerated theatrical bow.

"Your Majesty!" he cried. "How do the powers of my throne suit you? You thought you could replace me? Replace *ME*?"

Konstantin's screaming had subsided, and he now struggled to take shallow, measured breaths in a losing battle to minimize the razors' swath of damage. But every slight movement of his head, every pulse of his temples, caused the blades to slice further into his flesh. His eyes were pinched shut against the torrents of hot blood. By now he'd realized what I already had—the razors were going to sink ever deeper until their edges settled against his skull.

And, to my shock, Konstantin remained defiant.

"This does not matter."

"Excuse me?"

"This does not matter! My organization will crush you even faster because of my loss. They will avenge me, and you will fall as you have been destined to for some time."

"What organization are you referring to? Because you have none."

"The Far North Coalition will survive."

"Ah, but they have all been incinerated. Wait—not yet. They *will* be incinerated in...DAVID!"

The word was spoken as a threat, a death sentence if I didn't immediately understand his intent and respond at once.

I checked my watch.

"Two minutes, forty-nine seconds."

"Two minutes and forty-nine seconds," the Handler repeated, relishing every syllable. "Tell him why, David."

I blinked. This was absurd, all the more so because he was asking for my input.

But the Handler was not to be crossed right now, and so I drew closer to Konstantin before answering.

"I left a bomb in your compound. It's hidden well, inside a generator box."

"Ha!" Konstantin dismissed me. "The generators are at the far edge. Your bomb will not destroy my empire; it would take a nuke."

"I know," I said.

The Handler's eyes were glowing red in the light, darting from me to Konstantin, waiting until the moment was right to retake control of the dialogue.

But for now, he wanted Konstantin to hear my voice. To hear the truth from the man who'd emplaced the bomb, the steady, objective tone of the sole person who'd snatched him.

And in a perverse way, I wanted this too.

Konstantin dismissed me. "Bullshit. You do not have this technology."

"The Handler has had that technology for months. Until now, he just hasn't had the occasion to use it."

"I do not believe anything you say."

The Handler waved me away, and I stepped back.

Then he procured a towel and used it to wipe the blood from Konstantin's eyes.

"You will believe," the Handler said quickly, emphatically, "because you are going to bear witness. And the destruction of your empire will be the last thing you ever see. Not because you will die afterward—no, no, Your *Majesty*. You incurred a debt for what you did to my daughter, and you have not yet begun to repay it. I will have a medical staff ensuring your brain processes the horrors I will do to you long after your body gives up. I have an operating room set up to keep you alive, my liege, and alive you will stay until there is no more terror I can impart upon you."

The Handler gave a final, gentle dab of the towel against Konstantin's eyes, clearing his vision before draping the towel over his own shoulder like a butcher who would need it again soon. "The eradication of your kingdom will be the last thing you see, because when the nuclear fireball subsides, I am going to gouge out your eyes."

The view from the window turned from black to misty gray as we ascended through the clouds.

"Lower!" the Handler shouted at the cockpit. When the plane didn't immediately descend, he pointed to one of the guards, then the front of the plane.

The guard drew his handgun and advanced toward the cockpit. After he flung open the door separating the cockpit from the cabin, he disappeared inside.

His pistol must have made a convincing argument: the plane lurched downward so quickly my stomach lifted into my chest. I felt us bank into a tighter turn, and the clouds vanished to reveal the black Siberian night once more.

And then the misty streaks of clouds broke through again. This wasn't the pilots' fault—I would have felt the aircraft ascend if we'd gained altitude. The storm was closing in, and there was nothing they could do. Soon the entire sky would be filled with snowfall, whether the Handler accepted it or not. After all, he wasn't God; he merely thought he was.

A moment later the Handler noticed the change in view. Using an ice pick he had just procured from a drawer, he pointed at the same guard.

"Lower, *closer!* If I have to tell you again, the next one to occupy this chair will be you."

Once more, the guard drew his pistol and disappeared into the cockpit. And once more, the aircraft descended sharply, tightening its turn radius. Whatever initial flight path they'd planned, it was surely at the nearest survivable range. Now that the Handler was making them compromise this calculated radius, we were all in jeopardy. Konstantin would die, sure. But so would the rest of us. Rage had transformed the Handler into a mad dog, his psyche fractured completely. He'd always been crazy, but now his insanity had taken over all logic, reason, and emotional faculties that could guide a human being through life.

The Handler had long been working with terrorists; now, he had become one.

As he leaned close to taunt Konstantin, I moved toward Racegun.

"You okay with this?" I asked.

"The Outfit plane is trailing us."

"I'm not talking about his fucking security, Racegun. Your primary has gone insane."

"The Outfit plane is trailing us," he repeated. "The transfer point is secure."

His loyalty was immobile to the point of self-destruction—problematic at best, and nightmarish when he was taking his orders from a madman.

Another guard closed on me and grabbed my arm.

"Sit down."

"Fuck you."

He grabbed my jacket and shoved me down into the seat.

"You move from that chair, you're dead."

I pointed toward the Handler. "That's his call, not yours, fucker…"

My words trailed off as I heard my watch begin beeping, signaling the end of my timer.

Flinging my gaze out the window, I searched the night sky but saw only blackness.

And then, the nuclear device I'd planted in Konstantin's compound detonated.

I remembered seeing that device for the first time, after Sage was dead and I'd saved the Handler's life. It was the first time that I was unrestrained in his presence, though shadowed by Racegun as the Handler led me to a tall cabinet behind his desk, its walnut surfaces lavishly carved with the spiraling shapes of Oriental dragons.

When the Handler elegantly pulled the cabinet doors open, I saw an interior lined in deep purple silk. The smell of richly oiled wood and leather filled my nostrils as the internal display lights gradually brightened to reveal the contents within.

I remembered every sensory detail of that moment, was reliving the snapshot now just as I was once again feeling the emotions I'd encountered —whether from the memory or the current sight, I didn't know.

But it was there all the same, the strange pull of emotion twisting my stomach. Shame. Exhilaration. Enlightenment. An unnerving cocktail of emotions too powerful to control or come to peace with, then and now.

First when I'd seen the device inside the cabinet, when my hand had touched it and I'd lost the power of speech upon learning that this masterpiece before me had been created with the highly enriched uranium I'd recovered on my first Outfit mission.

You brought the heart back from Somalia, David. And now, she lives.

And now, I watched that device impart the greatest destructive power the human race was capable of.

The view out the window had been sheer blackness, a desolate void of nothingness. Then an impossibly bright flash turned the sky into a brilliant white eternity—an eternity that spanned but a split second before the blackness returned.

But there was a light in the darkness now, an infinitesimally small twinkle of coral glow in the distance. The glow shifted to a deep, flaming orange as it flared upward, a column of fire rising from the earth and striving to touch the universe beyond. Halos of moisture appeared and shuddered, first ringing the flames and then multiplying overhead in a cascading shockwave effect.

I could hear Konstantin sobbing now, but my eyes were riveted to the window. The blossoming ceiling of the blast was an undulating universe of every shade of fire, more complex and beautiful than any cloud ever seen. This was a display of what the power of nature was capable of when tampered with by man, the infinite bounds of destruction that could be unleashed. The sheer awe imparted by the sight was breathtaking, beautiful, awful. The ultimate display of death and life, of hope and horror.

But in the final seconds, as it withered to black, the last visible remnants of the blast looked sick and disturbing, a jellyfish from hell glowing with its final phosphorescence before it was washed away as carrion.

Konstantin screamed as the Handler gouged his left eye with the ice pick, then the right. The view outside my window went completely black again.

And then, the shockwave from the blast hit our plane.

The effect was like nothing I'd experienced midair—the ultimate turbulence, our plane simultaneously belted on its side and knocked sideways.

I was on my back and sliding across the ground to the far side of the plane before I realized what was happening. My view was of the metal aircraft floor, a skittering object careening toward my face.

It was the Handler's ice pick, its sharp point a roulette wheel closing with my eyes. I flung a hand up to block it, and the handle struck my palm like a blow from a hammer. I clutched it before it could do any more damage, my body whipping in a flat cartwheel until my feet hit the edge of a drop seat.

The pilots were struggling to control the plane's sideways yaw, and for a moment I levitated inches off the ground before slamming down again on my back.

Amid the maelstrom of blurry images, I registered two sounds above the metallic groan of the aircraft frame: Konstantin screaming himself hoarse, and a high-pitched maniacal laughter that could only be coming from the Handler.

A hard thump of turbulence sent me airborne and back down again, and I fearfully aimed the tip of the ice pick away from my body. Another hard sideways roll sent me sliding to the center of the plane. Christ, I was going to stab myself with this ice pick if I kept holding onto it. I made a move to throw it clear of my body, toward the tail. If it stabbed anyone else, better them than me.

But before I could toss it, I slid sideways and grunted as a body slammed into mine.

It was the Handler, still laughing gleefully—his eyes gazing upward as our plane was tossed in a turbulent sky. I caught a glimpse of his open mouth as he laughed, his amber eyes red in the flickering cabin lights.

His guards were crawling to him, but the pitching floor had turned us all into sailors thrown overboard, tossed by stormy waves.

Except we were all going down with the ship.

Gripping the handle of the ice pick with one hand, I used the other to grab the Handler's shoulder and rolled myself on top of him.

Using every ounce of my strength, and pushing hard with the full weight of my body, I drove the ice pick into his sternum.

The point penetrated his breastbone with a dull *pop* that I could feel resonating in the handle; beyond that was only his heart, and the ice pick descended through that too. The grip in my hands came to a stop at his chest, having been driven in to the hilt. I could feel the handle pressing against something in the pit of my own sternum—Konstantin's boar tusk, now a pendant reverberating with each rapid-fire heartbeat slamming in my chest.

Impossibly, the Handler didn't stop laughing.

Instead the last note of his rolling chuckle was suspended in time, drawing out into a long, wheezing cry. We were face to face now, his eyes locking onto mine, so close I could see the flecks of gold in his irises.

I was panting, breathless. It didn't occur to me whether I should speak, and if so, what I should say. My eyes were wide, a deer caught in the headlights a moment before impact, immobilized by an event I couldn't believe was happening.

The Handler had no such reservations.

His face relaxed from a laughing grimace into a look of peace, as if he was relieved to release his grip on life. I saw his lips purse to speak and I leaned in close to hear, fearing I wouldn't catch his words over Konstantin's anguished shrieking.

I needn't have worried.

The Handler's voice was clear, authoritative, as he spoke five unmistakable words.

"David...take care of Langley."

His last breath was used to speak the same request as Parvaneh—to protect a child I had yet to meet. My own response was spoken in a near-gasp, sounding like an echo amid Konstantin's screams.

"I hear, and I obey."

The Handler's eyes went still, locking into place on mine in a frozen, hollow void of death.

Then the aircraft twisted on its axis, the force causing me to fly off the Handler's body with the ice pick still clutched in my grasp. I was immediately fearful of stabbing myself, but the plane finally began to stabilize in a rocky, pitching equilibrium. The force of our plane pulling hard out of its descent kept my body glued to the floor, as if I weighed a thousand pounds.

Were we going to crash into the Siberian tundra? I thought we might, but the pressure lessened and was alleviated altogether as we leveled out. Then the bird began to climb.

I leapt to my feet while I had the chance, trying to determine the guards' location.

They were lifting themselves up too, using the drop seats and even Konstantin's chair for stability. Konstantin's voice had now gone raw from screaming, but he continued nonetheless, raspy cries of anguish that repeated with every breath. The crown of razors had embedded itself deep in his skull.

I looked down—the Handler was dead, both arms splayed out, his sternum marred by a single bloody puncture so small it was almost indistinguishable.

Looking up from his body, I saw the eyes of every standing man doing the same: evaluating the Handler, then meeting my eyes in a standoff.

They were arrayed before me—Racegun the closest, the trio of guards behind him. Racegun's stare fell to the ice pick in my hand. I held it with a death grip that I couldn't seem to release as it dripped blood onto the shuddering metal floor.

I waited for Racegun to make the first move; he'd drawn his pistol impulsively, but was only now absorbing the impact of what had occurred.

In truth, I was in as much disbelief as they were; I couldn't fathom that any of this was happening, that I'd just killed the Handler after all this time. I'd traveled the world in the pursuit of revenge, and now that I'd attained it, nothing felt real anymore. My head was swimming, I was standing amid a dreamlike delusion, my stomach airsick from turbulence. At any second, I was certain, I'd wake up back in my room at the Mist Palace.

One detail grounded me in reality, assuring me that this was no dream. In the midst of my fleeting standoff with the bodyguards, the doctor demonstrated the only mercy that would occur on that flight.

He grabbed a syringe from his equipment, strode quickly to Konstantin, and administered a dose of lethal medication through the IV injection port.

Konstantin's groaning cries faded at last, the rumble of the plane's engines continuing undisturbed. His death went unnoticed by Racegun, whose only reaction was to holster his modified pistol. He wanted to take me alive, I supposed, and had freed both hands for the attack. I widened my stance and turned the ice pick sideways, letting him see his master's blood spread across the metal point. *Come and get me.*

Racegun made a sudden crouching movement that made me flinch, and I braced myself to stab him before he finished tackling me. But Racegun only continued downward, settling into position on a knee.

Then he bowed his head.

At this, the other four men followed suit, quickly kneeling and lowering their heads as if before royalty.

I felt my death grip on the ice pick release, and it clattered to the floor at my feet as I gradually realized what was happening.

The Handler was dead.

And now, I had become him.

KINGDOM

Arcana imperii

-The secrets of power

14

The Mist Palace

The Gulfstream rolled to a stop on the Mist Palace tarmac.

I rose from my seat without looking out the window, steadying myself in anticipation of leaving the aircraft. In the shocking whirlwind of events from leaping out of a plane over Siberia to murdering the Handler, I'd learned perhaps the most impossible fact of all.

There were two reasons that Racegun—actual name Worthy Cottrill Junior, as I'd found out—hadn't shot me fifteen times upon recovering his balance to find the Handler dead. I knew the first reason from what Sage had taught me: the Organization was kept in check by assassination attempts, and when one succeeded, power transitioned to the victor. If that disenfranchised the Organization, then a new assassination conspiracy would quickly gain support and succeed. The Handler's incredible security apparatus existed not just to protect himself from external threats but from his own people.

But the second reason Racegun, now known to me as Worthy, had bowed in submission was inconceivable. I hadn't believed him when he told me, made him repeat the statement several times to be sure I understood.

The Handler had designated me as his successor.

This single incomprehensible truth had confounded me for the remainder of my journey to the Mist Palace. Why would the Handler designate me, of all people? Worthy didn't know. The Handler had told him shortly after I departed to infiltrate Konstantin's compound, and the vicars had learned of this succession plan only upon the Handler's death, when his final letter was revealed.

My assumption of the Handler throne was thus legitimate on two counts: I was not only the Handler's assassin but also the rightful heir to the Organization. My power was indisputable, though that meant little in the current situation. One of the vicars or their immediate staff had already proven disloyal, and by merit, one of them should have indisputably been the next Handler. And this made me certain that one of them would try to have me killed the second I stepped off the plane.

But Worthy had repeated what the Handler had told me in the garden: in the Organization's history, the vicars had never attempted to overthrow a sitting Handler. Many others had, to be sure, but the vicars' support had been unwavering and sacrosanct.

However, I reasoned, if there was ever a time for this edict to be broken, it was now. Even if the traitor was an aide rather than a vicar, all three vicars hated me, and the feeling was quite mutual. What's more, they'd voiced their displeasure in my presence, and were surely considering the possibility that I'd have one or more of them executed in the near future.

If an assassination attempt against me hadn't been plotted yet, then it wouldn't be long in coming.

The plane's clamshell stairs slowly lowered from the fuselage, the three bodyguards the first in line to descend. Worthy was next, disappearing down the steps.

Then I stepped out of the aircraft, stopping on the top step to assess the scene below.

The pines surrounding the Mist Palace stood inviolate as ever, black and unmoving, their tops vanishing into the pale morning fog. But the tarmac was transformed by a massive reception party—three vicars lined up at the bottom of the stairs, Fiona across from them, and two dozen others spread out across the tarmac. A few aides I didn't recognize, but most of them were guards. There was an exterior transport team with body armor and carbines, combined with bodyguards toting submachine guns for close work indoors.

As I walked down the stairs, the three vicars and Fiona began to kneel before me.

"Knock it off," I said as I set foot on the tarmac. "Get up."

After hesitating for a moment, they rose.

Fear was palpable in the eyes of Watts and Omari. Both had repeatedly recommended my banishment if not outright execution in my presence, and now that I had the power to kill them, they feared I might. Yosef had tried to accomplish much worse—sending me into vile deep cover assignments—but his eyes seemed impassive. He had a new master, and there was work to be done—it was as if the prospect of punishment hadn't even crossed his mind.

"Where is Parvaneh's daughter?" I asked.

Fiona adjusted her glasses, seemingly unperturbed by any discomfort of transitioning from the Handler's personal assistant to my own.

"Sir, Langley has just finished a tutoring session. She's in her room now."

"Take me there. I want to speak with her alone."

"Sir," Watts objected, "we have your critical briefs prepared for an emergency handover."

"The only emergency is if you don't take me to Langley this second."

I began walking across the tarmac, and they hurriedly followed as a group of men flooded in to enter the plane.

"Yes, sir," Watts said, his response delayed by what I could only assume was shock. Then a voice called out behind us.

"Sir?"

I turned to face the speaker, a gruff, unshaven man who'd jogged to catch me. He was manual labor, and behind him, his detail of people carried two body bags down the plane's steps.

"Sir, what should we do with the body of...of your predecessor?"

Ah, yes. That small matter of the Handler's corpse.

"Give him a proper burial, beside his daughter."

"And Konstantin's body, sir?"

I thought for a moment, suddenly troubled. I couldn't have him anywhere near Parvaneh.

"Take him to the wilderness and dump him. Let the predators have his body."

"I hear and I obey."

I turned and continued toward the Mist Palace, Fiona and the vicars scurrying after me.

* * *

Langley's room was located in the Handler's operations building, just a corridor removed from his office. I presumed this was because it was the most protected building on the compound, and planned to rectify it with Worthy later—she didn't need to be in the building most likely to withstand an attack; she needed to be in the building least likely to be attacked in the first place.

Worthy opened her door, starting to enter before me.

I grabbed his sleeve, then whispered, "I think I can defend myself against a five-year-old girl." Then I brushed past him, entering her room alone.

The sight of Langley stopped me in my tracks. I'd never seen her before, but for a moment, she looked eerily familiar.

I realized that the child before me reminded me of the girl I'd met in Rio.

And with this thought, I was transported back to the circumstances under which I'd met that girl in the favela—on the run from a kill team chasing me through the slums, hiding as I waited for them to pass. When they did, I was going to blow them away with my shotgun.

Until a little girl crossed before my hasty ambush position.

The sight of me bursting out of the cabinet had terrified her. I told her to run, using my limited Portuguese to tell her that monsters were coming. *Monstros.* But she was paralyzed with fear.

I had no choice—I yanked her into my hiding spot just as the kill team entered.

There were five of them, moving through the house with body armor and assault rifles. I held my palm over the girl's mouth, her hot tears flooding over my hand. If the kill team detected us, we'd both be caught in the crossfire.

But they swept through and continued moving through the back door. The last man on their team took a final glance in my direction, as if he detected something he couldn't explain.

And that's when I saw his face: Agustin.

I held the girl in place after the kill team was gone, terrified they'd return. Finally she threw my hands off her and burst out of our shared hiding spot. She wasn't scared anymore; at least, not outwardly. Instead she faced me boldly, and I, not knowing how to account for the trauma I'd just put her through, had watched her stare me down until I couldn't bear it any longer.

I'd cried then, blinking tears away before the little girl.

And I cried again now.

Langley was lying on her stomach, intently focused on her coloring book. She had her mother's dark hair, ending in curls. Her eyes were wide and chocolate brown, rather than Parvaneh's electric green. The mere sight of her reminded me of the obvious: she'd lost her father long ago, more recently lost her mother, and as of last night, her grandfather. I was central to both, and as much as that should have made me a villain in her eyes, there was no one else in this rat ship who would take care of her anymore.

And even as I felt my eyes fill with tears, the sight of her in a child's princess gown brought the first semblance of a smile to my face. She wore hot pink sneakers with white toe caps, her feet kicking in the air as she colored.

I lowered myself to the floor, sitting cross-legged across from her.

"Hello, Langley. My name's David."

Christ, I sounded like an idiot. How were you supposed to talk to kids?

She didn't look at me, didn't react at all. Just kept coloring.

"Hey there, sweetie?"

Nothing.

My eyes darted around the room. It was a heartbreaking sight—a little girl's domain, arrayed in pastel pinks and greens, the bed heaped with stuffed animals and baby dolls. But the dominating feature in the room was a bookshelf, packed with far more educational material than titles that would entertain a child or inspire their imagination with adventures in faraway lands.

She was being groomed, I reminded myself. Her entire education had been in isolation, the Handler's funds sufficient for the finest tutors but unable to provide her with a childhood. Even the room's lone window presented an almost imperceptibly distorted view: armored glass warping her view of the world beyond this place.

Unsure what to seize on by way of a conversation starter, I settled on the dress she wore.

"Princess Langley."

The crayon stopped moving in her hand. Langley's eyes met mine, and I smiled.

No longer did I see the rightfully angry face of the girl in the favela, traumatized by her exposure to danger. Now I was looking into the wide, inquisitive eyes of a bright child, and her gaze melted me at once.

"Princess, I'm David. It's very nice to meet you."

"Nice to meet you too." A soft, angelic child's voice. I smiled again.

"Do you mind if I talk to you for a minute?"

"Why are you crying?"

I swallowed dryly, cleared my throat.

"I was friends with your mom. She talked to me about you, a lot. She loves you very much."

"Loved."

"Excuse me?"

"She died. Just like my grandfather, and my dad. I don't have a mommy or a daddy."

This threw me off guard. I didn't know how to talk to a child about the weather, and now I was supposed to explain the death of her entire immediate family. My pity turned from her to myself. I longed for something easier, some casual distraction within my wheelhouse, like raiding a heavily defended building in a hostile land or maneuvering through a jungle gunfight. Something tangible, where the responses were clear-cut matters of tactical right and wrong, better or worse.

But I had to talk to this child about everything now; no one else was going to. Now that Parvaneh was gone, the closest thing to a nurturing presence would be the tutors preparing her to inherit the family dynasty.

I said, "You know who else lost both their parents as a child?"

"Who?"

"Me."

She abandoned her crayon, rolling to her side to face me.

"Really?"

I nodded. "My mom got very sick when I was young, and my dad was in a car accident. So I didn't have a mommy or a daddy when I was a kid, either. Sometimes it happens, and that's okay."

"Where do you think they are now?"

A lump swelled in my throat.

"You know, Langley, I remember asking my dad the same question after my mom died."

"What did he say?"

"He said no one knows. Different people believe different things, and that's okay too. But he thought we all go to a place of rest."

"Is that what you think?"

I shrugged. "I'm not sure. I suppose so. But you can come to your own belief, and that's just as good as mine or anyone else's. What do you think?"

She shrugged back. "I dunno."

I smiled, looking toward her window.

For once, the view outside looked less foggy criminal headquarters and more British Columbian wilderness. Usually this area was swathed in a shapeless white mist that pervaded the sky and forest, but the fog had lifted somewhat, allowing the sun's glow to filter through the trees.

The forest's gargantuan pines and moss-covered surfaces looked prehistoric, serene, reminding me not of the Mist Palace but of my isolation in Sage's cabin, where I'd sobered up in body and spirit in a landscape of staggering beauty. I thought of my daily ascent up the slope next to the cabin, past a view of the valley to the secluded hilltop lake where I'd felt the only peace since I first went to war.

Then I looked away from the window, back to Langley. She was watching me now, staring with the expectant gaze of a child whose entire universe hinged on a single adult they just met.

I asked her, "What do you want, Langley?"

"A playground."

"A...playground?"

Langley nodded solemnly, and the resoluteness in her stare made me break into a smile. This kid was gutsy, determined. The headquarters around us marshalled all the criminal resources in the world, and her dream was a heartbreakingly simple child's request.

"Well," I began, "I think I can make that happen. Let me see if we can—"

A single shot pierced the window and landed in the opposite wall with a *thwack*.

I dove atop Langley, forcing her to the ground as the sound that followed confirmed my worst fear. Holding Langley to my chest, I rolled sideways toward the door. Worthy was already inside the room, hoisting me up by my shoulders as Langley held tight.

That shot came from something high-caliber, probably a .50 cal with an extra armor-piercing round. It had managed to penetrate the glass, albeit inaccurately. But it wasn't a single sniper shot.

It was merely the first round from a sniper-initiated ambush.

Langley and I cleared the doorway just as machineguns outside began firing in unison. Their streams of bullets converged on her window with a sickening cacophony of noise. Each round's impact with the armored glass sounded like an explosion underwater, a deep, echoing resonance that sent vibrations rippling through the air.

Worthy pointed the way and I raced down the hall, Langley clinging to my chest as I tried to distance myself as far as I could from her room. The machineguns were firing viciously, in long bursts that paused only to steady their aim, focused solely on Langley's window.

And as I sprinted down the hall, holding Langley's face tight to my shoulder as she gripped me tightly, I knew the worst possible scenario was happening. The shooters outside weren't trying to kill anyone with the machineguns—they were trying to do something far more dangerous. Because the window in Langley's room was simply transparent armor, and like any armor it would fail when its ballistic rating was exceeded.

No glass in the world could withstand an infinite number of rounds, and judging from the hollow reverberation of rapid-fire bullet impacts, "infinite" was exactly what these attackers were going for.

I'd made it ten feet down the hall, fifteen, moving in great sprinting strides—this might work, I thought. I might save Langley, at least.

But I could tell the instant her window shattered. In a split second, the low drumbeat of impacts became a blaring thunderclap that seemed like it would never end. Until it did.

That silence was a terrifying interlude. Because I knew what would fill it before the searing hiss began, starting from nothing and transforming into an ear-splitting tidal wave of sound.

The sniper round and the streams of fire from multiple machineguns were just preludes to the main event: a single rocket, one that was at that very second on its way through the now-shattered window frame.

Time stretched then, my senses absorbing every infinitesimal movement of my body in slow motion as I pounded another footfall, launching forward for the next. Both arms held Langley as tightly as I could to my chest; her hair was flowing against my cheek, clinging to my lips as I heaved for breath. I was setting a track record right now, but that still might not be enough.

Because the simple fact was that the attackers would only get one shot at this— any element of surprise had evaporated in the seconds it took them to destroy the window. Their goal was to get that rocket on its way before I had much time to run, and while I didn't know any specifics of the payload, I knew it wouldn't be a precision weapon. Words like *thermite* and *anti-tank* flashed through my head as I ran.

Langley would get some protection from my body, my backside shielding her from the effects of whatever was about to happen. I cradled the back of her head with my hand, so if I was killed it would shield the impact of her tiny skull against the floor.

And that movement, that repositioning of my hand against her head, was the last thing I did before the blast.

With a great barking thunderclap of sound, the rocket detonated inside Langley's room.

The explosion seemed to suck all the air from the building at once, before expelling it at us in a blazing inferno of heat. I could hear the flames whistling down the hall behind us, coming to burn us alive. My last conscious decision before the flames arrived was whether to continue running or hit the ground. I didn't know what the right answer was, but my mind whispered a single coherent thought.

Heat rises.

I dropped to my knees and fell forward, rolling onto the shoulder opposite Langley's head. Bracing myself atop her, I tried to cover every inch of her flesh with my body.

The blast arrived then, roaring from my ankles to my head in a searing wash of flame. The sound was like newspaper being ripped all around me, an endless white noise of destruction as I waited for the skin on my back to blister.

And then, it was gone.

The heat and noise subsided to the blare of a fire alarm.

I looked up to see a scorched black ceiling, emergency strobes flashing down the hallway. Whatever overhead sprinklers remained functional sprayed water onto the floor.

"You okay, sweetie?" I rolled off Langley, taking her face in my hands as she blinked her eyes open.

"My toes hurt..."

"Your...toes?" I scanned her body for injuries, seeing nothing until I reached her shoes.

Her legs had been wrapped around my waist, her feet exposed along with my backside. The white rubber toe caps of her sneakers were warped with heat, and I pulled off her shoes and socks—her feet were mercifully untouched.

"Does that feel better?"

"Yeah. They were...hot."

"Okay." I stroked her hair, then pulled her into my chest. "You're okay, Langley. You're so brave. How are you so brave? You learn that from your mom?"

I felt her nodding against my chest.

I could hear distant gunfire and explosions outside now, the sounds of a battle raging as our security forces fought the attackers. And for the first time in my life, I didn't care about a gunfight.

Looking up, I saw Worthy kneeling behind me, his modified pistol leveled down the hall in the event that crazed attackers burst out of Langley's room.

I rose to my feet, lifting Langley and embracing her.

"Well that was...exciting, yeah?"

"Yeah."

"Let's get you someplace quiet."

Worthy led us into a windowless conference room adjoining the hall-way, where a cluster of bodyguards waited.

I addressed Worthy first.

"Mobilize the security forces to defend the Mist Palace against further attacks. If Agustin knows where we're at, it's only a matter of time before he sends an assault force. Find out how the assassins breached our perimeter, and fix it. Your top detail takes Langley somewhere safe. You're staying with me."

Worthy began issuing orders to the assembled bodyguards as I knelt to speak with Langley.

Her eyes were surprisingly curious, inquisitive even in the wake of the horrors around us. But the gunfire outside had ended, and I placed my hands on her shoulders and did the best I could to exude calm when I felt anything but.

"Okay, sweetie. I'm going to get you somewhere safe, and then I've got some work to do."

"What kind of work?" she asked.

My heart was thudding dully, a groundswell of rage that I knew would overtake me the second Langley was out of my sight. I reminded myself that I was speaking to a child, that I was the one voice of reason she had to listen to now that Parvaneh was gone.

I took a breath and said, "I know you're never naughty. But if you were, what would your mom do?"

"Put me on time-out."

"Good," I said. "Well, Mr. David has to go put some naughty people in time-out."

"For how long?"

"Trust me, Langley," I said, "they'll be on time-out a very long time."

"I mean, how long will you be gone?"

What could I say? How could I possibly know?

"Let me talk to some of my friends, and I'll figure it out. I'll come see you before I go anywhere."

"I want to go with you."

I smiled at her genuineness, then felt the expression fading as quickly as it occurred.

"Langley, you don't want to follow me where I'm going. I'll come see you as soon as I can."

Her eyes darkened at this promise. Judging by the look on her face, she'd heard this line before. Everyone who'd told her something similar was probably dead.

I kissed her head reassuringly, then stood.

"Who's in charge of Langley's detail?" I asked.

A tall bodyguard stepped forward. "I am, sir."

"Have someone load up a tablet with every children's book ever made, and let Langley relax while she waits for me to return."

"I hear and—"

"And stop saying that. Just do it."

"Yes, sir."

"One more thing." I stepped close to him so Langley wouldn't hear, then fixed my eyes on the man's irises, feeling a riptide of anger with an intensity unmatched by anything I'd felt in my life.

"If anything happens to her," I said, "you don't want to know what happens to you. Now go."

* * *

Worthy and I returned to the Handler's office, and he locked the door behind us.

I saw the place in an entirely new light now that its previous occupant was dead and it belonged to me. My view swept across the immobile wooden chair that I'd been strapped to for previous meetings with him, and the massive desk with the ornate cabinet beside it. That cabinet used to house his nuclear device, before I'd utilized it to wipe Konstantin's compound off the map.

"Sir," Worthy said, "there's something we need to do immediately."

I walked toward the Handler's desk, circling behind it while tracing a hand over the top of his chair.

"Stop calling me 'sir.' It's David."

"All right, David." He pointed upward and said, "See those red pipes lining the ceiling?"

They were hard to miss—I'd noticed them immediately on my first visit to this office. I'd naturally assumed the pipes comprised some kind of water or foam system to extinguish fires, until Sage told me otherwise.

The pipes aren't there to extinguish a fire; they're there to ensure it.

I spared Worthy the trouble of explaining them to me. "Sage told me all about the pipes. Instead of building a vault for sensitive information, the Handler built a vault around this office. If the Mist Palace is invaded, this is my safe room. And if we're overrun, I'm supposed to incinerate the office while I'm inside, right?"

"That's part of it—"

"The fire is initiated with an eight-digit code known only to you and me?"

I walked out from behind the desk as Worthy said, "Well, you're at least right about the code."

"Then what am I wrong about?"

"That system isn't just in this office. This place just gets torched first, and the most thoroughly, on account of the digital records."

"You're saying the entire headquarters building goes up in smoke?"

"No. I'm saying the whole Mist Palace gets burned. Every building, all at once."

"You're serious? Why, man?"

"I just work here. None of this fire bullshit was my idea. I need to change that code now—if your predecessor told anyone, that's his business. But no use testing our luck. If someone hacks the remote access and knows the code, my gun ain't gonna help."

He circled the desk and began typing on a keyboard. To my surprise, classical music began playing over the office speakers. Worthy was protecting this exchange from audio surveillance, and I approached him so we could speak quietly.

"Eight digits," he said. "Something you won't ever forget."

Well, that much was easy. I'd been reciting a set of digits in my head so often that it was forever etched in my memory—the satellite phone number that was my only contact with Sergio, Cancer, and Reilly in Argentina.

Then I realized that while I remembered the number, I'd almost forgotten about those men. This brought on a feeling of shame; I was their only lifeline to America, and now that I could retrieve them to safety, I must do so at once. If I was running this ship now, then no one would be able to contradict me.

First things first, I thought. Change the code, worry about the rest later. "62947908."

He typed the digits and said, "Confirm that again."

"62947908."

After repeating the keystrokes, he typed a final button.

"Done." He handed me an innocuous-looking cell phone. "This stays on your person at all times—if you're not at your desk, this is how you trigger the incineration. Now don't ever tell that code to anyone, understand?"

"Yeah, I got it." That part was easy enough. The only three people with that number were still in hiding somewhere in Argentina. I slipped the phone into my pocket.

"Next order of business—you've got to nominate a successor."

I shrugged indifferently. "How about you?"

"I'm serious."

"So am I."

"Well, I'm not leaving your side and I lack the constitution for betrayal, so if you go down then I'm going with you. This needs to be someone who's got a chance of surviving, a vicar or—"

"Fiona."

He stopped abruptly.

"You trust her?"

"At present, I trust her more than the vicars."

"Very well."

He typed at the keyboard once more before shutting down the screen. The classical music stopped playing. Then Worthy walked out from behind the desk, standing before me at a respectful distance and folding his hands to his front.

"Next up. We need to move you immediately to our offsite location."

"What offsite location?"

"It's a bunker we call Springfire North. Highly classified, located twelve miles from here. It's three stories underground, and can house your entire staff indefinitely. Full communications suite, so business can continue. Construction is corrugated steel with ten feet of concrete. It'd take military-grade explosives to come anywhere close to breaching the main door, and an entire army to get inside. Agustin has neither in North America, and that's why we need to take you and Langley there at once."

There was a sharp double knock at the office door, and Worthy went to answer it as I considered the prospect of fleeing to a secret bunker in the wilderness. Agustin was still hunting me after all this time. I felt like I was back in the favela, but this time, he and I were the only ones left.

Worthy opened the door to reveal a short guard. He began whispering a report.

"Come on in," I said. "Let's cut out the middleman. What do you got?"

The short guard looked nervous to be in my presence. "Sir, we've identified the security breach. They hacked a perimeter camera and then biased the ground sensors to—"

"I don't care how they did it. As long as it's fixed."

"It's fixed. There's something else, sir."

He was running his tongue along an inside cheek, as if wondering how I'd handle this next piece of information.

"Well, what? Spit it out, man."

"Sir, we've captured one assassin alive."

My pulse began racing.

"How is his medical condition? Can he talk?"

"He was knocked unconscious by a grenade detonation. But he's awake now, restrained. Interrogators from the Intelligence Directorate have started asking him questions. He hasn't said anything yet, but...he'll talk."

I clapped my hands to the guard's shoulders and gave him a shake. "This is *excellent*. Make sure whoever took him into custody alive is rewarded for their restraint. That's no small feat after a gunfight."

"Yes, sir."

"And have the interrogators stop questioning him immediately."

The guard's eyebrows wrinkled. "Sir, they're trained interrogators, and prepared to escalate to physical measures given your approval. They'll be able to get any information you need."

This, of course, was not an option. I didn't know who to trust, was certain of a high-level traitor and beyond positive that they'd helped engineer this assassination attempt that had nearly killed Langley. Information from any source was currently suspect—hell, I couldn't even be positive right now that Worthy was on my side.

But beneath all those shingles of logic was a smoldering furnace of wrath, and one that I intended to harness in the immediate future. I didn't care so much that someone had tried to kill me. That much was a frequent occurrence in this business. But involving a child was unforgivable. I was going to make the process of extracting information from the surviving assassin as painful and gruesome as humanly possible.

"I'll take care of this myself," I said. "I want the captured assassin restrained in a private location, and once he's restrained I want every implement of torture placed on a table for me." I was lightheaded with rage, almost dizzy with the effort of speaking in measured tones, and in complete disbelief that my voice sounded as calm as it did. "Believe me, he'll sing his life story at the opera if I tell him to."

The short guard said nothing.

"Well?"

"Yes, sir," he said at once, then turned to do my bidding.

I looked to Worthy. "Please leave. I need some time to think."

Worthy watched me a moment, looking pained as he nodded and left. The door closed with a dull *thud* like the distant blast of an artillery shell, and the noise was oddly comforting.

I turned to find myself alone for the first time in the Handler's office—no, in *my* office.

I strode to the desk, pulled back the chair, and took a seat.

This was it. The throne that all these murderous bastards had been fighting to attain or hold onto for so long, and now I occupied it by a bizarre cascade of circumstances. My eyes fell to an object atop the desk—the Handler's fountain pen, now mine. An immense, cigar-sized instrument with a swirling gold dragon. I picked it up, feeling its heft. This was the pen used to sign his every order into existence, the pen that had authorized my employment of the nuclear device against Konstantin. And with it, I could order whatever I chose, marshalling the Organization's seemingly limitless resources.

I removed the cap, examining the space beneath. This pen had been replicated at great expense in Myanmar, with the grip section covered in a thin sheet of transparent gel infused with an exotic, undetectable poison that would kill him within seconds. I fondly recalled the poisoned pen creator's words. *Acetyl fentanyl derivative... instant transdermal absorption... massive respiratory depression... the chemical equivalent of an atomic bomb against the body. Complete and total destruction, absolutely irreversible.*

But my fondly recalled memory was quickly erased by a troubling thought.

What had become of that poisoned replica pen? I had no idea...and that meant I could be holding it now. It was indistinguishable from the real pen. Someone would only have to replace it with the original on the desk, and as soon as I wrote with it I'd die, just as the Handler was supposed to. I lifted the pen close to my eyes, examining the grip section that normally resided beneath the cap. Was a transparent gel applied, or not?

I couldn't tell and capped the pen immediately, replacing it on the desk.

Then I reached beneath my collar, removing the necklace to hold the curving slice of boar ivory in my hand.

It was smooth, still warm with body heat as if my rage had given it life. I caressed it between my palms, turning it over as the leather thong twisted. I'd promised this to Susan once Konstantin was dead, but she was living in Colorado now, and I'd never see her again. So much the better. I'd keep this pendant as a memento for myself.

Before now, the tusk was a reminder of my hatred for Konstantin, and how he had to die for what he did to Parvaneh. Now Konstantin was dead, and with him the Handler—and my troubles had only gotten worse. I'd removed two enemies from the battlefield, and in doing so I'd made the third more powerful.

And let's not forget, my mind added, empowered the traitor within my Organization.

My Organization? Yes, I supposed it was in every sense of the word— after all, I'd become the leader by default, though that wouldn't last long under the current circumstances. An enemy within, allied with Agustin to bring me down and take control. I'd spent so long judging the Handler's every decision, and now here I was, in his throne, recalling his words to me just after I killed Sage and saved his life.

I sincerely believe that the more you see the way things work from my viewpoint, the more you will understand my rationale.

And now that I was here in his place, what did I think about his rationale? The violence, the endless bloodshed?

God help me, I was beginning to understand these people. Not just the Handler, but Konstantin and Agustin too. Because Langley's near-death had awakened a wrath within me, a dimension of rage with a ruthlessness that knew no bounds. I thought I'd seen into the far depths of my soul when I'd lusted for vengeance, when I'd killed with abandon in combat, shot men almost for the sport of it.

But the second I locked eyes with that child, something more powerful unlocked within me for the first time. It was a protective instinct, a paternal one, and the fact that Langley was not my biological child meant nothing. Had the attempt just been against me, I could have felt some semblance of objectivity. But no more. They'd almost killed that child, and the evolutionary instinct to protect her would drive me mad, if it hadn't done so already.

I understood my enemies now. And at that moment, I decided that I wasn't battling them. *They* were now battling *me*.

Because now I had the power, and I would burn a swath of destruction around my house so far and wide that it would be inconceivable to challenge me again. The Organization and all its resources had just become my playthings, and I'd use them to find and capture Agustin. The Handler had taught me much about terrorizing a human being, with electric chairs and implements of torture and crowns of spiraling razors, but I'd exceed those bounds to punish Agustin for what he did to Langley.

And in the process, I'd uncover his connection in my Organization. Once I had that name, the torture would begin anew—not just for the betrayer, but for anyone who worked in close proximity to them. For abetting or failing to detect the plot, I didn't care.

I began turning the boar tusk in my hands, feeling myself nodding. Sensing my lips sliding into a crooked grin for the first time since the attack. Because once Agustin and his conspirator in my ranks were dead and gone, the killing would begin in earnest.

I'd sentence every member of Agustin's organization to death. Anyone who served or ever had served would be hunted to the ends of the earth; anyone who had been recruited at any level would forever exist with a bounty on their head. The Outfit was going to circle the globe, and if there weren't enough shooters I'd hire more. I'd employ every mercenary from every country if that was what it took. The throne had been meaningless to me, but now I'd guard it with my life for no other reason than to continue the killing so I could keep Langley safe.

I rose from my seat, feeling tall, powerful. I was the Handler now, and my will was about to be done.

Pulling the leather thong around my neck, I tucked the boar tusk under my shirt until it rested against my skin.

Then I walked toward the door. Worthy would take me to check on Langley, and once I assured her everything was going to be fine, I would pay a visit to the captured assassin.

I could feel the wrath growing within me. My new prisoner would be the first of many to pay.

15

Langley was wearing headphones, watching a cartoon on a tablet when I entered. I ordered Worthy to wait outside, closed the door for privacy, and sat next to her on the couch.

As I tapped her on the shoulder, she removed her headphones and looked to me with concern. I was going to show this girl how well I could protect her by ensuring she was okay and then explaining that she wouldn't see me until it was safe for her.

But when she spoke, my brain stuttered to a confused halt.

"Mr. David, what's wrong?"

What's wrong? *What's wrong?* She must have been in shock, still rattled from the attack.

"Sweetheart, you may feel a little confused after what happened. But I'm going to fix it. I'm going to fix all of it, and you're going to be the safest little girl on the planet."

"Okay, but...what's wrong?"

"What do you mean?"

"You look...different. Are you okay?"

"Don't worry about me, Langley. Are *you* okay?"

Once again her features reminded me of the little girl I'd met in the Rio favela, but in that moment, I recalled another figure from that day—the pastor who had prayed a blessing over me.

God, this man is holding onto the power he came from, the power to pull the trigger. Show him that there's a power even greater than that.

There was a greater power than pulling the trigger, I thought. It was the power to marshal armies, to crush the enemies who'd endangered this little girl. Now I possessed the throne, and I was going to use it as my predecessor never had.

Then I heard Susan's voice in my head, partially echoing the pastor's words before the Outfit was ambushed in Russia.

The greatest power of all is our humanity.

But neither Susan nor the pastor in Rio had been responsible for a child as I was, had never felt the deep pull of protective instinct as I did.

Langley's hand fluttered to her throat as she looked down, avoiding eye contact. In that moment, I realized something that struck me as surreally odd.

Langley was afraid to look at me.

So I knelt in front of her, placing my hands on her tiny shoulders. She flinched with the contact, and I pulled my hands away.

"What's the matter, Langley? You have nothing to be scared of. Not anymore."

"You look like him, when he had one of his moods."

"Who?" I asked.

Her eyes looked haunted, terrified, as she replied, "My grandfather."

Alone in the Handler's office, I searched the Organization's database for the one phone number I needed. I entered it into a burner phone, then hesitated before dialing.

At my request, the office had been swept for surveillance devices; but I couldn't fully trust anyone right now, so I decided not to take the chance.

Selecting a Beethoven track to play from the Handler's computer, I turned the volume up and walked to the far corner of the office. The phone seemed to hover before me as I considered the words of a third figure from my past. This time it was Kun, the elderly crime lord from Myanmar. The day before he and I parted ways forever, he imparted one last piece of advice.

Revenge is futile—you cannot change the past. You can, however, alter the course of future events.

Those words weighed heavily on me now. I was about to risk it all, to place everything I knew and loved on the razor's edge of total annihilation. But every force in the universe was inextricably stacked against me, and if I couldn't alter the course of future events this second, then I'd never get another chance.

Finally dialing a number, I held the phone to my ear and waited. My pulse was roaring in my ears, my entire life distilled down to this final decision that would succeed or fail, either save Langley or condemn her forever.

I heard the line ring three times before the ringing stopped—but no one answered.

I breathed a sigh of relief, speaking quietly as Beethoven played in the background. "It's me. David."

No response.

"I need your help. Please. I wouldn't call if it wasn't important."

Still nothing.

"Listen, this isn't a trap or a ploy and I can fucking guarantee that. But if I told you why, you wouldn't believe me. For now, take my word for it. Just answer me."

Finally, after a pause that seemed to span an eternity, a voice responded.

The voice was nasal, intellectual in its precision. It was the voice of my past, the voice of someone I'd met on Boss's team and who had been my partner in crime for my every attempt on the Handler's life. Since then I'd saved his life and he'd saved mine, though the last time I saw him I'd been departing for Argentina.

Ian answered me. "I'm here, David."

I was gripping the phone so hard my hand hurt, and at the sound of his voice my hold loosened, my eyes pinching shut against stinging tears.

"Thank you," I almost gasped.

"Are you okay?"

"I am now." I blinked my eyes open, lashes wet and vision blurry. "But I need your help. The end is in sight."

"The end of what?"

"Everything."

"Okay...what do you need me to do?"

I almost laughed as I considered my response. Sniffling, I answered his question as honestly as I could.

"Everything, Ian. I need you to do everything."

PERIL

Aut consiliis aut ense

-Either by meeting or the sword

16

Worthy and I walked down the hallway toward three metal doors. The middle one was open, with a half-dozen guards posted outside it.

One of them was the short guard who'd entered my office earlier, and he swiftly addressed me.

"Everything is ready, sir. We've identified the captured assassin as Lajos Silva, former Brazilian Special Forces."

I nodded, then told Worthy to have Fiona stand by outside the room. He nodded, and I walked through the open door.

Of course, I knew what I'd see before I saw it. And when I entered, my memory didn't disappoint.

I knew this room well; I'd been here twice before, both times under what could be conservatively termed two of the most memorable experiences of my life. The Handler had been present both times, which meant that those memories, of course, were of horror.

The entire room was a shower of sorts. The floor was marked by a large drain, and the walls were tiled. One of the walls held a red telephone and a switch box with a long, Y-shaped handle. But the primary fixture was a huge chair made of thick golden wood arranged into right angles, a throne beset by leather restraint straps designed to hold the most uncooperative occupant. A man sat in the chair, immobilized by restraints and rigid with terror.

When I'd first entered this room upon returning from Somalia, a different man had been strapped to the chair: the Indian, an intelligence source who had helped me infiltrate the Outfit to get closer to the Handler. The Handler had known this all along, as I came to find out; but at the time, he wasn't interested in divulging all the details. He'd simply interrogated me as to whether I knew the Indian. I denied, the Indian denied, and then the Handler flipped the switch to electrocute him before my eyes. Then Racegun had belted me over the head with a leather sap, knocking me unconscious.

When I awoke from the blow, I had taken the Indian's place in the electric chair.

Now I was the Handler, whether I wanted to be or not. I approached the electric chair slowly, my eyes drifting to the room's new additions: a metal folding chair in front of a stainless-steel table, its surface covered with everything I'd asked for. A miniature vise with what looked like a wine opener that I took to be a thumbscrew. Needle-nose and locking pliers. A power drill with various bit attachments. Tourniquets. Cloths, tape, and gallons of distilled water. Blowtorch and lighter. A set of knives for field dressing game. Coils of rope, chain, and fishing wire. A portable power station unit, complete with clamps. Hacksaws of varying sizes, and an electric knife for carving meat. Sets of instruments that looked suited to a dental office, and surgical implements like scalpels and clamps. Two red handles connected by the steel chain for a chainsaw.

Pausing, I ran my fingertips across the cool brushed stainless steel of the table. This was the type of stuff my predecessor had lying around his palace, and now I understood why. I gazed at the implements longingly, thinking of how the man in the chair was willing to kill Langley to get me. I wanted to cut his head off. I wanted to carve his heart out.

But neither would help Langley now.

None of these torture devices had been present when I'd been in the chair. I'd woken from Racegun's blow to find my head had been shaved and crowned by a metal cap holding a wet sponge against my bare scalp. It was clear there would be no torture, beyond psychological; if the Handler chose to kill me, he'd merely flip the switch and send electricity surging into my brain. But instead, he let me live in order to serve his other ends, a manipulation representing the closest he would ever come to benevolence.

And the second time I'd been in this room, Ishway was strapped to the chair. His head was also shaved, the metal cap once more in place. I knew the terror he felt, had been there myself; but this was in the aftermath of his and Sage's assassination attempt, when I'd learned how they planned to detonate the Handler's nuclear device in Rio. I thought about the ground zero they selected, the favela where I'd been on the run with Parvaneh and Micah. But most of all I thought of the little girl I encountered as Agustin hunted me down, how she would have died, incinerated by Ishway's plan had I not stopped it.

The Handler hadn't needed to flip the switch and electrocute Ishway.

I'd done it for him.

And now here I was, the Handler himself, in the same room, approaching a man strapped to the chair just as the Indian, just as Ishway, just as I once was. Now I held the Handler's power. I hadn't asked for it, but I held it nonetheless. I could no sooner refuse it than walk out of the Mist Palace forever; now I was inseparably tied to the throne, with no way out but death. And death for me meant death for Langley. Her face became convoluted in my mind, juxtaposed with that little girl in Rio. I'd already saved one; now, I had to save the other.

But how to accomplish that?

For most of my mercenary career, I'd succeeded due to my ruthless inhumanity. Taken to the next logical step, endowed with the Handler's powers, I could extend that natural instinct to kill for as long as it took. Given my history, this was the most logical path to ensure Langley's safety.

But when I couldn't bear Langley's terror at the sight of me, I'd asked myself another question.

What if I reversed my methods and leveraged not my inhumanity...but my humanity?

People like the assassin before me, like Agustin, didn't deal in humanity. Before today, neither had I. Truth be told, I had no idea whether my current ploy was going to work.

But I had to try.

Gripping the folding chair, I dragged it toward the captive with a metallic shriek of its legs against the ground. Then I thumped it into place directly across from the electric chair and took a seat. Resting my hands on my knees, I examined the assassin for the first time.

He looked unassuming, his youthful features standing in contrast to short-cropped chestnut hair and a thin beard with no mustache. This was no assassin, no child-killer. Were it not for his camouflage fatigues, now soaked in sweat from what was probably a long overland movement toward the Mist Palace, he would have looked like a young waiter picking up overtime shifts to help pay for college.

But when his gray eyes met mine, I saw a cold lifelessness within. It was the same detached, appraising stare that Sage had held. And Sage had been one hell of an assassin. To be selected for Agustin's crack team assigned to the first attack on the Mist Palace, this man must have been, too.

I began, "Clearly you know who I am, Lajos."

He said nothing. Of course he didn't. He'd been forged by that strongest form of negative reinforcement perpetuated by criminal organizations: the fear that your own boss would do worse to you for betrayal than any enemy could.

"I'll bet you were at the ambush outside Yakutsk, too. You guys almost had us dead to rights. I didn't think I'd make it out alive. That was a hell of a fight, and any man who made it out of that has my respect."

I could see in his eyes that he knew exactly what I was talking about. He had been one of the fleeting shadows in the woods, one of the many who got away.

But still, he refused to speak.

"Here's what we're going to do, Lajos. We're going to leave this place, you and me, together. Just you and me. No bodyguards, no surveillance, no bullshit. And you're going to take me to Agustin."

Lajos opened his mouth, and for a moment I thought he was going to say something. Then he closed it, waiting for me to go on. But his eyes were alight with interest now, and while he didn't yet believe me, he was ready to latch onto any alternative that didn't involve the implements lined up across the stainless steel table beside him.

"You've got a recovery network, a number you can call. You're going to tell them that you got me alive. I'll follow their instructions on where to go and let them take custody of me. They can take me through a surveillance detection route of their choosing until they're convinced I'm not being followed, and then you'll bring me to Agustin. I want a face-to-face meeting with him."

Lajos spoke for the first time.

"He will fear a trap."

Now I had to admit something I didn't want to for fear of being overheard. My glance slid toward the metal door, which was still closed. I considered whether the room might be wiretapped, and couldn't rule it out. I spoke anyway.

"I am going to give an order that no surveillance efforts follow me, and my people will follow this order. You and I both know Agustin has a mole within my Organization who will be able to verify this. He'll know it's not a trap. Tell them I will fly us both to the charter terminal of any airport worldwide. You and I will walk out the front door, get into a car, and follow any instructions we receive. You will deliver me to Agustin alive. Acceptable?"

He pursed his lips, considering my offer. But he didn't answer.

"I'll rephrase," I said. "If not 'acceptable,' is my proposal preferable to having your body dismantled in this room by my predecessor's collection of torture devices?"

Lajos nodded quickly. "Yes. Preferable to this."

"Good. Then make the fucking call."

I stood and left the room, finding that Fiona had joined the bodyguards outside. I addressed them all.

"Lajos Silva will be treated as my personal guest, and provided every courtesy. He will be afforded the opportunity to shower, dine, and dress in new clothes. Most importantly, he will be provided a phone and allowed to make and receive calls on it. He will provide the name of an airport, and as soon as we have it I want my jet prepared to fly there. Questions?"

There were none.

"Fiona, come with me."

I led her away from the guards, stopping her in the hall once we were out of earshot.

She stood attentively, her tablet held at the ready with one hand hovering over the screen, ready to type. Her hazel eyes were bright and unblinking behind her glasses, and I considered how to phrase my question.

"Fiona," I said quietly, "what kind of funding do I have access to?"

"Sir, allow me to get the current report from the Directorate of Finance. I can have the exact figures in thirty seconds."

She made a move to type into her tablet.

"That won't be necessary," I said, holding up a hand for her to stop. She lowered the tablet and tilted her head, lips pursed, watching me closely as if trying to anticipate my next words.

"What I mean is," I began tentatively, "what kind of funds can I personally access, right now?"

"Sir, Vicar Omari controls the distribution of funds in accordance with your directives. He'll provide all the details during your finance transition brief. But as for your immediate personal access..."

Her voice trailed off as her eyes flitted to either side of the hall. Then she took a half-step toward me, now standing so close I could smell her perfume.

In a low voice, she explained, "Your predecessor maintained a modest black fund."

"What is that—a slush fund?"

She nodded solemnly. "It's completely off the books. Only he and I had access. Currently it's at $8.6 million."

"Did you report this to the vicars?"

Her eyes went wide. "No, sir, I—I didn't want to do anything until I informed you."

I watched her closely, trying to ferret out any lies. Fiona seemed genuine, and if she was being truthful, then my respect for her was growing by the second. But for all I knew, she could be the inside traitor who had gotten the Outfit ambushed in Russia. Until I'd definitely ruled her free from suspicion, I couldn't risk trying to access those funds.

I gave her a warm smile.

"You did the right thing, Fiona. Keep this between us."

She nodded and took a step back, returning to normal speaking distance.

Then I said, "Now listen carefully. I want you to have Watts meet me in the conference room. He is to bring any and all materials related to our ties with terrorist organizations."

She gave me a quizzical look.

"Sir," she replied, "the Organization doesn't deal with terrorists."

"Just tell him, Fiona."

"Yes, sir."

* * *

Watts entered the conference room within minutes, and the group of bodyguards parted to let him pass.

He held a tablet at his side and stopped before me, almost at the position of attention, as I rose to hear his Boston-accented greeting.

"Sir, my deepest apologies for the attempt on your life. Our security forces have established a layered defense to cover repairs of the security breach. That being said, as your Chief Vicar of Defense I take full responsibility for this assault and stand ready to provide my resignation or my life as you see fit."

I watched him closely. Was he the traitor? I'd suspected him before, and even though I saw no indication of it now, these people were so good at lying that I would never be able to tell. Even Sage had beaten a polygraph.

Watts appeared unflappably cool, maintaining unbroken eye contact and a solemn expression. This was especially impressive given the rage that I could feel radiating from my every pore, the thoughts that I knew my eyes were projecting at this very second.

If anything happens to Langley, if she so much as gets a papercut reading children's books, if she catches the common cold while in her safe room, I will string you up and burn this entire place to the fucking ground.

"Vicar Watts, I appreciate your candor and your accountability. I am not a zero-defect person, and I don't expect anyone in this Organization to be, either. As long as the problem is fixed going forward, you have an absolutely clean slate. Please, have a seat."

"Thank you, sir." He lowered himself into a chair across from me, folding his hands across the tablet in his lap. I sat back down.

"Besides," I continued cheerily, my mood lightening at once, "we have work to do."

There were precious few silver linings in this job, and I was about to cash in on the biggest one of all.

"Yes, sir?"

"I want to be briefed on any and all terrorist ties maintained by this Organization. I already know we have them."

Watts looked uneasily toward Fiona, seated in the chair next to me.

"Sir, that's the LIONTAIL Program. It's compartmentalized, for the eyes of the sitting Handler, his personal guards, and the chief vicars only."

"Consider Fiona added to that list, effective immediately."

"Your briefing is scheduled for later today along with—"

"My briefing got advanced to right now. Show me."

He quickly began operating his tablet. Swiping and tapping across the screen, he finally handed it to me.

"Here, sir. This is every operative and leader known to be affiliated with terrorist organizations. Two hundred and ninety-three individuals in sixty-seven countries."

I felt bile burning in the back of my throat as I accepted the tablet. The roster of names was expandable to files containing a picture, current address and list of safehouses in the operative's network, numbers to satellite and burner phones, and email accounts.

Watts nervously continued, "I'll add, sir, that any interaction with these individuals must be approved by you on a case-by-case basis. This list represents nothing more than a network we can call upon if the requirement presents itself."

I didn't reply. There was only one individual I knew by name to check. Scrolling down the alphabet, I located Sasa, the Yemeni Al-Qaeda officer I'd encountered, and just barely survived meeting, on my first Outfit mission to Somalia. Opening his file, I saw his information listed. Current location was Aden.

"Thank you." I handed the tablet back to Watts. "Now listen carefully, because this part is very important. Your immediate priority, at the exclusion of all else, is to ensure the death of all 293 individuals on that list."

"Sir, the targeting matrix alone would take the Outfit months to—"

"The Outfit will have nothing to do with this. They're not going to bear the risk of killing these pieces of shit. Our criminal network is."

Watts crossed his legs, then recrossed them.

"Sir, if I may."

"I'm listening, Vicar Watts."

"Sir, any use of our global criminal network to eliminate present allies is a strategic decision. To do so once greatly risks destabilizing our power base with any associated organizations."

"Anything else?"

He gave a brittle, disbelieving laugh.

"Sir, ordering the deaths of even a dozen names on this list could result in repercussions that we're not currently prepared to handle. Now if there's an individual or two that you'd like removed, we can perhaps arrange it. But putting the entire LIONTAIL Program on a blacklist is killing a mosquito with a crop duster."

I paused, feeling the blood rushing in my ears.

"Let me be very clear: I don't want to send in a crop duster."

Watts's posture visibly relaxed.

"I want to drop a nuke."

Watts was leaning forward now, his eyelids fluttering as if he hadn't understood me.

"Look," I said, "I'm the Handler now. I don't know who I can trust, I don't know if I can trust you, and now you're either going to prove your loyalty or not. You will call in every favor and bribe, clear every debt, pay, cajole, coerce, threaten, and, if necessary, terrorize our global criminal network to achieve the deaths of as many people on this terrorist list as possible." I checked my watch. "In twenty-four hours, you will brief me on your current progress. And if more than a half-dozen names on this list remain alive, our next conversation will be considerably less amicable. I say that so there's no confusion, Vicar Watts. What are your questions?"

His face had paled considerably, his mouth opening and closing.

"No questions, sir." He rose to leave, and I stopped him at the door.

"One more thing, Vicar Watts. To ensure this task is performed with the maximum enthusiasm on your part, I'm going to have three people from my personal security detail shadow you while you do it." I looked to Worthy, who tapped an index finger toward three of his men, then swung it toward Watts.

The trio of bodyguards strode briskly over to the Vicar of Defense, who stood slack-jawed at the door. But he gave a nod and a weak, "Yes, sir," before departing for good.

As he left, Fiona's phone chimed.

She checked the display. "Sir, there's a message from the captured assassin."

"Did he make his phone call already?"

"Yes, sir. It appears so."

"Great. What's the message?"

She lowered the phone.

"Sir, the airport selected for your drop-off is...I'm sorry."

"Sorry for what?"

"You're going to Newark, New Jersey."

17

Newark Airport, New Jersey

I stepped outside the Newark Airport to blaring car horns as vehicles jockeyed to cut one another off outside the terminal. Even the pigeons trawling the sidewalk seemed pissed off. Could I blame them? This was New Jersey, after all.

I looked to Lajos standing beside me. He didn't seem troubled in the least by our cross-country flight to New Jersey. Quite the opposite, in fact. Lajos now had some spring in his step, was bright and happy at becoming a free man once again. But to me this was a bad joke, a cruel trick of fate on two immediately obvious grounds.

First, the airport.

Given the option of any airport in the world, and a fully fueled Gulfstream to take me and my would-be assassin there, Agustin had chosen Newark. As far as I was concerned, Newark was the armpit of New Jersey, and New Jersey was the armpit of America. When the smell of jet and vehicle exhaust faded from my nostrils, it would be replaced by the rotten-egg odor of chemical plants and landfills that pervaded Newark proper.

Second, the city itself.

Newark was, I recalled all too clearly, the site of my Outfit tryout. Given a location—Kontio's Tavern—and a freezing night to go there, I had met Sergio for the first time.

Sergio had given me very simple instructions: if I mentioned his name, I was out. If I got arrested or detained in the course of the proceedings, I was out. Until then, my job was to do whatever I was told. Simple enough, I'd thought.

And when we entered the tavern, he'd simply pointed out the biggest guy in the room. Your first test, he'd said, is to knock him unconscious and escape. So I ordered a bottle of beer, then smashed it over the man's head. But the bottle didn't break, and that man turned out to be Viggs, a herculean fighter who succeeded in kicking my ass before I was dragged away by bouncers.

Instead of tossing me out, the bouncers had taken me down a back hall and thrown me down a flight of stairs.

At the bottom was Cancer.

He was fully committed to his role as a wiseguy in the local mob, and I was handcuffed to a pipe while Cancer delighted in putting out cigarettes on my flesh. I refused to speak Sergio's name, and so Viggs and Cancer took me to a harbor and stuffed me into a steel drum with holes cut in the side. There, facing the prospect of drowning if I didn't reveal why I walked into the tavern, I still refused to mention Sergio's name.

So they'd tilted my steel drum on its side and rolled me into the freezing water.

I frantically tried to escape, to no avail—the icy water quickly filled the drum, my restraints were unbreakable, and I couldn't force off the lid of the drum due to a ratchet strap holding it in place.

Within seconds I lost all feeling and mobility in my limbs. Then, with a final thought of Karma, I slipped into death.

When I awoke, I was on a backboard with a medical team forcing air into my lungs through a mask until I vomited water. They raced me to a heated medical unit concealed among the harbor's many structures and nursed me back to life. Once I recovered, I'd suffered an all-night evaluation by a psychologist.

That was my first day in the Outfit.

So the prospect of returning to Newark for any reason, least of all to traipse into the jaws of death at Agustin's hands, left me more than a little disturbed.

After a few minutes, I asked Lajos, "Where's this car we're supposed to be waiting for?"

Lajos shrugged.

"When they are here, they will let us know." He looked forward, scanning the traffic.

I shouldn't have been in a hurry for our transport to arrive. But I didn't want to wait any longer. My plan was ambitious to say the least, but if it didn't work, I was doomed and so was Langley. The next assassination attempt against me would come from within the Organization, whether the perpetrator was allied with Agustin or not. All three vicars hated me unconditionally, and all certainly considered themselves better capable of running the Organization.

And they were probably all correct.

But I wasn't interested in what they wanted or what was warranted by the rules of this abhorrent criminal underground. I was only concerned with what happened to me and Langley, and only one possible path had the slightest chance of working out well for us. It was the plan I was now executing, and Agustin was about to cast his vote on the proceedings.

A late-model van pulled to a stop at the curb, the sliding door opening to reveal a trio of men inside. They were all athletic-looking Latinos, none of whom seemed too happy to have received the assignment of transporting me. I could tell they expected this was an ambush of some kind, and wouldn't believe otherwise until I'd been swept for tracking devices and completed their surveillance detection route.

Lajos bounded inside the van with glee. My entry was considerably less enthusiastic. By the time I stepped into the cargo hold, Lajos was sliding the door shut behind me. Two of the others descended on me, pulling a black hood over my head and handcuffing my wrists behind my back.

They threw me to the floor, and I felt my own hot breath against my face within the hood. Then the van accelerated and I stared forward into blackness.

Agustin's people suspected the worst.

I felt them checking every inch of my body for tracking devices, running scanners over my clothes before frisking me for weapons. Since I had no tracking devices on me, I came up clean—but this was just the beginning.

They conducted two vehicle changes separated by twenty minutes of driving, roughly moving me from the van to the trunk of a car, then to another vehicle I presumed to be a new van. My hood stayed on the entire time, and I made no attempt to dislodge it. I didn't want to give them the slightest reason to doubt my intentions or have any excuse to cancel the meeting.

After completing countless street turns across three vehicles, and all this after they determined I wasn't carrying a tracking device, they stopped the vehicle and pulled me out of it.

A man at each side held my arms, escorting me from the vehicle to a building, then into an elevator. I felt us ascend five floors, and they led me off the elevator, down a hall, and through a doorway.

Then I was thrust downward into a chair, still handcuffed, and the hood was ripped off my head.

I squinted in the sudden light, blinking to determine my surroundings.

I was seated at a conference table and surrounded by five men with submachine guns. Lajos pulled out a chair at the end of the table and sat down.

And seated directly across from me, calmly spinning a pen between his fingers, was Agustin.

He looked like he'd put on weight since I'd seen him in Konstantin's compound last month. His shoulders were bulkier, face rounder. Though I supposed he'd had some pounds to put back on after his time in the Argentinian jungles— I know I did.

"Thank you for meeting with me, Agustin."

He smiled. "You are quite welcome. Insane, and ludicrously so, but quite welcome."

Off to a bad start, I thought.

Agustin went on. "Look at the two of us...as I told you in Rio, David, maybe one day it will be the two of us behind closed doors."

"And now we are."

"Yes. Pity that only I will walk out alive."

I shook my head. "I am not dying today."

"You are wrong about that, David Rivers. I've heard that you were nick-named Suicide. But this is an interesting way to do it."

I looked to the door behind me, heart hammering in my throat, but my voice sounded impossibly calm as I said, "You're going to let me walk right out that door, and you're going to pray that no harm befalls me on my way back to the Mist Palace."

"Why is that, my friend?"

"Because I can give you everything you've ever wanted."

"I've already got that. Your predecessor thought his organization impen-etrable. I've proven that it's not, and now I will take everything from you."

"I know that you've been working with a traitor in my Organization. I also know there is an active fire destruction system wired within the Mist Palace's infrastructure. You think your traitor will volunteer that information to you? Do you trust them not to kill you if and when it plays to their advantage?"

"Oh, but I should trust you?"

"You should, and here's why: I ordered no surveillance to follow me to meet you. You know this is true because your inside source, whoever that may be, has confirmed it. If they hadn't, you wouldn't have taken this meet-ing. My life is in your hands, and I wouldn't have stepped out on this gang-plank unless I had something worth assuring my safe return."

"This would mean something if I could take you at your word. But from what I have heard"—he gave an apologetic shrug—"I am not sure I can believe you."

"Of course. By now you've probably heard the rumors that I infiltrated the Organization to kill its leader."

"No organization is free from wanton hearsay, but yes, I have—"

"It's true."

He was briefly silent, tilting his head in confusion. "Go on."

"I worked for a paramilitary team that served the Handler. He betrayed us, and killed everyone but me. From that moment on, my mission in life was to kill the Handler—and ever since, I've strived for nothing else. I've traveled the world for this sole pursuit, and when I had the chance to plunge an ice pick into his heart, I took it."

"This is...interesting. But it changes nothing about our circumstances."

"It changes everything. Because I have no interest in retaining power or running the Organization. I joined and ascended the ranks solely to kill the Handler, and since that's done, I wish to retire. Now I already nominated a successor in the event I don't return from this meeting, and it's someone whose hatred for you is absolute. Their first order of business will be to kill every possible traitor—thus eliminating your inside source—and then leverage every possible asset against you. So if you kill me now, your fight will continue. For how long, through how many double-crosses, and at the cost of how many lives, no one can say."

Agustin gave a kindhearted shrug. "If I were squeamish about the cost, David, I would not have entered this arena."

"But you're smarter than Konstantin. You know your goal, and you'll take the quickest route to get there. And I can offer you the quickest route of all."

"I am listening."

"Upon my return, I propose to nominate you as my successor. I will remain in power as the Handler only to grant you secure entry into the Mist Palace under my sole protection. I will then conduct a handover of my Organization to your exclusive control, completely, indisputably, and in full. No one will be able to contest your reign, and instead of having only a chance of taking the throne amid the chaos of war, you will begin your reign with certainty and from a position of absolute power."

Agustin's eyebrows were wrinkled in confusion. "What do you get out of this?"

"Two things. First, I will leave the Organization to you, but not to my betrayer. Someone within my ranks gave you the information on exactly where and how to ambush the Outfit in Russia, and then to make the assassination attempt against me. I want their name, and twenty-four hours to make them suffer like they've never suffered before."

He chuckled at this, his laughter rising in volume until it became momentarily uproarious. Finally he managed, "And the second?"

"My goal was to kill the Handler, and I did. I am mission success, and when I transition control to you, I want a lifelong protective order that ensures I live out my days in peace. With, of course, a modest severance package."

Now his expression sobered. "Define 'modest,' Mr. Rivers."

"Ten million dollars has a nice ring to it. Clean money, in an offshore account."

For a moment I thought he hadn't heard me.

But he blew out a long breath and smiled, then replied with an almost mocking tone. "I've often heard the price of treason can be quite small. But given your assets, I would have expected a much higher cost for you to betray your entire organization."

"It's not my Organization. I killed the Handler; now I'm done fighting. Forever. The question is, are you? Your inside source is expecting what I imagine is a significant cut of power, or money, or both. Maybe you double-cross them, maybe they double-cross you. But my plan puts you legitimately and directly in the Handler's throne, exactly twenty-four hours after I return to the Mist Palace. Instead of fighting the Outfit, you will assume command of them. And," I added, "are you really going to notice the loss of ten million dollars?"

He sat back in his chair, crossing his arms, then uncrossed them and leaned forward.

"That is all you want?"

"That's it."

Agustin clapped his hands together.

"All right, Mr. Rivers. I will agree to your plan."

"Good. The name of your source, please."

"Mr. Rivers, a word of caution. You will not believe me if I tell you—"

"Try me."

"—so you must take me at my word. Agreed?"

"I will take you at your word, just as you have taken me at mine. The name, Agustin."

"Very well. First, you are completely wrong about your betrayal."

"I am not. You could not have blown up the plane outside Yakutsk or staged my assassination at the Mist Palace through any means but a high-ranking traitor. I want the name."

"There is not one name."

"There is."

He paused, smiling politely. Then, folding his hands across his stomach like a man who had just consumed a satisfying meal, he went on, "Please allow me to finish. Your predecessor could not control his rage, and look where that got him."

My jaw was clenched, blood pressure rising. After what they'd almost done to Langley, I wanted to rip his throat out with my hands, wanted to drive my thumbs into his eyes like that poor bastard I'd brutalized in Argentina.

But I forced myself to remain silent until Agustin spoke again.

"As I said, there is not one name."

I felt my body tense, every muscle ready to support an enraged leap across the table.

"There are several."

My rage faded almost completely. I felt suddenly deflated, emotionally fatigued at his words.

"Okay," I breathed. "Let's hear it."

"Yosef. Chief Vicar of Intelligence."

Slimy little fuck. Of course he was in on it.

"Who else?"

"Omari. Chief Vicar of Finance."

That figures, I thought. He'd made no concessions about his hatred for me.

"And?"

"And Watts. Chief Vicar of Defense."

That name, completing the trinity of vicars, made my blood go a bit cold in my veins. It was one thing to have a rogue vicar or assistant, perhaps even a combination of them; but all three of the Organization's top advisors had joined a unified effort to merge with Agustin, a man who wanted to increase the power of international terrorism, a man who was unarguably more evil than the Handler had been. Even in their hatred for me, this should never have happened—they could have enacted their own assassination plot to remove me from power and then split the kingdom however they chose.

Unless...

"Did these three unify before or after I assumed the Handler's throne?"

"I was not finished, Mr. Rivers. The chief aide for each vicar is also aware, though they have not had direct communications with me."

"When did they ally with you?"

"At first it was only Omari. He approached me before we killed Parvaneh."

"Did he know it would happen?"

"Of course he knew. This was not done to remove an heir as we told you. It was done to drive the Handler mad, to break his mind, before commencing the complete takeover of his Organization. And it worked."

My eyes pinched shut, and I tried to let this nonchalant statement pass over me. There was nothing I could do for Parvaneh now. But Langley was still alive, and relying on me.

I opened my eyes again. "What about the others?"

"Omari was joined by Watts and Yosef the moment you killed the Handler and assumed the throne. My assassins were on their way to the Mist Palace before you had returned with Konstantin's body."

The Organization was totally corrupt now, rotten from the inside out.

And Omari, that heartless motherfucker, had known about Parvaneh in advance.

"Can you prove this?" I asked.

He gave me a small grin, then waved two fingers at one of the guards.

The man retrieved a small laptop, setting it in front of me and playing a video. The screen was filled with the view of a conference table, around which sat Watts, Omari, and Yosef. In a square at the lower left-hand corner was Agustin's face. It was a teleconference recording, the sound muted but the body language clear: they were negotiating.

"Who else is in the conspiracy?"

"No one else, Mr. Rivers. I give you my word."

"My bodyguards?"

"No."

"Fiona?"

"No."

"Good," I breathed. "Here is how we must proceed. Once I leave, tell the vicars everything with one exception: instead of accusing them, you accused Fiona. She's our patsy. I'll verify this information upon my return, and confide in the vicars that I'm going to deal with Fiona—but this will be a ploy to capture the vicars and their chief aides simultaneously. And once I do"—I took a measured breath—"my twenty-four hours of torture begin. Agreed?"

"Very well."

"Do you require any of them alive? Because if so, they won't be alive by much."

"I will replace them with my own people whether the vicars are alive or dead. But I do," he cautioned, "require full access to all files and continuity records."

"That's easy. I will give you the Handler's master key, capable of accessing everything."

"Very well. Then do with the traitors what you wish."

"I will," I said, relishing the thought of what was to come. "I'll be in touch."

He waved a hand at a man behind me.

"Until we meet again, Mr. Rivers."

Before I could reply, the black bag was pulled over my head, and Agustin vanished from view.

18

Someone ripped off the hood, leaving me standing on a sidewalk, facing a building exterior staffed with an audience of one.

The homeless man sat against a brick wall, limply holding a guitar, an old fried chicken bucket serving as his cash collection point. He was left to question his own sobriety as the van pulled away behind me.

I turned to see it drive down the street and turn the corner at a dry cleaner. Placing my hands on my hips, I looked at the run-down brick buildings lining the cracked streets.

Facing the homeless man, I asked, "This still Newark?"

He nodded.

"Shit," I muttered.

"You're telling me. I gotta live here, pal. Then again, I ain't the one just stepped out of no damn rape van."

I procured my wallet and looked inside. They'd been decent enough to leave my cash, so I pulled out a few twenties and dropped them into the man's bucket.

"I'll survive. Bar around here?"

He pointed down the street.

"Thanks. Have a good one."

He didn't reply, instead opting to watch me depart with either silent awe or disgust, I wasn't sure which. Quickly walking a block and a half, I found the dive bar he'd indicated and entered.

No one was smoking, but this place had been filled with cigarettes for so long they'd never get the smell out. A row of old-timers was lined up along the stools, watching sports and nursing pints of beer.

I walked to the end of the bar and took a seat.

"Woodford rocks."

"We only got Jack."

Fucking Newark.

"Jack rocks," I corrected myself.

"Single or a double?"

"Life is short. Let's make it a double."

I directed my attention to a flat screen as I waited, feigning interest in the game until my drink was ready.

As the bartender set down my glass of whiskey, I asked, "Mind if I use your bar phone? Need to check in with the wife, and my cell battery just died."

"Sure." He returned a moment later with a cordless phone before attending to his other patrons.

I picked up the phone, the cheap plastic feeling impossibly heavy in my hand. Then I turned it over, staring at it as if it held every answer in the world. In a way it did, because everything—absolutely everything that had been building since I stepped off the path and became a mercenary—hinged on the call I was about to make.

My ribs seemed tight, my body fatigued. I'd never held so much power, and yet, I'd never felt so powerless. The Organization used to strike me as something out of a movie: a transnational criminal syndicate existing above the law, with unlimited resources. But the higher I got, the more unstable and tenuous the Organization became, the more apparent it became that I sat atop an enormous house of cards. Its power was in its legacy. In that regard, the Organization was a rattlesnake: you could lop off the head and the collective power would cause it to continue functioning indefinitely before the tail knew it was dead.

This was the moment it all came down to; the outcome of the call I was about to make would be life or death, not just for me but for Langley as well.

With a pulse that made my fingers tremble, I dialed a number and raised the phone to my ear.

The call connected, and I spat out my question before the answering party had a chance to speak.

"Did we get him?"

Ian sounded casually offended by the inquiry. "Do you even have to ask? You're talking about me and my buddies from the old life. Did we ever let Boss's team down? Did I let you die in Argentina? Come on, man. Who else could have coded a message like that—"

"Ian," I cut him off. "I love you. Now shoot me straight."

"We had a five-car rotation trail you from the airport to the meeting. As soon as you were out of the building, Agustin and his entourage returned to their bed-down site. That's where they are now."

"Your people are babysitting them?"

"No. My guys are setting up the site blueprint, staging area, and picking up your hardware. But there's only one real way out, and Susan is watching it. Believe me, though—Agustin's not leaving until tomorrow."

I almost collapsed atop the bar. If Ian couldn't deliver, I'd have had nothing; yet given an impossible task, he'd delivered. Yet again. I still had a chance—not much of one, but a chance—and given the circumstances, that was more than I could ask for.

"What are we dealing with? A bunker in the Catskills or what?"

"They're not in a bunker, David. Apparently they're pretty certain they've got this takeover nailed."

"What do you mean?"

"Agustin is in the presidential suite at the Infinity Manhattan. He's got the entire 55th floor to himself, and judging by the caviar order he just put in with room service, his executive staff is up there with him. Working or celebrating, who knows, but when you've got 360 views of Lower Manhattan, does it really matter?"

My mind spun into the tactical realm, momentarily considering how I'd begin to plan an assault on a high-rise floor of an ultra-luxury hotel.

But none of that would matter, I thought, if everything else hadn't fallen into place.

"What about everything else?"

"Four hours, and we're all set."

I checked my watch—that put us near sunset on a Saturday night. The city would be buzzing with nightlife, the streets packed, and NYPD probably at maximum presence. So be it. If Agustin and his people were on the 55th floor, then that's where I was going.

"Got it. I'll call you back from a landline in a few hours. I've got some business to take care of first."

"What kind of business is more important than this?"

I spun the whiskey glass on the bar's lacquered surface.

"My favorite kind. I'll fill you in later. And thanks, Ian."

I hung up, dropped a twenty next to my drink, and left without taking a sip.

19

The Handler's personal jet had three passenger compartments.

As I walked up the clamshell stairs, greeted at once by Worthy, I entered the first seating area.

This was more or less a lounge, filled with black leather couches and cream surfaces, where Parvaneh had given her briefing before her delegation landed in Norilsk, Russia. More recently, this was where Lajos Silva, my would-be assassin, was transported on our flight from the Mist Palace to Newark. He'd received no VIP treatment—instead he'd been administered a blindfold, earplugs, and handcuffs. Lajos had then passed the flight in a sensory blackout while Worthy ensured he didn't feel the sudden urge to move. He wasn't freed until we debarked onto the tarmac, and when the blindfold came off, his eyes darted about in an attempt to uncover some trick. But our arrival in Newark was indisputable, and by the time we exited the terminal to await the van's arrival, Lajos was in a positively carefree mood.

The jet's middle section, separated by a glossy wood partition and sliding door, held a conference table and flat screens. Worthy trailed me as I passed through this and entered the third and final passenger compartment at the far rear of the plane. Beyond the last partition, the open door revealed the one secret I'd kept not only from Lajos but from my vicars as well.

I'd brought two stowaways.

They looked up at me now, the table between them covered by a child's board game.

Fiona faced me from one seat. Across from her, turning in her leather chair to see me enter, was Langley.

I knelt before her.

"How are you, Langley? Being good for Ms. Fiona?"

Langley nodded. "Yeah. She's not very good at this game."

I shot a stern glare at Fiona.

"No throwing the game for her, Fiona. Make her work for it."

"Yes, sir—er, David. But I'm not throwing it. Langley's got a hot hand for dice."

I stood. "Then you won't mind taking a break."

"Of course not," Fiona replied. "What do you need?"

I felt a wave of gratitude. For the first time, I could address Fiona with total trust.

"You still have access to the black fund?"

She nodded quickly. "I do. I can transfer or distribute those funds immediately, if you wish."

"Let's discuss that in a bit. For now, please get me a call with Watts right away."

Fiona moved to the front compartment to set up the video teleconference. I assumed her place in the chair, looking across the table at the little girl.

Bringing Langley was a bit of a risk, to be sure, but far less of one than leaving her behind at the Mist Palace. While the vicars, and therefore Agustin, had surely been able to figure out that I'd taken Langley with me by now, she was safe here for the time being. Her jet sat parked on the tarmac of Newark Liberty International Airport, roughly ten miles from Ground Zero and in the middle of so many concentric rings of post-9/11 security that it was the best option for leaving her unsupervised. At least while Agustin and the vicars were still alive.

After that, our options would expand considerably.

"So you're pretty good at this game?"

She nodded.

"Think you can give me some of that luck, Langley?"

"I guess."

"Good. Because Mr. David's going to need all the help he can get."

"Are you almost done with your work?"

"Almost, sweetheart."

"Where are we going after that?"

I sat back, considering the question.

"I don't know," I said at last. "I hadn't really thought about it. But it's a beautiful country, and a beautiful world. Where do you want to go?"

"Somewhere with a playground."

"You've made your point about the playground, sweetheart. What else?"

"Someplace sunny, maybe. I'm tired of fog all the time."

I wrinkled my nose in distaste. "Yeah, the Pacific Northwest isn't the sunniest. I think we can handle that. Anything else?"

"No. Not really."

Fiona appeared in the doorway.

"David," she said, "I've got Watts on the line."

"Thanks. Langley, I need to borrow Ms. Fiona for a few minutes, okay? It won't take long."

"Okay." Langley nodded.

I followed Fiona to the front compartment of the plane, sliding the partition shut and taking a seat before a video monitor.

Watts was visible on the display, and I could see at once that he had been burning the midnight oil.

The silver-haired Chief Vicar of Defense was unshaven for the first time since I'd met him, wearing the same clothes as twenty-four hours ago. His face was pale with fatigue, making his scars stand out against his skin. Watts didn't agree with my order to have every possible terrorist killed as quickly as we could, but like a good little trooper he'd carried it out nonetheless.

I leaned in toward the screen. "Where do we stand?"

He spoke, but I couldn't hear anything. Fiona handed me a pair of headphones, and I donned them to hear Watts's Boston accent as clearly as if he were sitting across from me.

"...with standing orders—"

"Sorry," I said, "can you start over."

Watts shifted uneasily in his seat.

"Sir, in the past twenty-four we have confirmed the deaths of 168 known terrorist operatives and leadership. That leaves 125 souls alive, with standing orders on the kill list."

"I want to see the list. Did you send it to Fiona?"

As he answered in the affirmative, Fiona handed me a tablet. I swiped through the list, seeing the names now divided between red text—dead— and green—still alive. Scrolling down, I saw that Sasa, the Yemeni Al-Qaeda officer I'd narrowly escaped in Somalia, was still alive.

I said to Watts, "I thought we established that my minimum threshold was a half-dozen survivors. Why are half of these cocksuckers still processing oxygen into carbon dioxide?"

"Sir, you must understand...some of these people are extremely well-protected, and went underground the second their colleagues were getting slaughtered. Others aren't at the locations we have on file for them, for one reason or another. They might take months to locate, maybe a year or more. And frankly, sir, your Organization doesn't have the resources to track all these people down at once, no matter how much you want to."

"You're right," I admitted, "my Organization doesn't have those resources."

He nodded.

I lifted the tablet, holding it in the air until Fiona took it from me.

"Fiona, ensure the contents of these files—all known terrorists, living and deceased, with all contact and address information—are immediately sent to the foreign and domestic intelligence services of the US, UK, Canada, Australia, and New Zealand."

Fiona nodded. "Yes, sir."

On the screen before me, Watts folded an arm across his stomach as if suddenly feeling ill. "Sir, that's a breach of compartmentalized information. That violates every rule of—"

"It's egregious, I agree. Fiona, do you agree?"

"Yes, sir. Egregious."

"Good. Do it anyway."

"Yes, sir." She walked to the center cabin as I called after her, "And close the door!"

Then I leaned in close to the screen and whispered, "Listen closely, Watts. Fiona is the traitor—she's been working with Agustin, set us up in

Russia, got our Outfit shooters killed. Now I don't want you to tell a soul. But I need you to have the torture chamber set up upon my return. I'm going to take twenty-four hours to make Fiona pay for what she did to us."

"Twenty-four hours...before what, sir?"

I hesitated. "I'll tell you the rest when I get back."

"And when will that be, sir?"

"I'm taking Langley to a show in the city. We'll fly back tonight."

I removed my headphones and ended the call with Watts. His concerned, perplexed expression turned to black, and I looked over to see it replaced by another: Worthy.

He tilted his head and asked, "What's this talk about a show?"

"Oh, there'll be a show all right," I said. "Get your ammo ready. You're going to meet a few of my friends."

VERDICT

Amat victoria Caedite eos. Novit enim Dominus qui sunt eius.

-Kill them all. For the Lord knows those who are his.

20

Night had fallen by the time Worthy and I walked the streets of Lower Manhattan.

The sidewalks were bustling with people, the Saturday night in full swing. While I was unarmed, Worthy concealed his heavily modified competition pistol under his jacket. A police frisk would be enough to derail our night. And as unlikely as that may have been in the current crowd, the odds or lack thereof couldn't completely alleviate the feeling of guilty adrenaline. The forbidden kind and, in many ways, the best kind.

I was well acquainted with this sensation, indeed in this same setting: as a West Point cadet, many weekend evenings had been spent on BASE jumping excursions in the city. My mentor Jackson would take me to apartment buildings along the Harlem River or the World Fair towers, some new high-rise construction site, or some combination thereof in a single night. We traveled the city by car and subway, wearing stash bags concealing BASE rigs until we'd infiltrated the site. Sometimes we jumped, sometimes the winds turned against us, and sometimes we ended up running from cops or security guards.

And looking up at the Infinity Manhattan, I couldn't help but think how perfect that building would be for a jump.

The high rise was a towering, tiered silo rising seven hundred feet over Lower Manhattan. Its pinnacle was a brightly spotlighted crown, and I searched for the beveled corners just below it: the four balconies of the presidential suite, marking the 55th floor and the location where Agustin and his top people were now gathered. And if all went according to plan, it was the place where they'd die tonight.

Worthy and I made our way toward the hotel. Once the entrance was in sight, we could hear singing and guitar music from a female street performer sitting cross-legged and wearing a hoodie. Her guitar case was open before her, having amassed a fair collection of crumpled green bills. As I got closer, I could hear why.

She was playing to the crowd, singing the US national anthem and doing a decent job of it. She was cleaning house with the patriotic tourists and locals alike, and a small crowd of admirers had begun to form around her.

I reached into my pocket, found the object there, and tossed it atop the green bills and change filling her guitar case.

Konstantin's boar tusk landed amid the bills, and the woman's voice momentarily stuttered before her music stopped altogether.

She ended her song and changed her tune, loudly belting out the Russian national anthem. From beneath the hood, Susan Fox's eyes momentarily met mine.

I knew Susan had been watching the hotel, making sure that Agustin didn't come or go unnoticed. But this was a novel way to do it, I thought, impressed by her resourcefulness—she could stay out here on the street for hours, hidden in plain sight.

I gave Susan a nod and a smile, and she sang louder in response.

Worthy and I continued walking, mounting the steps to the Infinity Manhattan's grand entrance.

The lobby was a whirlwind of gleaming marble surfaces and discrete interior landscaping. Guests heading into the hotel carried shopping bags or had a porter doing it for them, and well-dressed couples swept outside on their way to dinner. Amid the flux of people, I recognized one stationary figure whose head nodded in a polite bow as he saw us: Ian.

True to form, Ian blended with his surroundings perfectly. Tonight he was instantly identifiable as a personal assistant banished to the lobby to wait for the arrival of his master's guests. He wore sober business attire, a phone earpiece, and politely clutched a leather-bound ledger that was probably filled with blank pages.

He approached us and said, "Gentlemen, welcome. How was your trip today?"

"Eventful," I replied. "You're looking quite well, Ian. This is my colleague, Worthy—"

I looked over to see Worthy not listening, instead looking about the lobby in awe. It had been some time since I'd BASE jumped for recreation, but his naivety annoyed me. He was violating the first two rules of infiltrating a public site—always look like you're supposed to be exactly where you are, and always look like you know exactly where you're going next.

"Please forgive my friend," I said. "He is but a simple man from the Deep South, and unaccustomed to our Yankee ways."

Worthy raised an eyebrow at me. "Fuck you say?"

Ian quickly intervened, extending a graceful arm toward the elevator. "I understand completely. Please, follow me. Your party is waiting upstairs. You arrived just in time for cocktails."

* * *

As Ian, Worthy, and I strolled down the carpeted corridors of the 47th floor, I realized that I'd conducted mission preparations at a hotel once before, albeit in far less glamorous surroundings. At the time I was with Boss's team, and we gathered in a hotel room to await the appearance of their intelligence operative. Finally he'd arrived, and that was how I'd met Ian for the first time.

How far he and I had both come since then.

My stomach tightened as Ian stopped in front of a door and rapped lightly on the wood. I'd once looked forward to this moment, but now I dreaded it, feeling only guilt and shame that it had taken me so long.

But as Ian opened the door and allowed me to enter, the emotions were quickly banished from my mind. Inside the room were three men I hadn't seen since leaving Argentina, and the sight of them felt like I was coming home.

Sergio, Cancer, and Reilly all smiled upon seeing me, and I barely had time to brace for impact before Reilly rolled me up in a bear hug.

"Thanks for bringing us home, boss!" he said, releasing me.

Reilly was a study in opposites. His upper body was as muscled as an amateur bodybuilder, but his face was boyish. In combat he fought as well as any of us, but his character held a deep compassion for those affected by the fight. In war, I'd lost my humanity, but Reilly's had only deepened.

And he was a first-rate combat medic. It never hurt to have one of those around.

"Good to see you too, Reilly—"

My words were cut off by Cancer stepping forward, but rather than hugging me, he thwacked his knuckles against my testicles.

"Shit!" I hissed, doubling over with pain.

"Shoulda called us back sooner, asshole," he said in a raspy Jersey slant before balling me up in a hug as well.

I hadn't expected Cancer to be capable of any affection, much less a hug. The deeply tanned man with close-cropped silver hair looked like your average older, slightly trashy Jersey native. The reality couldn't have been further from the truth.

Unlike Reilly, Cancer hadn't maintained his innocence; instead, he'd seen the dark side and embraced it fully. By reputation he was a skilled sniper and an Outfit legend with multiple valor bonuses to his name. But by my experience with him in Argentina, he was a true killer with few scruples beyond those dictated by operational necessity. Cancer was a reef shark, swimming dreamily beneath the surface until the slightest chance of combat was presented like blood in the water. Once that happened, he'd kill with bullet and blade until there was no one left, just as he had in Argentina.

And on this mission, I needed him desperately.

He released me from his hug, thrusting an index finger toward my face.

"And don't even think about trying to get me back for the balltap, 'cause I'll fuckin' kill ya."

"Okay," I groaned. "I believe you."

Sergio approached, his Latino face bearing its trademark goatee. Instead of hugging me, he stopped and extended his hand. Of course he did, I thought. Compared to Reilly's and Cancer's enthusiastic reactions, Sergio's demeanor marked him as what he was: an old, wise soul.

I reached for Sergio's hand, gripped it tightly, and then pulled him into a hug of my own.

His body stiffened momentarily, then relaxed.

Sergio had been hardened by combat, by life, and by the job. Once a staunch loyalist for the Organization, he'd been initially unwilling to accept that the Handler was trying to have him killed with the rest of us. Now he was a man between worlds, who'd given many years of his life to Outfit service only to find himself betrayed with nothing to show for it.

But he'd been my second-in-command in Argentina, and had been indispensable both as an advisor and a warrior. It was one thing to make the right strategic call for the mission, and I seemed capable of that. But it was entirely another to translate that directive into myriad tactical orders that leveraged the strengths of each man while drawing upon an immense base of experience, and in that regard, Sergio was without equal.

Seeing him brought an immense feeling of assurance. I'd made impossible decisions on a wing and a prayer in Argentina, and Sergio had ensured that each one had the greatest possible chance of success. Granted, they all paled in comparison to what we'd be attempting now. But if anyone could turn my harebrained ideas into results, it was the man standing before me. I embraced Sergio with genuine gratitude, squeezing him more tightly than I intended.

Then I released him and said, "So you guys have already met Ian, I see."

"Fuckin' A," Reilly replied. "When someone besides you called our sat phone, he had to answer every piece of paramilitary trivia about Boss's and Jimmy's teams before we believed he wasn't one of the Handler's people."

I said, "I'm glad you believed him. Moving on with introductions—Worthy, this is Sergio, Cancer, and Reilly. Guys, meet Worthy. He's a country bumpkin simpleton, but for tonight he's *our* country bumpkin simpleton. And he's not half-bad with a pistol."

"Pistol?" Cancer said, disgusted. "How's he going to do with a rifle, because that's what we're carrying through the door upstairs."

Worthy pulled his jacket back to show them the 1911 holstered there: barrel extension, reflex sight, and a double-stacked high-capacity magazine. Reilly audibly gasped at the sight.

Worthy said, "I'm quicker with this cowboy piece, boys. Four-time President's Hundred in pistol, one-time finalist for IPSC Handgun World Shoot."

"Yeah?" Sergio asked. "How much of a fight do those paper targets put up?"

I cut off the response. "The dick-measuring contest has been canceled due to lack of interest. So let's talk about the guy we're here to kill tonight."

Now Sergio cut me off. "Let's kit up first, boss. Ian's got to get any extra gear out before we can bang the target."

There was plenty of kit to choose from.

Pieces of luggage were strewn about the bed and floor, all open to reveal the contents of their foam-lined interiors. I was awestruck at the sight—it was a funhouse of weapons, ammunition, body armor, and explosives.

Sergio pointed to a plate carrier on the bed. "That set is yours, boss."

I examined it, and had to do a double-take. I'd never seen this particular plate carrier before, but it had all its pouches configured just the way I liked them. Six magazines across the front, radio to the left for easy operation with my non-firing hand, the antenna routed to the back of the carrier.

Then I picked up the suppressed M4 assault rifle lying beside it, marveling at the configuration. It was spec'd out just like the weapon I'd used in Argentina—no pistol grip, taclight mounted on the right side of the barrel as far forward as the rails would allow, connected to a pressure switch on the top handguard that I could activate with my thumb. Even the holographic reflex sight was mounted where I preferred it, the lead edge flush with the front of the ejection port.

I set it down and looked up to find my recon team smiling at me, quite proud of themselves and rightfully so.

"Aw," I said, blushing. "You guys remembered."

"'Course we did," Cancer said kindly. "And there's something else. Ian?"

Ian stepped forward and presented me with a shoebox-sized container. I accepted it and, sensing from its heft that a considerable object was within, set it on the bed and opened it.

The sight took my breath away.

A folded pistol belt rested within, its tactical webbing bearing an incongruous leather holster. I reached for the holster and snatched out the massive revolver stuffed within, the textured rubber grip falling naturally into my grasp.

The revolver weighed nearly three pounds. I nearly shouted, "The Ruger Super Redhawk Alaskan chambered in .454!"

Ian gave a sheepish nod. "The bear gun you almost killed yourself with before meeting Boss's team. Who knows where the original is, but I wanted you to have it for this hit."

I opened the cylinder, saw the six rounds stamped *.454 CASULL*.

"This piece is so hard to find... where did you... how did you... and on such short notice," I gasped. "Guys, I...I can't accept this."

Reilly put a hand on my shoulder. "You deserve the best."

I swallowed, holstering the revolver and putting on the pistol belt. Cancer stepped out of the way so I could see myself in the long closet mirror, and I turned in a circle.

Sergio said, "It looks great on you."

I put my hands on my hips and looked at each of them in turn. "You guys—look at all this. Weapons, explosives, enemies to vanquish...it's all too much."

We all donned our gear, and then re-packed the excess equipment before helping Ian stack the empty cases atop the luggage cart.

Ian addressed us a final time. "It'll take me about ten minutes to get these out of the building. I'll call you once they're loaded in the car, and then you'll be clear to launch."

"Thanks, Ian," I said, giving him a hug before he left. "See you at the safehouse."

"Be careful up there, David. You're running out of lives."

Cancer slapped him on the ass as he left, and with that, we were alone as a five-man assault force, and a motley one at that. Cancer, Reilly, and I had tried to kill the Handler. Sergio had served him. Worthy had protected him, all the way up to the point that I shoved an ice pick in his chest. Were it not for the Handler I never would have met these men, and that fact felt like an obscure privilege as we stood together, united against a common enemy.

"Okay, boss," Sergio said, laying out a blueprint of the presidential suite. "Let's go over the plan."

* * *

Our team ascended the stairs quietly, flowing as smoothly as if not a day had passed since we'd maneuvered together in Argentina. Cancer was in the lead, his rifle slung in favor of a suppressed pistol for the quietest possible means of sentry removal. The only other man in our stack with his rifle slung was Worthy, who carried his namesake as the last man in our order of movement.

I felt honored and humbled to be in the company of these men. Each had volunteered to participate in tonight's mission; we were still outnumbered, but would have been critically so if any man had refused to go. None of them had any self-serving motivations—all but Worthy had just returned from Argentina, where they'd nearly been slaughtered by the Organization they were now protecting by attacking its chief opponent. Worthy should have been masterless after the Handler's death; he either suspected or knew outright that I wouldn't last at the helm.

And yet we'd all assembled because of the simple facts at hand.

Agustin was at the tipping point of successfully taking over the Handler's Organization. He had inside conspirators on his side, powerful allies in his pocket, and his ultimate goal was to maximize profit through the fusion of criminal enterprise and terrorism.

That much was already happening around the world. We'd gotten a taste of it in Argentina, where Hezbollah funded terror by helping the cartels move drugs. Ideology was taking a backseat to money on an international scale. Even the Handler forbid those unions—at least officially—but Agustin sought to galvanize them. He intended to create a global economy with no distinction between crime and terror, and if he assumed control over the Organization's resources, there'd be nothing left to stop him.

As we rounded a landing two stories beneath Agustin's suite, a member of his guard force called to us.

"That's far enough," the Latino voice said. "Go back down. Now."

"Sir," Cancer said, "this is a routine check of the fire escape."

"It works," the man replied, growing louder as he descended toward us. "Now go back down, or I'll have your job."

With that, Cancer rounded the corner and fired his suppressed pistol twice.

I heard a body tumbling down the stairs, and Cancer ducked backward as it crashed to a stop at the landing.

Cancer whispered to the corpse, "Your dick ain't big enough to take my job, pal."

Then he continued forward, stepping over the body as we followed him up the final steps to the suite's sole door access.

We formed a stack on the stairwell, stopping our movement. Cancer holstered his pistol in favor of his suppressed M4, and then Worthy moved forward with his explosive breaching charge.

Worthy had drawn the short straw here—as breacher, he would have to blow the charge, then transition to his weapon while the rest of us flowed into the suite before he did. Worthy would be the last man through the door.

But he'd begrudgingly accepted this role, and presently unrolled a long strip of flexible linear charge and peeled off the adhesive backing. Then he applied the end of the strip beside the door's top hinge, unrolling it down until its length was exhausted at the bottom edge of the door.

A length of det cord emerged from the bottom of the charge, and Worthy reached into a cargo pocket to tie into it with his detonator attachment.

It was at that moment, with Worthy kneeling at the door's bottom hinge and the rest of us braced against the wall, that the door swung inward.

In the open doorway stood a man with a submachine gun, looking as perplexed as I felt—had he heard something on the stairwell? Was he conducting a routine shift change? It didn't matter now. Cancer dropped him with his rifle, administering a tight group of three rounds to the chest.

Our deliberate approach just got upgraded to an emergency assault, and Cancer charged up the final steps with the rest of us in tow.

The suite was split into four quadrants: living room, library, spa, and master bedroom. We rightfully assumed Agustin and his staff would be holding their meeting in the living room or library, and our entire stack cut left toward those two quadrants.

The first segment of the suite was the living room, and my view of it was obscured by huge rectangular marble columns.

When it came into view, I saw a deep extension ending in a vaulted glass archway overlooking the city. The fireplace was blazing, room packed with coffee tables surrounded by couches and chairs from which suited men were leaping up in alarm.

Cancer and Reilly posted themselves behind a pair of marble columns and commenced a mostly one-way firefight, systematically slaughtering every occupant with rapid shots.

Their roaring semi-automatic fire sent a shower of expended shells arcing into the hallway. Sergio and I ran through the barrage, getting pelted by the hot brass on our way toward the library. I took a quick glance sideways, not seeing Agustin among the bodies falling amid the withering gunfire mowing them down to a man.

Sergio continued moving along the suite's central wall, and I staggered myself to his right to keep my barrel oriented in our direction of movement. But he was exposed to the library corner before I was, and when he began shooting, I couldn't make out his target.

And before I could, Sergio's head whipped back in a cloud of pink mist.

I was already driving my M4 left, and began firing as soon as Sergio fell out of view.

My reflexive shots struck Sergio's killer, a long-haired guard whose submachine gun gave a final burst of automatic fire as he fell. I saw a spark of bullets on marble and a spray of scalding debris pelted my neck.

Vaulting Sergio's body, I drove my barrel into the library and thought, this is where it all ends.

These men had more notice of our arrival than their partners in the living room, and their weapons were aimed accordingly. Four of them took aim against me as it became apparent their bodyguard just got salted.

I fired from right to left, trying to achieve a single torso hit on each man before reversing the sweep to finish them off. My mind processed the scene before me at an impossibly fast rate, my every sense hyper-acute. I wouldn't be able to kill these people before they got me; there were too many, and I could still hear Cancer and Reilly firing in the living room quadrant. I scored another chest shot and swung my sights to the next man, squeezing my trigger before he could complete his aim. But the two men to the left were drawing a bead on me too quickly; I may have been able to hit one but not both, and as I made this realization I saw a previously unnoticed rifle directed by a man who'd taken cover behind a leather chair.

One second to go before the rounds tore into me, no choice but to continue shooting, and my last thought was a profound sense of disappointment that none of these men was Agustin.

Then something very peculiar happened—the two men on the far left recoiled with a bullet impact to their chest in near-succession, the double strikes separated by a fraction of a second. I registered that the man behind the chair was trying to shift his aim away from me when a round caught him dead-center between his eyes. Then the two men I'd already shot were hit again, both to the chest, and by the time I squeezed off a third round on my sweep, the shots continued—this time moving the other way, as each of the four men were hit with a headshot as they fell.

By now I was barely managing to nail the fourth man with a glancing shot as he fell.

I looked left to see Worthy beside me. He'd arrived after I began shooting, ripped off nine direct hits in the time it had taken me to fire four times, and was completing a tactical reload by the time the last man hit the ground.

My senses compressed reality back to real time in a sudden rush, and I looked over to see Cancer and Reilly continuing their clearance. By the time Worthy and I had cleared the corner, they were clearing the empty spa quadrant.

Then Cancer barreled toward the door to the master bedroom, bypassing all else in a hate-filled rush to reach Agustin. Reilly broke into a dead sprint to back him up—not that Cancer needed it. That son of a bitch would bag Agustin before I could even reach the bedroom.

Then I caught a whiff of something else over the gunpowder, recognizing it after a second's delay.

Cigar smoke.

Whirling toward the smell, I moved toward a closed wooden panel and nodded to Worthy.

He threw the door open and I rushed inside, M4 at the ready.

This was the master bathroom, every surface from floor to ceiling built from a quarry's worth of mottled gold onyx.

Then I saw the source of the cigar smoke—a bathtub faced the far window, and Agustin blew a stream of smoke before setting the cigar into a glass ashtray perched at the edge.

Spigots continued pouring into the tub, which appeared at first to be overflowing.

But a wider basin caught the runoff; this was an infinity tub placed to overlook the view of Lower Manhattan. The glimmering city lights beyond created a stunning backdrop of glamour, wealth, and power, and Agustin languidly stared into that abyss without so much as a sideways glance at me.

I kept my rifle barrel aimed at him, sidestepping to his front, my finger poised against the trigger to fire at the slightest provocation. He surely had a gun beneath the placid surface of that water, and I wasn't going to let him get a shot off.

But as I stepped to the side of the tub, facing him with my rifle, I saw he was naked, his hands empty.

Worthy saw the same, and he darted out of the bathroom to continue clearing with Cancer and Reilly.

"No gun?" I asked Agustin. "You're many things, but no coward."

He looked to me for the first time, emitting a laugh of disbelief.

"So that was your plan, David? Secretly track me from our meeting?" He pulled a hand from the water, whipping off the droplets to pluck a cigar from the glass ashtray at his side. Taking a puff, he waved the cigar idly about his surroundings. "We were not exactly lying low."

"And that's going to cost you everything. Right. Now."

But Agustin appeared calm, gazing out the window with an expression of contentment.

"The most important indication of a man's character is how he faces his final moments. I choose this." He gestured toward the window. "Do you remember what I told you about my past, when we met in Rio de Janeiro?"

"I remember. You were taunting me, thinking I'd be killed within the hour."

"Naturally." He assumed a stern tone, as if correcting me. "But not *lying*. I did arrive to Rio as a boy of eight. With nothing, not even family. I did see Christ the Redeemer glowing atop the hill that first night. It was the beginning of the only life I wished to remember. And seeing the glow of New York will be the end of that life. So be it."

"For once, you and I are in agreement."

He spoke quickly. "But you will never be able to leave this behind,

David. Men like you and me...it is in our nature. The end you deliver me is the end you will face yourself. There is no retirement in this adventure—only reaching the summit of power, or dying on the way."

"I thought I had reached the summit."

Another puff of his cigar, a long stream of smoke momentarily obscuring his face.

"You took a shortcut, and that will cost you your kingdom of shit. The vicars will eat you alive. This is happening already, whether you know it or not. You will return to nothing, and they will hunt you for as long as it takes. Your one way out was through me."

"Maybe you're right about that. Maybe you're not. But I'm going to be the only one of us to find out."

I lowered the rifle on its sling and drew my .454 revolver from its holster.

"I was going to kill myself with this gun, once. It's about the *only* weapon I haven't killed people with over the last few years. But you've taught me a valuable lesson: as long as there are people like you, it's up to people like me to put our bullets to better use."

I aimed the revolver at his face, assuming the two-handed stance necessary to control the hand cannon.

"Do you see *my* redeemer, Agustin?"

His eyes were lazy, vanishing behind a cloud of cigar smoke that he blew up at me.

I fired the pistol, the heavy revolver bucking so hard that it felt like I'd slammed my right hand in a door.

The .454 round had cut a vortex through the cloud, now a foggy smoke ring spreading away from Agustin's face.

Or, rather, what was left of his face.

His body was sliding slowly into the tub, the water blossoming scarlet as it overflowed the main tub and sloshed out of the hole where the bullet had ripped clean through.

I holstered the pistol on my third attempt, my right hand half-numb from the shot. Not a great tactical weapon, this hunk of steel, but it was sufficient to get the job done.

Then I looked up, shocked to see Reilly watching me from the doorway.

"Sergio's dead. It's time to go, boss."

* * *

We charged up the remaining stairwell, reaching the final door labeled *ROOF ACCESS*. I pushed the red bar to open it, and an ear-splitting alarm began to sound.

A strong wind buffeted us on the roof, and I turned to scan the night sky. All around us was a glittering universe of city lights, and before I could orient myself to which side of the roof I stood on, my eyes fell on a sight that stopped me in my tracks.

Far below amid the packed urban structures was a barren city block packed with trees. Apart from a short triangular building there were only two staggered squares in the ground, each a hole of waterfalls cascading to a glistening pool of water. At the center of each was a black square that the water disappeared into, the two final voids staring upward like eyes in the night.

It took me a moment to realize that I was looking at Ground Zero from above. I'd seen it once before, under far different circumstances.

The first time had been upon returning from my first deployment to Afghanistan in 2002. The pilots had received clearance to fly our military transport aircraft over the city. Back then, I recalled seeing little more than a massive dirt pit packed with construction equipment. Now the site was a staggering reminder of the event that had propelled me and my country into war, a morning that changed the trajectory of the world forever.

Now, I was carrying my team out of that raid at tremendous cost—we bore Sergio's body on our collective shoulders, and that blame fell on me. He'd been recovered from Argentina only to fall in battle, and the fight was not yet over. I felt an enormous guilt about bringing these men together and asking so much of them; but the sight of Ground Zero was a reminder that the cause was just, perhaps the only inviolable cause there was. We had fought that night to kill terrorists, pure and simple. Whether none of us died or all of us did, we had pursued the most noble calling I knew.

"David!" Cancer shouted, shaking my shoulder. "Get your fucking ass over here."

I turned to see the rest of my team lined up at the adjacent corner of the roof, kneeling to brace themselves against the wind whose intensity and noise were increasing to a fever pitch.

I shielded my face from the whipping maelstrom and followed Cancer toward the others, taking the last place in line. Worthy shouted something at me but I could no longer hear him—the churning howl of rotors was too loud, and I squinted upward to see a single unlit helicopter descending toward us on its final approach.

The helicopter gently eased to a halt atop the helipad, and my team stood to race aboard. I counted each man as they climbed through the open doors—Worthy, Reilly with Sergio's body over his shoulders, assisted by Cancer before he leapt inside himself.

I was the last aboard, clambering onto a seat beside Reilly and giving a thumbs up to the cockpit.

The pilot nodded, and we immediately lifted upward and then dipped in an accelerating roar away from the rooftop. But in the second I saw his profile, I felt the odd reassurance that he too had been involved in everything that followed 9/11. I craned my head to catch a final glimpse of Ground Zero, knowing that the pilot was doing the same.

I recalled meeting him for the first time, seeing him beside a Cessna Caravan as Boss, Matz, and Ophie prepared to load our equipment for a cross-country flight to our next mission. At the time I thought he was an unremarkable sixty-something pilot with trim silver hair and jug ears. Boss had scolded me immediately thereafter.

Joe is a living legend. Thirty-five years of service before he went private sector, and he's seen more trouble than the rest of us combined. Remember that when you get a few jobs under your belt and start to think you're tough.

The wind and rotor wash whipped against my face as Ground Zero slid from view, barricaded behind a glittering wall of buildings rising up from New York. I leaned back and looked at the faces of the survivors around me —Cancer, looking bored; Reilly, his eyes downcast to Sergio's body on the helicopter floor; and Worthy, watching me intently and giving me an affirming nod.

I nodded back at him, but the gesture felt empty with Sergio's body between us.

Before I could dwell on Sergio's loss, the helicopter banked into a hard right turn. I braced to hold on as Joe whipped our chopper between two skyscrapers, leveled out, and then increased the throttle to fly us away from the final mission.

We just had to make one last stop.

Joe flew us northeast of the city, toward the Long Island Sound. And when the view beneath our helicopter was nothing but a sheer expanse of placid nighttime water, Sergio got his burial at sea.

As his body bag splashed into the jet-black surface and began its descent through the depths, Joe banked left and began the flight to Ian's safehouse.

Where that safehouse was, I had no idea.

I hadn't wanted to know, and had specifically told Ian to keep it a mystery to everyone but the pilot. All I needed was a place where Langley and Fiona would be safe, and a communications suite to include video tele-conference with the Mist Palace. Both were satisfied aboard the Handler's jet, but with our recent mission all over the news and everyone in the world searching for our helicopter, we couldn't go back to Newark.

Instead, Joe flew us along a northwest arc over land, across the Hudson River, and toward rolling hills extending beyond the lights of towns below. Soon there were no lights at all, save one: a flashing red strobe, blinking at the edge of a field ringing a small lake.

We descended toward that field as the red light extinguished. The lake's formerly placid surface rippled with fury, and when our helicopter thumped to a stop in the field, it was only for a moment—Cancer, Reilly, Worthy, and I leapt onto the expanse of long grass whipping in furious objection to the rotor wash. We'd barely made landfall before the heli-copter was lifting off again, its engine howling to a fever pitch as Joe guided it skyward.

The aircraft disappeared quickly amid the night sky, the only evidence of its presence the throb of rotors receding in the distance. I knew I'd see Joe again, though where or under what circumstances, I had no idea.

A red light flashed at the edge of the field, and we moved toward it in a file. As I approached, I saw Ian holding the light. He searched our faces in the dim red glow, ticking off the survivors by way of determining who hadn't made it back.

"Sorry about Sergio," he said.

"So am I. How's Langley?"

"She's sleeping. Come on, I'll brief you on the way."

With the red lens flashlight, Ian guided us up a trail through the woods. As he did so, he spoke quietly to me.

"The vicars initiated a total evacuation of the Mist Palace."

"I guess that was a matter of time."

"You think? New boss holds the incineration code to burn the Mist Palace to the ground, then flees and conducts an unsanctioned hit against Agustin. It doesn't take an analyst to figure out their chances of survival are better in the bunker."

"Are you sure that's where they're at?"

"Positive. Fiona's established communications with the bunker, but they won't talk to her. Seems the only person they want to speak with is you."

"Well," I said, "let's not keep them waiting."

The trail ended at a small cabin nestled in the woods.

Between the pre-sunrise glow beginning to tinge the night sky and the red light of Ian's flashlight, I couldn't make out much of the cabin's exterior. But the appearance of the wooden walls gave me a strange sense of déjà vu that took me a moment to account for.

Maybe it was the adrenal fatigue from the mission, or simply a trick of the light in the early morning's dim glow, but I had the eerie sense that I was approaching Sage's cabin. That dilapidated structure was on the opposite side of the continent, though after living there for six months in near-total isolation I was probably doomed to recall it anytime I saw a cabin.

We entered to find a sparsely furnished interior, with Fiona waiting.

"Langley?"

"Asleep in the bedroom," she said in a distant tone. Her eyes were searching me and the others up and down, as if she was in shock. I realized she'd probably never seen anyone in tactical kit, much less four men who'd just emerged from a bloodbath.

"How soon can I speak with the vicars?"

She swept a hand toward a short hallway. "Communications suite is set up in the back room. The video teleconference link to the bunker is up and running. The vicars are waiting to talk to you."

I checked my watch.

"All right. Let's get this over with before Langley wakes up."

* * *

I closed the door for privacy, then took a seat before the computer monitor. Its screen glowed with a single camera image of a conference room.

Watts, Yosef, and Omari were seated closest to the camera, and

lining the rest of the table, culminating in a row of chairs against the back of the room, were people I'd never seen before. These were the top assistants, willing parties to Agustin's plans.

The setting was the bunker's interior conference room: the deepest depths of the Springfire North site, which I had never seen before now.

I put on my headphones so I could hear and transmit, feeling my shoulders swell.

Then I said, "I don't recall authorizing an evacuation of the Mist Palace. What do you have to say for yourselves?"

On the screen, Omari shook his head slowly and said, "You have been too deep in our Organization for too long. This is your one and only opportunity to defect from the role of Handler and appoint a successor from among the vicars."

"A noble offer. You traitorous little motherfuckers couldn't kill me before and now you don't know where I'm at, so your next play is a legitimate transition of power. What's the matter, Omari, you don't think I'm capable of leading the Organization?"

Watts answered for him. "None of us do, David. But you don't have to. All you have to do is defect."

"Or else what?"

"Don't let it come to that, David. We have already faced the unfortunate necessity of betraying the sitting Handler. Your predecessor went insane, and chose an heir who is unfit to lead. You can legitimately transition power to one of the vicars, or we will disown you and rule as a council."

"As a council?" I scoffed. "You power-hungry backstabbers would eat each other alive, and the Organization would fall apart. And forgive my mistrust, but I don't believe any of you would respect my safety in retirement. So, I propose a different plan." I picked up the phone beside me, holding it before the camera so they could see, and concluded, "I burn this entire ratship to the ground."

Watts spoke quickly. "Don't do anything rash. There's no one left at the Mist Palace."

"We are all in the bunker," Omari agreed. "You would accomplish nothing but burning down the buildings, and nothing will stop us from rebuilding."

"Well," I said casually, "let's put that to the test."

Holding the phone with both hands, I typed 62947908. The first eight digits of the number to the satellite phone that I'd recited in my head dozens of times a day, fearful that I'd forget my only means of contacting the team in Argentina.

Yosef spoke for the first time, his Israeli accent raspy. "If you burn the Mist Palace, David, it will not just mean death to you. We will order Langley's death as well. Neither of you will survive a single week."

My phone's screen blinked with a confirmation message. I confirmed.

"What was that?" I asked. "Sorry, I was busy entering the code. Did it work?"

There were gasps of horror from the room, aides consulting tablets and whispering in what appeared to be a state of aggrieved shock.

"Looks like it did," I said, setting the phone down. "How about that?"

Omari slammed a fist on the table. "You still have no control. All your contacts and information become obsolete within days if the money stops changing hands. And you have no money, Rivers. I've made quite sure of that."

"Aside from a small black fund left behind by my predecessor, I'd have to agree with you. But you're assuming I care about money. Or the Organization."

Watts addressed me in a stern tone, a father reprimanding his son.

"You had better care, insofar as you plan on you or Langley surviving. I maintain a direct line of communications with the Outfit commander—"

"Orlando?" I interrupted. "Yeah, funny thing about that. I have a direct line of communication with him, too."

Then I picked up a radio hand mic from the desk and waved it in front of the screen. "Want me to prove it to you?"

A stunned silence had fallen over their assembly, a few nervous glances toward one another. None could tell for certain whether I was bluffing.

Yosef spoke now. "Even if you try to contact the Outfit commander, he will honor his Organization. Not the orders of a rogue leader who set his own headquarters aflame."

I shook my head. "You three are cunning, I'll give you that. But you're not seeing your situation clearly. I saved Orlando's life in Russia, fighting alongside his men. You three? None of you has spent a day in the Outfit. And for years you've been sending their shooters to spill their blood and give their lives and limbs on your behalf. Meanwhile you've all sat in your ivory tower, pulling the strings and counting your cash. So who do you think the Outfit is going to listen to—me, or you?"

"Every government in the world," Watts said, "has their political and military elements separated. Many of them are just as criminal as we are. So don't give me the sob story when these Outfit men know what they've signed up for."

I felt a sting of pride for the control in my voice when I responded.

"Well, today the power balance has shifted."

Omari shook his head. "The power balance remains with the Handler's throne. And after incinerating the Mist Palace, not one among our staff concedes to your reign." He lifted his hands helplessly. "You have no Organization. You sit alone in an empty house. You are not the Handler."

"Well, it seems nobody sent that memo to the Outfit boys. Because they've borne sacrifices on your behalf for some time, and they seemed pretty ecstatic to return the favor."

The vicars were silent for a moment before Watts asked, "What—what does that mean, 'return the favor?'"

I picked up the radio mic. "I told you I had a direct line with the Outfit. Well, I also set up an insurance policy in case I didn't make it out of New York alive. By now you're all wondering if I'm bluffing, so let's find out."

I transmitted into the mic. "Leopard Six, the order I am about to give you is final. You will acknowledge no mission abort, even from me."

Orlando replied, "*Copy all, Suicide. Send your order.*"

"Initiate terminal objective."

"*Roger that. Enjoy the fireworks.*"

I set the radio mic down, watching the screen intently. Just then, the people in the conference room heard a sound—I did too. It was just a distant thump, its origin unclear.

"You know," I addressed them, "my predecessor once entered negotiations with his domestic opposition, just to consolidate them for a decapitation strike."

Now there was a second blast, this one a deep booming echo. Some of the staff members jumped in their seats, looking to the camera in alarm. I continued.

"The team he sent to kill his enemies was mine. I completed the mission with Boss, Matz, Ophie, and Karma."

I could hear a spattering of gunshots through the speakers—the Outfit was now eliminating guards within the bunker.

"Then the Handler killed everyone but me. So today, I'm doing the same thing—"

Another explosion sounded through the speakers—the Outfit was blowing the interior bunker doors now.

"—consolidating my enemies, and sending in the warriors to kill them. Not even I can call them off now. But there's one important difference: this time, the warriors get to retire."

I heard more bursts of gunfire from just beyond the conference room, and the sound of Outfit shooters shouting to one another. It was too late now; too late to stop anything.

Yosef shouted at me, the last act he'd do in life.

"Burn in hell, Rivers—"

At that moment, the final explosive breach detonated. The camera blurred with the momentary concussion, which knocked out the audio recording. From that point on, the footage continued in silence.

The view came into focus in time to capture the reinforced conference room door flying into the room with blinding speed. It struck Yosef, crushing him where he sat before coming to rest against the heavy table.

Watts leapt to his feet, both arms outstretched in a defensive posture, and shouted orders toward the momentarily empty doorway.

Omari threw himself out of his chair, attempting to dive beneath the table.

The row of assistants seated on the far wall had varying reactions. Some were frozen, others trying to shield their faces in the wake of the blast.

Then the Outfit shooters entered the room.

They flowed through the doorway with fluid precision, the operators breaking in both directions as they moved to the corners.

Puffs of mist obscured the view of the assistants in the back of the room, and Watts's head. The opening salvo of Outfit shooters firing dropped every visible person like a puppet with the strings cut, their bodies crumpling in place. Watts's face was gone in a flash, and his skull bounced off the conference table on his way to the floor.

Omari survived the longest.

He was under the table, unseen by the camera until two of the Outfit shooters dropped to a knee and engaged him in a crossfire. On the far side of the table, a chair moved as Omari's arm flung into view before going motionless.

By this time seven Outfit shooters lined two walls of the room, sweeping their barrels for living targets and finding none.

So they engaged the bodies instead, firing into the head of each corpse and removing any possibility of a survivor—with one exception.

The reinforced door remained angled across the table. A pair of shooters approached each side of it, and together they hoisted it from the table and let it fall back onto the floor.

Only then was Yosef visible once more.

His mangled body was slumped over the conference table. His spine was shattered, ribs crushed, his corpse a grotesque half-flattened image of death soaking in blood and entrails.

Two of the Outfit shooters closed in, standing almost shoulder to shoulder as they raised their automatic rifles in unison. The ends of their barrels disappeared in bright muzzle flashes as they fired, and Yosef's head was transformed into a pile of brain matter and skull fragments blasted across the surface of the table.

The shooters reloaded their rifles in two alternating volleys, but no one moved. Instead they lowered their barrels as Orlando entered the room.

He was clad in tactical equipment, like the rest of the Outfit operators, save three details: dual long-whip radio antennas rose from his rear armored plate, he carried no weapon beyond a sidearm on his hip, and he moved with the assistance of crutches.

After Orlando entered, he pivoted left and right on his crutches to survey the carnage. Then he spoke a few words, and the Outfit shooters began flowing out of the room back the way they came.

Orlando remained in the room after they left, nodding to himself as if satisfied by the outcome.

Then he unslung a bulky satchel from his shoulder and set it on the table. He opened a flap, reached beneath it, and then patted the satchel reassuringly. Turning to face the camera, he raised a fist with middle finger extended. After a momentary pause, he used his crutches to maneuver himself out of the room. For a full minute afterward, nothing happened.

Then, in a blinding flash of light, the satchel exploded.

I pulled off my headphones as the screen went black. Then I sat back in my chair, stomach tense, mind racing for answers. I felt like I was watching myself in a movie, and had to assure myself that this wasn't a dream. It was all over, finally and at last.

Orlando's voice crackled over the radio hand mic. "*Suicide, this is Leopard Six. Mission complete.*"

I picked up the radio mic. "Yeah, I can see that. Your guys okay?"

"*I got two malingerers bitching they got shot in the plate. Other than that, we're good to hook.*"

"Fiona's got the bank accounts set up with an even split. Each man will get his number at the rendezvous. Congratulations; the Outfit is officially retired."

"*Good,*" he replied, "*I need a fucking drink. Over.*"

"Story of my life. Suicide, over and out." I released the transmit button, then keyed it again and added, "Forever," before setting down the mic.

The sound of Reilly's voice made me jump.

"How does it feel to destroy your own Organization?"

I turned to see him standing in the now-open doorway beside me.

"Not bad," I admitted. "If anything needed to be destroyed, it was—"

Cancer cut me off, forcing his way past Reilly and into the room.

"How was the video?"

"Pretty gnarly—"

Worthy forced his way into the room next, crowding next to the computer. "If you forgot to hit 'record,' I'll kill you."

"Relax," I said, rising from the chair. "I got it all on tape."

The men let out a collective cheer.

"I'll even give you guys some time to watch it before we destroy the only recording."

A collective groan.

I headed for the door, stopped at my discarded equipment to retrieve the .454 revolver, and stuffed it in my belt.

Cancer saw me doing this and asked, "Where you going with that bear gun?"

I pulled my shirt over the pistol. "Don't worry about it."

"Pro tip, David: you need to file the front sight post off the barrel."

"Why?"

"So when the bear shoves it up your ass, it won't hurt as much."

I grinned, leaving the men to replay the video of the Outfit's final raid. Then I exited the cabin, walking down the stairs and into the early morning sunlight.

The small clearing around the cabin was thick with dew-soaked grass, and the morning chill hit me at once. The early glow of sunrise bathed the forest around me, tinting my surroundings with the dim hue of dawn. I scanned for the path we'd followed to reach the cabin, locating the trail-head winding its way through the trees.

Then I followed it, walking the path's every winding curve toward the spot where our helicopter had deposited us. I needed to think, needed to purge myself of the nervous energy that hadn't dissipated with the slaughter of the Organization's last remaining leadership. Once again I was reminded of being in isolation at Sage's cabin, when every sunrise found me climbing a hillside toward a crystal lake. The view was incredible, sure; but more than anything it was a place to reflect and find peace, however momentary.

But unlike the British Columbian wilderness, I wasn't passing through tremendous vistas of lush valleys and distant snow-capped mountains. Instead I was walking through...well, woods. An ordinary forest, no different than those of my childhood. This was life after war, I thought. Nothing striking, nothing significant. Just...woods. The ordinary and the banal, a reality we all survived to reach. Now there would be no return to combat, and I sensed that before long, we'd all miss the thrill.

On the far side of the continent, the Mist Palace was still smoldering. Before long the entire place would turn to ash and be reclaimed by the wilderness, just as it had when the original mining settlement was abandoned in the mid-1800s. I briefly wondered what would be built next at that site, and what those occupants would think of the ruins they found. Hopefully it was forgotten for good; that piece of land would be better off in nature's hands. Parvaneh would rest there in peace, laid to earth beside her father.

And twelve miles north of the Mist Palace, smoking piles of charred bodies were forever entombed in the bunker. Those people had been willing to project war but not bear it themselves, and when war had found them, they'd perished just as the countless men and women they'd sent to death on their behalf. Good riddance, I thought. This shit was finally over.

I emerged at the field and crossed its overgrown grass toward the lake.

There was no breathtaking landscape here, just a field and a small lake as ordinary as any other. I stopped at the edge of the water.

With the exception of a lone assassin, Lajos Silva, everyone who needed to be dead was. Unfortunately, so too were many good people who should have survived—all of them deserved it far more than I did.

I removed the .454 from my belt. The pistol was heavy in my hand, the chosen instrument of my self-destruction when I thought about little else. I opened the cylinder, seeing the six rounds stamped .454 *CASULL*, each capable of killing any big game on the planet. Then I spun the cylinder, seeing it rotate cleanly with the centrifugal weight of the steel, a marvel of precision American engineering. The action felt natural; it was an act I'd performed during untold rounds of Russian roulette after losing Boss's team.

I saw their faces then, mind lost in thought as the cylinder stopped spinning. Rather than snap it back into place with a practiced flip of my wrist, I withdrew a single massive bullet. It looked cartoonishly large in my open palm, as ludicrous as the mindset that had pervaded my thinking before now. This round could bring down a cape buffalo, and I'd spent years of my life compulsively fantasizing about firing one through my brain.

That's what the fuck I'm talking about, Suicide.

Matz's voice in my head, from the moments before we assaulted a building to kill everyone. My first terminal objective, from an eternity ago when I was a virginal young mercenary. Matz was the first one to nickname me Suicide.

I stared absently at the bullet in my hand, seeing Matz in my mind. The perpetual look of barely suppressed intensity within his dark-circled eyes, the way an assault rifle looked like a toy slung across his chest. His delight in the thrill of combat, the way he masterfully orchestrated an assault against impossible odds.

Whipping my arm in an arc, I threw the bullet into the pond.

Its surface rippled with the *plop* of impact, but the disturbance quickly subsided to a glassy smooth mirror that reflected the treetops rising around it.

I withdrew another round from the chamber, wondering how Matz, with his superior abilities, died, while I, alone with my infinite death wish, had lived. The same went for the rest of the team, all better men than me—why? Why did I, of all people, survive that day? Because I deserved it and they didn't?

I knew what Ophie would say, what he had said in response to this question asked by combat vets the world over.

It's all random and meaningless, boy, and I think you know that much by now.

I thought of him now, tall and lean, his straw-colored hair, his drawl, how laidback he was no matter the circumstance. Ophie had been the first to accept me as a teammate, had seen some spark of potential and discreetly coached me long before I had anything to offer.

Yet he'd also seen enough of the chaos of combat to believe, firmly and with the full conviction of his soul, that there was no cosmic order. That, in his own words, *God doesn't care about us.* Combat was all random, all meaningless.

Maybe it was, I thought; maybe life itself was. That's what my experience seemed to indicate—a meaningless void from which meaning had to be extracted, or built, and then maintained at all costs. A spouse, a child, some passionate life's work to sustain us through the cosmic insanity in which we existed. I hurled the second bullet into the pond, absentmindedly pulling a third bullet from the revolver's cylinder.

Then I realized I'd heard Ophie's notion before. I recalled my father saying much the same, his Irish-accented voice raw with effort: *Make your mark with the triumph of your spirit over the absurd and meaningless void we've been born into.*

He was on his deathbed. I remember him weeping as he spoke his final words, his sole concern to impart some final wisdom upon his only child.

It's never too late to become a better person, and the only failure in life is a failure to change for the better, every day and in whatever way one finds possible...Look at what I meant to you, look at the man I raised, and you go do the same.

Go do the same, I thought. What had he meant—to raise a kid as he had? The thought seemed ludicrous, and I flung the third bullet into the pond with disgust. Given the unspeakable atrocities I'd committed since killing a human being for the first time in the wake of 9/11, what right did I have to mold a child?

But as I plucked a fourth bullet from the cylinder, I had a new thought. Boss had told me the same thing, hadn't he? I thought of the last night I'd seen him alive. He was sitting on the corner of his bed with a picture of his twin girls in his hands. Boss's face was weary, bearing the pain of a lifetime as he spoke.

Get married, have a family, and put everything you've done with us in that place inside that your wife won't know about, along with everything you've already got from Afghanistan and Iraq. Veterans have been doing that since the dawn of war, and now it's your turn.

I pitched the fourth bullet helplessly into the water. Having a family was inconceivable at the time, just as it was now.

But now, I didn't have a choice.

Langley had long ago lost her father, then more recently her mother and grandfather. Protecting her, giving her the childhood she'd been denied so far, was my current purpose in life whether I liked it or not. And truth be told, I did like it; I wanted to protect her, and raise her, and see Parvaneh's spirit shining through her eyes. Langley was everything I wasn't: pure, innocent, full of joy. I didn't deserve to be her father. Instead, it was a lucky privilege that I'd spend the rest of my life trying to earn.

My throat felt constricted as I extracted the fifth bullet.

Langley would need a mother eventually. Hell, I'd probably excel at being the fun parent, but she needed a strong female role model.

In that instant, I realized that Langley would have adored Karma.

I was enraptured with Karma from the moment I laid eyes on her, smoking a cigarette with her petite gymnast's frame leaning against a truck.

Shoulder-length blonde hair, I fondly recalled, jetted with streaks of dark pink. Her tattoos, her pale lipstick, and above all her clear, lucid blue eyes. With a tugging sensation in the center of my chest, I threw the round into the pond, then hastily pulled the last round from the cylinder. But I found no bullet; instead, there was only an empty shell casing from the round that had slain Agustin. I pulled that out instead.

Karma was gone now. So too was Langley's mother.

What would Parvaneh want me to do?

Her death should have been too recent to contemplate, but in a strange way it felt as if she hadn't been gone any longer than everyone else I'd lost. She seemed to understand me from the beginning, and I thought of what she said upon my return from Argentina.

You've just returned from war. And retired as a warrior. Either one is an immensely difficult adjustment; both at once, even more so...But I'm here for you, and I always will be. You understand?

Except, of course, she wasn't. Not anymore. I was on my own, left to figure out how to raise Langley on my own.

With a frustrated grunt, I hurled the last shell toward the water.

If only Parvaneh were still here, with her impossibly quick responses and razor-sharp logic, telling me what to do. Her brunette hair, so dark it appeared almost black. How she never wore makeup on her heart-shaped face, aside from dark eye shadow and eyeliner that highlighted her electric green irises...

This thought made the breath hitch in my throat as I remembered another girl I'd once known with those eyes.

Of course, I thought. It was obvious, wasn't it? Yet I'd been so consumed with the events since I'd met Boss's team that I'd forgotten all that had come before.

I hurled the pistol in a long arc toward the center of the water.

By the time it splashed through the surface and began its weighted descent to the depths of the pond, I was running back down the trail toward the cabin.

When I arrived, I strode up to Ian.

"Ian," I gasped, still out of breath from running, "there's one last person I need you to locate for me."

OPPORTUNITY

Faber est suae quisque fortunae

-Every man is the artisan of his own fortune

21

Charlottesville, Virginia

Our long journey had come to an end in a most unlikely place: East Coast, upper-middle-class suburbia.

I sat on one of the park benches overlooking the playground, watching Langley flit about the conjoined obstacles with a feverish intensity. If I could bottle that child's energy, I'd carry an eyedropper filled with it at all times. Just a drop under the tongue every three to five days, and I'd never need an adrenaline rush again.

The ground was mottled by shade from the overhead treetops, providing cool respite from the blazing sun. The squeaks, chirps, and cries of children echoed like birdcalls around me. I had joined a new species of adult male: the dad. That meant carrying a water bottle and watch, cutting the kid loose at a park, and then resigning myself to being a joint hydration station and referee of time remaining for the child to run like mad with her peers.

I'd adapted fairly well to this, I supposed.

Langley had wanted to live someplace sunny, and Virginia was both sunny and about as far as we could get from the British Columbian wilderness that harbored enough negative associations for her and me both. Plus, we could spend one weekend in the mountains and the next at the beach, and a reasonable driving radius took us to any number of East Coast cities where Langley—and I—could see how regular people lived in this new, normal world we'd been missing out on all these years.

I'd chosen Charlottesville for another specific reason, and time would soon tell if my instincts would pay out.

There were, however, more than enough pragmatic justifications to move to our neighborhood in Charlottesville. It was virtually dead-center among all the kids' parks, playgrounds, and museums of the surrounding area. Its streets were tree-lined and packed with great schools, constant family activities, and parks like this one scattered throughout the city.

True, it was going to require some adjustment on my part.

I'll admit that my blood pressure frequently soared while trying to achieve even the speed limit while fighting my way through a sea of mint green hybrid vehicles wafting about at inoffensive speeds. But Langley loved the area, and that was all I needed.

Yes, the entire town couldn't have been more yuppie if it were baptized in soy milk. It was, however, the perfect place to raise a child.

And sure, a short time ago I'd been shooting motherfuckers in the face in a New York high rise. Now, I had grocery store clerks looking at me like I clubbed a baby seal if I didn't bring in a reusable shopping bag.

But this wasn't about me; it was about Langley.

She clambered down the ladder and ran up to me in her trademark uniform—princess dress and sneakers—to snatch her water bottle and slurp down a few hydrating gulps.

"How much longer, Daddy?"

I checked my watch. "Five more minutes, honey."

She took another sip and set her bottle down, turning to sprint back to the playground.

A female voice spoke beside me. "Mind if I have a seat?"

Looking over, I saw an African American woman in her fifties. I picked up Langley's pink water bottle, quickly clearing the bench for her to sit down.

"Thank you, young man," she said in a courtly voice. "How are you on this fine day?"

"Never better, ma'am. Yourself?"

"I'm good, thank you for asking."

She was too old to be supervising her own child on the playground, and I took her for a young grandmother. Playground conversation with other adults here in Charlottesville was fairly predictable—they worked in any number of white-collar jobs with a pension or tenure or both, and I braced myself for a banal conversation about the weather.

This time there was a long pause, and I continued watching Langley race about the playground with the other children.

She asked, "So, are you from around here?"

"Just moved to town. You?"

"I'm not too far away—I'm from the Agency."

"There's a lot of agencies."

"Well, mine shares its name with your beautiful daughter."

Shit. The CIA was headquartered in Langley, Virginia, and the town's name was a ubiquitous underhanded reference to the massive intelligence organization.

"Nice meeting you," I said, rising to leave.

"Relax, Mr. Rivers, and let me tell you a story."

I sat back down, suddenly feeling overheated. Speaking curtly, I said, "Make it quick. I've got an appointment to keep."

She smiled kindly, but there was a coldness in her voice that made me hang on every word as she continued speaking. "For years now, my division has heard tales of a certain transnational crime syndicate. One whose leader is known only as the Handler, regardless of who held the seat. Sound familiar?"

"No," I said, my stomach fluttering.

"Well, the Russian equivalent of this organization had its entire leadership obliterated in a rogue nuclear explosion. We tracked an aircraft flight pattern to British Columbia. And there were some interesting occurrences afterwards."

"Such as?"

"Such as someone starting quite a ruckus at the Infinity Manhattan in New York. It seems the South American equivalent of this syndicate had its entire leadership annihilated by a team of men who left by helicopter."

"I think I saw something about that on the news."

"Well, a survivor was arrested trying to flee the hotel. Lajos Silva."

I swung my head toward her, staring forcefully into her calm brown eyes. "And?"

"Well," she sighed, "he was quite averse to cooperating with local law enforcement. But we arranged to accommodate him at a site for wayward miscreants. And for whatever reason, once he became the beneficiary of some proper hospitality, he found himself motivated to spontaneously confess everything he knew."

"Must have been something in the water."

She didn't seem to find the humor in my comment, despite what I thought was a massively witty double entendre to waterboarding.

Then she continued, "Well, this Lajos Silva character had quite a wild story. He claimed that the transnational criminal syndicate we were seeking had been infiltrated by a kid in his twenties who climbed to the top of the organization and became the Handler."

"Sounds pretty far-fetched."

"That's what we thought, too. But he provided some information that checked out."

"Such as?"

"He provided a location for the Handler's syndicate in the British Columbian wilderness—which, as you recall, was where we last tracked the flight pattern associated with that mysterious nuclear explosion. Our Canadian friends looked into it and found a couple pretty comprehensive facilities, along with a lot of dead criminals."

"Weird."

"He had a name for the young kid who took over the organization— David Rivers."

"It's a common name."

"I'm sure it is."

"What happened to Lajos Silva—is he still alive?"

She gave a mournful cluck of her tongue. "Succumbed to a nasty case of pneumonia. Passed away in custody, I'm afraid."

I turned my gaze back to Langley on the playground, unable to suppress a grin spreading across my face. "Too bad."

"Quite unfortunate, indeed."

She suddenly turned to me, her eyes darting between mine. "There's one thing I need to know, Mr. Rivers. Are there any other nuclear devices or materials in play?"

I shot her an angry glare, saying nothing.

She continued, "I'm afraid that not answering isn't an option."

The fate of Lajos Silva flashed across my mind. Leaning toward her, I spoke in a low and sincere tone.

"No. If I had any knowledge of an active nuclear device, or *any* terrorist activity unknown to US intelligence, I would have called you people already." I nodded toward the playground. "Jesus, woman, I've got a kid. Think I'm interested in letting a bunch of shitheads try and kill civilians when I have a chance to stop it?"

She had been staring at me intently, probably watching for subliminal signs of deception. Then she leaned back on the bench, seeming to relax. "So I take it you were responsible for the list."

"What list?"

"One hundred and twenty-five terrorist identities leaked to the intelligence agencies of US, UK, Australia, Canada, and New Zealand. A leak that coincided with a sudden and worldwide massacre of suspected terrorists."

"I don't know what you're talking about."

She gave an understanding nod. "At any rate, I'm very glad to hear that there's no other nuclear material out there. Because otherwise our conversation would be taking a very different direction than it's about to."

"And where, exactly, is this conversation headed?"

"It's a big world out there, Mr. Rivers, and it's filled with innocent people like your daughter, and bad people doing bad things." Her face wrinkled in contempt. "You call them 'shitheads,' but my organization calls them terrorists. As you know, there's no eradicating terrorism. All we can do is cut the grass, knowing it will grow back; keeping terrorism at a manageable level at an acceptable cost." She frowned, then added, "An endless cycle of people to be killed."

"Stop it. You're giving me an erection."

Rather than offending her, my comment elicited a warm, grandmotherly smile. "Then perhaps you'd be interested in playing a part."

I shook my head. "My daughter's in school. I'm not moving her anywhere."

"I wouldn't dream of asking you to. About that, though...you could have gone anywhere in the world. Why did you choose to settle in Char-lottesville?"

I considered telling her, then decided I had better not. Whoever she was, this woman had enough dirt to go around; she didn't need any extra ammo.

I settled for a diplomatic response, one that would have made Parvaneh proud.

"Let's chalk that up to 'none of your fucking business.'"

She tilted her head toward me, then spoke in a near-whisper. "Well, how would you like to stand up a new Outfit?"

I tried to reply, found the words stuck in my throat.

"Not as large as the previous Outfit, you understand," she quickly added. "Just a small team for now. People you know and trust."

"What kind of work are we talking?"

She gave a noncommittal shrug. "Perhaps it could be the type of team that would require only a little intelligence, funding, and logistics in order to go a long way in furthering"—she chose her words carefully—"select national security objectives. As far as terrorism goes, we have people to cut the grass. We're good at it. I need someone who can pull the weeds. Namely, the tier of up-and-coming terrorist leaders who can be quietly removed from the global battlefield before they become major players. The true believers. Interested?"

"Am I correct in assuming this would be contractor status, so you don't have to involve DoD personnel?"

"You would, Mr. Rivers. We provide the targets. You choose your own people."

The faces raced through my mind—Cancer and Reilly, for starters, then Worthy, Ian, and Orlando...maybe even Joe and Fiona. The survivors who had navigated the Organization's swath of crime and horror and come out alive on the other side.

I asked, "Why do you guys need another team of contractors? I thought you had enough of those already."

"If we need something to go boom, and we want it to look and smell like the US Government, we've got an app for that already. You and I are having this conversation for two reasons. First, it seems that everywhere you go, bad guys mysteriously die. You seem to be rather good at it. Second, my bosses are tired of the memoirs, of the classified operations that become major motion pictures five minutes later. On the other hand"—she gave an appreciative smile—"I had a hard enough time finding you. Discretion is a job qualification that is exceedingly hard to find. It is also an absolute requirement for this offer. So, are you interested?"

I didn't look at her. I was watching Langley race across the playground bridge and back to the slide.

"Langley, sweetheart," I called. "It's time to go."

The woman handed me a business card, holding it in the air between us until I took it from her. A single phone number was printed on it, and nothing else.

"Think about it. I'll be waiting for your call."

"What's your name?"

She shot me a dismayed look, as if I should have known better. But her expression quickly softened and she said, "Let's go with Duchess."

"Nice meeting you, Duchess."

"And it was nice meeting you, Mr. Rivers," she said, fixing me with a stern glance and adding, "in person."

Then she stood to leave, and I remained alone on the bench. I glanced over my shoulder to see her disappear toward the parking lot.

Langley ran up to me, face flushed and out of breath. Tendrils of wet hair stuck to her forehead. I handed her the water bottle.

"Who was that lady?" she gasped between gulps. "Where's her kid?"

I turned the card over in my hand. "I think I'm her kid, sweetheart."

"Can we go to Bumble Brews later? You could get a beer while I play."

"Good negotiation skills," I admitted. "But we'll discuss it after your appointment. And only if you're very, *very* good for the nice doctor. You remember what we talked about?"

"Yeah. I've been practicing."

We left the park, heading back toward the parking lot. The woman was gone. I saw a trash can on the way, and stopped to deposit the business card inside. My life was about making Langley happy now, not chasing some visions of glory from my distant past. Then I hesitated. The card felt super-glued to my hand, my fingertips pinching it with resolute determination. What the hell, I thought. I'd think about it.

I slid the card into my pocket beside my phone, took Langley's hand,

and walked to my truck.

* * *

After a nurse took Langley's vitals, she escorted us to one of the examination rooms and said the doctor would be with us shortly.

Langley knelt at a toy road racing set in the corner and began maneuvering the toy cars around the plastic track. I took a seat and looked about the room, every wall adorned with teddy bears and hearts painted against a bright blue sky. A rainbow arced across the top of the wall opposite me, and on that rainbow was written *UVA Children's*.

The door opened, and the doctor entered.

She was an attractive blonde woman in her late twenties, and her face brightened at the sight of Langley.

Kneeling down, the doctor said, "You must be Langley! So nice to meet you."

Langley returned a high five, and then the doctor rose and looked at me for the first time.

"And you must be—"

She stopped mid-sentence, her jaw dropping as she stared at me with electric green eyes.

"Hi, Laila," I said.

Before she could respond, Langley asked, "You know her?"

"I sure do, sweetheart," I said without taking my eyes off Laila's. "Daddy and Dr. Laila knew each other back in college. She must be doing her pediatric residency right here in Charlottesville. What a coincidence."

This was an understatement, of course. Laila and I had dated while she was a medical student at Ohio State and I was a cadet at West Point. We'd hit it off from the start, and had every intention of staying together—until she discovered the staggering depth of my depression, and the self-destructive lengths to which I taunted death as a result. Having lost her own father to suicide, she could no longer bear the sight of me.

Now Laila's eyes were wide with shock, but she managed an exaggerated nod for Langley's benefit. "Yes. What a...coincidence, that you would relocate to Virginia from...where have you been, exactly?"

"Oh, here and there."

"I was wondering," she played along, "because I've tried to look you up a few times since our college days. Seems no one knew where you were."

"Well, now I'm back. With my daughter, Langley."

Laila's eyes drifted to her, and then back to me. Langley was much older than the amount of time that had elapsed since she'd last seen me, so it was obvious she'd been adopted. But Laila's shock spoke to an inability to reconcile those two facts—me disappearing as a suicidal, alcoholic vet, and reappearing in her town with a child in tow.

Suddenly Langley barked, "Will you go to dinner with us?"

"Langley," I stammered, "that's very...forward of you." She was supposed to wait until the end of the appointment. Also, to sound more spontaneous and less rehearsed.

"But," I quickly added, looking to Laila, "I suppose we do have room for a third. If, you know, you're free later. I know you MDs get busy."

She watched me closely, tapping a manicured fingernail against her lip and trying to discern who I was anymore.

So I said, "The man you knew is gone. You can see that in my eyes. When we last saw each other, I told you I was going to start over. Well, now I finally have. So?"

Laila blushed, her eyes finding her clipboard.

"Okay...I suppose dinner wouldn't hurt. Why don't you give me a call later?"

"Sure." I retrieved the phone from my pocket, quickly entering a new contact. "What's your number?"

As I saved the digits, I caught a flash of movement beneath my phone.

A scrap of paper must have stuck to my phone when I pulled it out.

Now the white card fluttered to the floor, landing to stare at me with a single phone number printed across its face.

Laila stopped speaking abruptly.

"What is that?"

"It's nothing," I quickly replied, hoisting my phone toward her. "You were saying?"

But Langley had already retrieved the card, and now held it out to me.

"Here you go, Daddy! You dropped this."

I pretended not to hear her, looking instead to Laila's confused eyes.

And then, I smiled.

THE ENEMIES OF MY COUNTRY: SHADOW STRIKE #1

On a mission to assassinate a Syrian operative, a young CIA contractor uncovers a shocking terrorist plot that threatens his wife and daughter.

David Rivers is very good at killing people.

He's an expert in the art of violence—first as a Ranger, then as a mercenary, and now as a CIA contractor conducting covert action around the world.

But he's never had a family to protect...until now.

Newly married, and with a five-year old adopted daughter, David thinks his family is safe in Charlottesville, Virginia as he risks his life abroad. But when his mission to assassinate a Syrian operative reveals an imminent terrorist attack on US soil, nothing can prepare him for what he discovers.

The attack will occur in one week. The target is in his hometown.

And his wife and daughter are mentioned by name.

Get your copy today at
severnriverbooks.com/series/shadow-strike-series

ACKNOWLEDGMENTS

I owe my thanks to the following people for their support with *Terminal Objective*.

My pre-beta readers Codename: Duchess, JT, and Julie helped me immensely in revising the initial draft.

Beta readers for this book were: Becky Stilwell, Bob Waterfield (Senior Chief, USN Ret.), Bourbon Delta, Dean "OZ" Fukawa, Derek Burt, Dr. Earl, Janet B, Jim Flagg, Jon Suttle, M Julien, MK, and Raymond Dennis.

My editor, Cara Quinlan, has been tirelessly fixing my manuscripts since the very first book. Once again, her careful attention to detail and suggestions to content elevated the finished manuscript to a much higher level than it was when she received it.

Finally, thank you to my beautiful and long-suffering wife Amy—her unwavering support never ceases to inspire, and I couldn't be more grateful.

ABOUT THE AUTHOR

Jason Kasper is the USA Today bestselling author of the Spider Heist, American Mercenary, and Shadow Strike thriller series. Before his writing career he served in the US Army, beginning as a Ranger private and ending as a Green Beret captain. Jason is a West Point graduate and a veteran of the Afghanistan and Iraq wars, and was an avid ultramarathon runner, skydiver, and BASE jumper, all of which inspire his fiction.

Sign up for Jason Kasper's reader list at
severnriverbooks.com/authors/jason-kasper

jasonkasper@severnriverbooks.com

Printed in the United States
by Baker & Taylor Publisher Services